CW01510536

MURDER AT THE COLOSSEUM

By Jim Eldridge

MURDER AT THE COLOSSEUM

JIM ELDRIDGE

Allison & Busby Limited
11 Wardour Mews
London W1F 8AN
allisonandbusby.com

First published in Great Britain by Allison & Busby in 2025.

Copyright © 2025 by JIM ELDRIDGE

The moral right of the author is hereby asserted in accordance with
the Copyright, Designs and Patents Act 1988.

All characters and events in this publication,
other than those clearly in the public domain,
are fictitious and any resemblance to actual persons,
living or dead, is purely coincidental.

All rights reserved. No part of this publication may be reproduced,
stored in a retrieval system, or transmitted, in any form or by
any means without the prior written permission of the publisher,
nor be otherwise circulated in any form of binding or cover
other than that in which it is published and without a similar
condition being imposed on the subsequent buyer.
A CIP catalogue record for this book is available from
the British Library.

First Edition

ISBN 978-0-7490-3215-9

Typeset in 11.5/16.5 pt Adobe Garamond Pro by
Allison & Busby Ltd.

By choosing this product, you help take care of the world's forests.
Learn more: www.fsc.org.

Printed and bound in Great Britain by Clays Ltd. Elcograf S.p.A

EU GPSR Authorised Representative
LOGOS EUROPE, 9 rue Nicolas Poussin, 17000, LA ROCHELLE, France
E-mail: Contact@logoseurope.eu

To Lynne, who makes my heart quicken every time I look at her.

CHAPTER ONE

Tuesday 7th August, 1900

Thirty-seven-year-old Vincenzo Sulli and his younger brother, Edoardo, sat in the office of Salvatore Fuschetti, at the yard where Fuschetti stabled the horses that pulled the carriages and taxis in the Celian and Palatine Hill areas of Rome. It was a good and profitable business, with most of the city carriage drivers unable to afford their own stables. Their horses were kept fed and watered and groomed. The result was not only that Salvatore Fuschetti earned a good income from the services he offered, but he also benefited from the information passed to him by the drivers themselves: the addresses of the wealthy who were going to be away from home for a few days, indiscreet whispered conversations between passengers with verification of rumours and gossip that would be worth good money to certain interested parties. Salvatore Fuschetti was not just a successful and rich stable owner, he was also a key figure in the Celian Hill Cosa Nostra, second only to the local *capo*, Massimo Cassani. Fuschetti was the one to whom disgruntled locals brought their grievances. It was up to Fuschetti to decide on the importance of the particular grievance, the fairness or lack of it in the situation and, most importantly, the money. The cost of settling a dispute depended on what was required. Physical pressure, perhaps. An arm broken. At the extreme end, a bullet or two.

'This Giovanni Maduro,' said Vincenzo angrily, 'threatens to ruin us.'

'His rantings in the press could persuade the authorities to close down our shops!' snarled Edoardo. 'And we know they read him, because only recently some interfering council man quoted him in the Chamber of Deputies.'

The Sulli brothers owned a series of dingy sweatshops where women laboured for long hours and little pay over ancient sewing machines, producing clothes for the city's most expensive shops.

Vincenzo produced a few newspapers, which he slammed down on the table.

'Read them for yourself!' he thundered, outraged. 'He even names us in one of these scurrilous articles. We should sue him.'

'But we can't,' said Edoardo unhappily. 'If we did, it would only publicise us to the kind of people who buy the clothes we make, the rich, whereas at the moment it's the left-wing rabble and the poor who read the so-called newspapers and magazines his articles appear in. But, sooner or later, what he says will be out in public for everyone to read.'

'He has to be stopped,' said Vincenzo. 'He must be stopped.'

Fuschetti nodded. He picked up the newspapers.

'Leave this to me,' he said. Then he looked at them questioningly. 'There will be a cost, of course.'

'Whatever it takes!' roared Vincenzo.

'But within reason,' added Edoardo, bringing in a note of caution.

'Of course,' said Fuschetti.

CHAPTER TWO

Thursday 9th August

The Rome Express bearing Daniel and Abigail Wilson was finally approaching the Italian capital. It had been a long and tiring journey from London – a train to the south coast, then a ferry across the English Channel to Calais-Maritime, where they'd caught the express train that travelled the length of France before crossing into Italy and going through Turin, Genoa, Pisa and Florence before arriving in Rome. The journey had taken three days.

'Did it take you this long when you were here before?' asked Daniel.

'Longer, I'm afraid,' said Abigail. 'We were held up by some unfortunate rail accidents.'

Abigail was referring to her first visit to Rome fifteen years earlier, in 1885. After graduating from Girton College in Classics, Abigail, then aged twenty-five, had joined a group undertaking an archaeological dig at the Colosseum in Rome. It had been the start of her career in archaeology. Now, in August 1900, she was internationally recognised as one of the pre-eminent archaeologists of her generation, mainly for her work in Egypt at the pyramids. Recently she'd led an expedition sponsored by Arthur Conan Doyle to Abusir, in particular to explore the pyramid of Niuserre, and the work she'd done there was still being studied by Egyptologists and written about in magazines. But ever since that first experience of working at the ancient Colosseum, she'd had an enduring love for all things classically Roman, so when she was invited to take part in a festival in Rome on the classical era, she'd leapt at it.

'You will love it,' she'd assured Daniel. 'It will be our first real holiday in continental Europe.'

'We were in Paris not so long ago,' Daniel reminded her,

'That was not really a holiday,' Abigail pointed out. 'It began with my being imprisoned and threatened with the guillotine and then developed into a mystery for us to solve.'

As well as Abigail's career as an archaeologist, for the last six years she and Daniel had established a reputation as the Museum Detectives, starting when they'd solved a series of murders at the Fitzwilliam Museum in Cambridge together, and as a result received similar commission from most of the other famous museums – the British Museum, the Ashmolean, the Natural History and, most recently, the Louvre in Paris. Daniel had been a detective at Scotland Yard, working with the famous Inspector Abberline on the Jack the Ripper investigations, before becoming a private investigator. Now he and Abigail were not just partners in detection, but also partners in life, having married.

Abigail took a letter from her handbag and passed it to Daniel.

'This is what Giuseppe sent me,' she said, referring to Giuseppe Saredo, the organiser of the Classical Rome Festival, someone she'd first met and worked with on the original dig at the Colosseum fifteen years before. 'It's the programme for the Festival.'

'You showed it to me before,' Daniel reminded her. 'Remember, I pointed out that it's in Italian.'

Abigail took it back from him and proceeded to go through the programme.

'It begins Friday, tomorrow. The morning starts with a blessing, followed by processions and displays by local schoolchildren.'

'A blessing?' said Daniel.

'This is Rome, the most Catholic city in the world,' said Abigail. 'The Church is omnipresent. Nothing important happens here without the involvement of the Church. Using the schoolchildren is a brilliant idea of Giuseppe's. It means their parents and grandparents will turn up, and so everyone will be made aware of what's going on at the Festival. Giuseppe says the displays by the children will include presentations depicting the great heroes of Rome: Romulus and Remus, and Castor and Pollux.'

'I have no idea who they are,' said Daniel.

'Surely you know about Romulus and Remus?' said Abigail, surprised.

'You forget, my education was in a workhouse,' Daniel reminded her. 'Picking oakum, and reading and writing, and numbers, but at a very basic level. Everything I know, I learnt after I left the workhouse, so basically, I'm self-taught. And that didn't include the history of Rome, or of Egypt. What I do know about them I've picked up from you.'

'Rome is named after Romulus. Romulus and Remus were the twin sons of the god Mars and the daughter of a King

11

of Alba, after Mars had taken advantage of her while she was asleep.'

'The cad!' said Daniel.

'Exactly. The girl's father was not impressed, so the twin baby boys were put in a basket and set afloat on the River Tiber. The basket came ashore beside a grotto, where a she-wolf found them and suckled them. A shepherd and his wife came along and took the boys in. As the boys became older they became rivals, and Romulus killed Remus. There is a longer version of the tale, but I won't go into it now. I'll explain more as we watch the procession. In short, Romulus survived and founded the city of Rome. As for Castor and Pollux . . .'

Daniel held up his hand. 'Again, later,' he said. 'I can only cope with a certain amount of classical history at a time. So, that's Friday morning.'

'And on Friday afternoon, I do my guided tour of the Colosseum,' said Abigail. 'I'll be showing the audience where we did our original dig, where the Roman audiences sat, and the underground cells where the gladiators were kept prior to them going into the arena. Then, on Saturday, my old friend Giovanni Maduro will be doing the same kind of thing at the Forum. On Monday someone, who I don't know, will be doing the same at the Palatine Hill. What's good about it is that, unlike archaeological conferences, which usually consist of people in halls talking and pointing at pictures, all the events at this are taking place at the classical sites with a guided tour, where the person leading the sessions takes the audience around, pointing out and describing places of particular interest.'

'There's nothing on Sunday,' commented Daniel.

'It's the sabbath. It's no different to back in Britain,' said

Abigail. 'Nothing happens except church events. No shops open except newsagents, and then only in the morning. It's even more so here because Rome – as I said – is the most religious city in the world as far as Catholics are concerned. So, on Sunday the population goes to church and takes part in solemn masses and processions.'

'So that's Friday, Saturday and Monday at the Festival,' said Daniel.

'Then on Tuesday, back at the Colosseum, we have a troupe of actors and acrobats recreating gladiatorial contests. I bet you that will be very popular. Then, on Wednesday, the universities have been invited to take part in debates at the Forum. That's where the original debates took place back in classical times.'

'I bet that won't be as popular as the gladiators,' said Daniel.

'Possibly, but they're adding a short drama about the assassination of Julius Caesar. Lots of stabbing going on. And then, on Thursday, Giovanni and I swap. He will do his take on the Colosseum, while I do my own tour of the Forum. Then, on Friday, there will be a big parade around the Forum and the Palatine Hill, ending at the Colosseum, at which Giuseppe Saracco, the Prime Minister of Italy, will be present, along with other dignitaries, to close the Festival.'

Daniel looked out of the window. 'It looks as if we're coming into the station,' he said.

Abigail began putting the letter and other things away.

'In his letter, Giuseppe suggested rather than his meeting us off the train, we go to the Colosseum and he'll meet us there.' She checked her watch. 'That makes sense – the train's running about an hour late, which isn't bad considering how long the whole journey is.'

'It's no different to catching a train back home,' commented Daniel.

'I suggest we leave our luggage at the railway station and walk to the Colosseum,' said Abigail. 'It's not far.'

'Excellent idea,' said Daniel enthusiastically, who always advocated walking around new places to learn about them.

CHAPTER THREE

Their route to the Colosseum took them along via Cavour, a long wide street with houses and shops on either side.

'The Romans were very keen on straight, wide main roads,' said Abigail. 'They liked to move the Roman army quickly from place to place. That's why so many of our major roads in Britain are like that, the product of the Roman occupation.'

Their walk took them past two ornate churches – 'Santa Maria Maggiore', Abigail informed him of the first; then 'San Pietro in Vincoli' as they passed the second.

'They look very old,' said Daniel.

'They are, but compared to what you'll see when we get to the Colosseum and the Forum, they're relatively modern. San Pietro is about a thousand and a half years old.'

They turned off the main wide road at the church of San Pietro and made their way along a narrower street, and saw directly ahead of them the magnificence of the Colosseum towering high into the air above.

'My God, it's huge!' said Daniel, awed as he looked at the ancient, high brown stone circular walls, with what appeared to be the spaces for open windows every few feet along the bottom three levels, and smaller window spaces running at intervals all the way along the highest section.

'It's the largest amphitheatre in the world,' said Abigail. 'Construction began under the Emperor Vespasian in 72 AD and it was finally completed in 80 AD. It held up to eighty thousand spectators.'

'And this is where the gladiators fought?'

'Gladiators, and animal hunts, executions, re-enactments of famous battles. What makes it special is that many Roman theatres were built into hillsides. The Colosseum is entirely free-standing, which makes it a masterpiece of building construction. Come with me and I'll show you the arena.'

Daniel followed her through one of the many arches and found himself in an enormous open space of sandy ground surrounded by ascending rows where the audience must have sat, or stood. The area was filled with people milling around, many of them tourists, but there was one small group being addressed energetically by a stout middle-aged man, with lots of gestures, pointing at various aspects of the enormous ruined building.

'I think that might be Giuseppe Saredo,' said Abigail.

'You don't recognise him?'

'It's fifteen years since I saw him, and people change. The Giuseppe I knew was tall, thin and clean-shaven. If it is Giuseppe, he's certainly put on weight and developed a bushy beard.'

The man she was talking about swung round to point to another part of the ruins and suddenly saw Daniel and Abigail. Immediately he hurried towards them, his arms outstretched in welcome, shouting, 'Abigail!'

'I think we can conclude it is him,' murmured Daniel.

Giuseppe Saredo's face bore a huge, happy smile as he neared them.

'Abigail!' he boomed. 'And this must be Daniel, *il marito*!'

'He is indeed,' said Abigail as Giuseppe swamped her in an affectionate bear hug. Stepping back from Giuseppe, she introduced them. 'Giuseppe, this is Daniel Wilson, my husband. Daniel, this is Giuseppe Saredo, whom I worked with at this place fifteen years ago and who's organising this festival.'

'*Buongiorno*,' said Daniel, shaking Giuseppe's hand, to which the delighted Giuseppe responded with a long burst of excited Italian.

'Forgive me,' said Daniel apologetically. 'Currently my Italian is limited to a few basic phrases such as *buongiorno*, *grazie* and *arrivederci*, but I'm determined to improve while I'm here.'

'Then we converse in English,' smiled Giuseppe. He turned to Abigail and asked, 'How does it feel to be here again after fifteen years?'

'In fact, I was here some eight years ago. I stopped over while on my way back from Egypt. I wanted to catch up with Sarah and Giovanni.' She turned to Daniel. 'Remember, I told you about them?'

'Indeed. Sarah, the young woman you were here with in 1885.'

'Who fell in love with a young Italian archaeology student on the same dig, Giovanni Maduro, and married him and still lives in Italy.' She turned to Giuseppe and said, 'As Giovanni's in your programme, I assume you still see them.'

'Of course!' said Giuseppe. 'The past few years they have been busy at the Forum, which Giovanni will be giving a talk about at the Festival. I told them you would be arriving today and Sarah particularly was very excited to see you. She said they would make a point of coming here today.'

'That will be wonderful!' said Abigail.

Giuseppe looked around them, then asked: 'Where is your luggage?'

'We left it at the Roma Termini left luggage office so we could walk here unencumbered. If you tell us where we'll be staying, we'll collect it later.'

'We can do better than that,' said Giuseppe. 'We'll walk together to the Termini later and I'll come with you to the hotel. It's the Miazzo, very close to the Termini.'

'That will be ideal,' said Abigail.

Giuseppe gestured towards the group of people he'd been addressing. 'I have to talk to these people. They will be acting as stewards at the Festival and I need them to know what their duties are, and where they will be located. Do you have everything you need for your talk tomorrow afternoon? If there's anything I can get for you . . .'

'No, thank you.' She waved a hand at the vast ruined site. 'These are all the illustrations I'll need.'

'In that case, I'll see you at the Forum later. We have an office there for administrating the Festival. I'm about to take these stewards there to hand out details for them.' He sighed. 'Paperwork, always paperwork.' Giuseppe shook hands with them, then rejoined his small crowd of stewards and led them away.

'He's very energetic,' commented Daniel.

'He always was,' said Abigail. 'He's passionate about archaeology and classical Rome. He's the perfect person to be in charge of organising this festival. Now, let me show you the Colosseum. A guided tour.'

'Are you sure?' asked Daniel. 'Wouldn't you rather save yourself for tomorrow?'

'No. For one thing, it's been many years since I was last here. I need to see what's changed so I'm not caught unprepared when I take the people around. And I'll be giving tomorrow's talk in Italian, so you won't be able to understand a word.'

From their position in the middle of the arena, Abigail pointed to the ascending tiers which rose up.

'The seating at arena level is where the most important people sat. The senatorial class, who were allowed to bring their own chairs. The level above that was for the non-senatorial nobles, and the next level up was for ordinary Roman citizens, but even that was subdivided according to class. The lower part was for wealthy citizens, and the upper part was where the poor sat. Roman society was rigidly organised according to rank and wealth. The seats were made of stone for the poorest, and marble for the elite, who would bring their own cushions. The highest level of all was a separate gallery for the common poor, slaves and women. That would have been standing only, no seats.'

'It doesn't sound much different to the arrangements in London theatres,' commented Daniel.

'Interestingly, some people were banned from the Colosseum completely,' added Abigail. 'That included actors, gravediggers and former gladiators.' She gestured at the sandy ground they were standing on. 'Beneath the sand is a wooden floor, and beneath that is a two-level network of tunnels where gladiators and wild animals were kept. You can imagine how large the tunnels were when the animals included elephants. Incidentally, the Latin word for sand is *harena*, or arena.'

'Abigail!'

They turned and saw a woman in her late thirties waving at them. She was accompanied by a man in his forties and a young woman who looked to be in her teens.

'It's Sarah and Giovanni,' exclaimed Abigail delightedly.

'Who's the girl?' asked Daniel.

'I've no idea,' said Abigail.

'Their daughter?' suggested Daniel.

'No,' said Abigail. 'Sarah and Giovanni did have a daughter, but sadly she died some years ago. This is possibly a relative of Giovanni's. I'll leave the rest of our tour for later.'

Daniel and Abigail moved forward to greet the three newcomers. Sarah and Giovanni were all welcoming smiles, but the young woman with them looked at Abigail and Daniel with what appeared to be overt hostility.

'Whoever she is, her face says she doesn't like us,' murmured Daniel.

'Shh,' Abigail murmured back.

Abigail and Sarah embraced warmly, then Abigail and Giovanni. For his part, Daniel shook hands with Sarah and Giovanni as Sarah did the introductions.

'This is my sister, Julia,' said Sarah, indicating the young woman. 'She's come to stay with us for a few months to get the flavour of Italy.'

'Hello,' smiled Abigail to the young woman. The young woman, who now they were closer to her appeared to be about seventeen, merely nodded at her, unsmiling and sullen.

'Giuseppe said you'd be here today,' said Sarah. 'This is such a delight!'

'An enormous pleasure to see you again, Abigail,' added Giovanni. 'And to meet your husband. How was your journey?'

'Long,' said Daniel ruefully.

Giovanni pointed to where a coffee stall had been set up, along with a few chairs.

'Let us talk over coffee,' he said.

They walked towards the coffee stall, and saw that there were only three chairs available.

'I will sit on the ground,' said Giovanni. 'I'm used to it.'

'I will join you,' offered Daniel. 'Let the ladies have the chairs.'

'There's no need,' said Julia. 'I want to go to the Vatican to take a proper look at the Sistine Chapel.'

'If you wait till we've had coffee, we'll go with you,' said Sarah.

'Thank you, but I'm happy on my own. I know my way around Rome. I speak Italian. I'll be fine.'

With that, Julia made her exit. Sarah let out a sigh.

'I'm sorry about my sister,' she apologised to Abigail and Daniel. 'I don't think she realises she's being rude.'

Oh yes she does, thought Abigail. Aloud, she said, 'She's young, and I can understand her wanting to see Rome for herself, rather than sit and listen to four old friends gabble away about things of which she knows nothing.'

Sarah and Abigail settled themselves down on a chair each. Daniel looked enquiringly at Giovanni, who shook his head. 'Please, sit,' he said. 'After so many years working as an archaeologist, dusty ground is a second home to me.'

21

'Giovanni is currently engaged in excavations at the Forum,' said Sarah.

'I've yet to show Daniel the Forum,' said Abigail.

'I'll be happy to show you,' said Giovanni. 'Possibly tomorrow, after you've given your talk.'

'That will be excellent,' said Abigail. 'How is Paolo?'

'Paolo?' asked Daniel.

'Sarah and Giovanni's son,' explained Abigail. 'He must be quite grown up by now.'

'Indeed he is,' said Sarah. 'He's seventeen.'

'He's working for Pirelli in Milan,' added Giovanni. 'The tyre company. He wants to work in the motor industry and most of the firms involved are in Milan or other parts of the north.'

'Yes, cars have started to appear in Britain,' said Abigail. 'Everyone says they are the transport of the future, but I'm not so sure.'

'Here in Italy we see it as the big industry with lots of work for the young generation,' said Giovanni animatedly. 'Up till now most work in Italy has been in farming. Olives, tomatoes, very labour intensive, but poorly paid. It's led to large parts of the country losing people because they're too poor to stay and support a family. Instead, they are emigrating to America.'

Sarah smiled affectionately at her husband as she said gently but firmly, 'That's enough politics, Gio.'

Giovanni gave them a rueful smile and said, 'I apologise, but it's something as a country we cannot ignore.'

'How about you?' asked Sarah, discreetly changing the subject. 'No children of your own?'

'Alas, no,' said Abigail.

She didn't tell them that soon after they'd returned from Paris the previous year, Abigail had discovered she was pregnant. Sadly, their joy was short-lived. At four months, Abigail had suffered a miscarriage, and her doctor had cautioned against Abigail becoming pregnant again. Abigail also remembered that Sarah and Giovanni's daughter, Lucrezia, had died at the age of ten, eight years before, and she was concerned that telling the couple about her miscarriage might bring back sad memories for them of their daughter. Instead, their talk turned to Sarah's and Giovanni's work as archaeologists, though most of Sarah's now seemed to be writing articles on the subject for magazine and newspapers.

'That's how I know about your expedition to Niuserre,' Sarah said. 'It was in one of the magazines I write for. It caused quite a stir, a woman leading an archaeological expedition. Will you be talking about that?'

Abigail shook her head. 'As the subject of the Festival is classical Rome, I shall be concentrating on the dig here in 1885.'

'Ah, such happy memories,' said Sarah.

'Actually, we'd better get to our hotel and recover from our long journey,' said Abigail. 'We said we'd meet Giuseppe at the Forum and he'd take us to it. We're staying at the Miazzo near the Termini.'

'Very comfortable,' said Sarah.

'We'll walk with you to the Forum,' said Giovanni. 'I need to check that everything's in place for my talk.'

CHAPTER FOUR

The four of them rose and Giovanni led the way to the Forum, Sarah and Abigail chatting excitedly, swapping memories. At the Forum, once Giovanni had been reassured by Giuseppe that everything was in place for his talk, Abigail and Daniel repeated the long walk along the via Cavour, this time in reverse, to the Termini. Once there, they reclaimed their luggage, and Giuseppe helped them carry it to their hotel.

'Thank you, Giuseppe,' said Daniel warmly. 'I really don't know what we'd have done without your help today.'

'You'd have done perfectly well, because you have Abigail with you,' said Giuseppe cheerily. 'She is one of the greatest organisers and survivors I've ever known.' To Abigail, he said, 'If you'd like to arrive at the Colosseum tomorrow late morning, I'll introduce you to the stewards. At least, to the key ones.'

'I'm looking forward to it,' said Abigail.

'One important thing for tomorrow,' said Giuseppe. 'The tunnels beneath the arena. You were possibly planning to take your audience down to them to give them the experience of what it was like being there?'

'Yes,' said Abigail.

'It's a wonderful idea, but the organising committee are worried about it. There's more chance of an accident happening down there with a group of people who are novices, rather than when there are just a handful of experienced archaeologists. Someone could get lost in the tunnels, for example. A child running off from their parents.'

'Yes, that's a good point,' said Abigail, but unable to hide her disappointment. 'So, keep everything above ground?'

'Thank you,' said Giuseppe, obviously relieved.

Once Giuseppe had departed, they both slumped down onto comfortable armchairs.

'My God, I'm exhausted,' said Daniel. 'Not just the journey, but today, walking everywhere, meeting people.'

'At least we have the evening and tomorrow morning to ourselves,' said Abigail.

'It's disappointing about the underground areas,' said Daniel, 'I was looking forward to that.'

'It makes sense,' admitted Abigail. 'All sorts of things can go wrong in underground areas – tunnels caving in, people getting lost. It happens all the time at digs in the pyramids. But don't worry, I'll arrange with Giuseppe to take you into the tunnels. When we did the original excavation, we found an entrance to them. Hopefully, it's still there and hasn't been blocked off.'

'You're sure you have everything ready for tomorrow?' asked Daniel. 'You're confident about using Italian?'

'The same as I was when I gave a talk at the Louvre in French,' Abigail reminded him.

'How many languages do you actually speak?' asked Daniel.

'French, obviously. Arabic. Italian. And Greek, at a pinch.'

'That's so impressive,' said Daniel, awed.

'That comes from being an archaeologist who travels.'

'Yes, but these last few years you haven't travelled like you used to.'

'It doesn't matter. When I'm in a country like Italy, or France, it sort of comes back to me. I'm often rusty at first, but having spent the last few days on a train where the staff spoke either Italian or French gave me plenty of time to practise. What did you think of Sarah and Giovanni?'

'I liked them very much. And Giuseppe. The only one I wasn't keen on was Julia. I thought she was quite hostile towards us. Glowering.'

'Maybe she was shy about meeting new people,' said Abigail. 'She is quite young.'

'Yes, that's another thing. How old is Sarah?'

'Thirty-seven.'

'And Julia looks about seventeen.'

'There's a reason for that,' said Abigail. 'Julia's the daughter by their father's second wife. Sarah's mother died when she was fifteen. Her father married again three years later, when Sarah was eighteen. Sarah was twenty-one when she came out to volunteer on the original dig at the Colosseum, and that's where she met Giovanni. Sarah and Giovanni had a back-and-forth relationship between England and Italy over the next couple of years before they married. Sarah then moved permanently to Italy, but every couple of years she travels to England to visit her father and sister.'

'And now Julia's come to stay.'

'Not permanently. As Sarah said, it's to get to know Italy. Lots of young people spend time abroad as part of their education.'

* * *

Francesco Bastigna, the trusted adviser to the seventy-eight-year-old Prime Minister of Italy, Giuseppe Saracco, entered the Legato and Company's small shop in Rome's industrial quarter and made his way towards the office at the back. The large man standing guard nodded in recognition and knocked on the door, then opened it and announced quietly, 'Your expected visitor is here, Signor Legato.'

The large man then stood to one side to allow Bastigna to enter the office.

Rocco Legato, an elegantly dressed man in his early forties, rose from his chair behind his desk and stepped forward, his hand outstretched, and the two men shook hands.

'Welcome, Signor Bastigna,' said Legato. 'Thank you for coming here.'

'I believe it is the safer option,' said Bastigna. 'The fewer people who know about our association the better, in order to protect us and our project. That is why I have come alone. Regrettably, I can trust no one in my own offices.'

'I understand,' said Legato, gesturing Bastigna to take the chair opposite.

Bastigna sat. This was the second meeting between the two men. The first had come about after Bastigna had expressed his doubts about the Prime Minister's future to an old political friend. 'It's not just his age,' Bastigna had told his friend. 'Although people have expressed doubts as to whether a man approaching his eighties can successfully run a country as dysfunctional as Italy. We have the extreme left, the socialists, communists, republicans and radicals, causing chaos in the Chamber of Deputies. We have strike after strike across the country. The assassination of the King was just an extreme example of how chaotic this country has become. If we are not careful, another election will see Giuseppe Zanardelli and Giovanni Giolitti sweeping in with a landslide, which will be a disaster for our side. They've already forced General Pelloux out.'

His friend nodded. General Luigi Pelloux had been prime minister until he and his party had been forced out of office following a series of political and social upheavals which had led to the government being deemed unstable. The King, Umberto, had asked Saracco, who was seen as a moderate, to form a new unifying government. Unfortunately, it hadn't had the desired effect. Society was in the same chaos as before, possibly even worse. Even some of Saracco's supporters were muttering that the old man was out of his depth.

'We have to make him look electable,' said Bastigna. 'And not just by his own side, but the people as a whole. We have to get the people unified behind Saracco, and we have to do it now ahead of the election.'

'You really believe an election will be called?' asked his friend. 'Saracco has only been in power for less than two months.'

'There will be one, I am sure of it,' said Bastigna. 'The country cannot survive if things go on this way.'

His friend fell into a thoughtful silence, then said quietly, 'You may need to use unorthodox tactics.'

'I'll use any tactics, orthodox or otherwise,' said Bastigna fervently.

'In that case, it might well be worth your meeting an acquaintance of mine. He gets things done, although his methods are often unorthodox.'

And so a meeting had been arranged at his friend's house between Bastigna and Rocco Legato, a businessman who ran an olive oil export business.

'But olive oil is, shall we say, a cloak for his real business,' his friend told Bastigna. 'His real business is sorting out difficult problems. His fees are expensive, but when conventional methods fail, sometimes there is little alternative.'

At that first meeting, Legato had listened as Bastigna explained the predicament he and his political and business colleagues found themselves in.

'I understand,' said Legato. 'I will need to think this over, but I believe I may have a solution. Can I suggest we meet again. Perhaps it might be best to meet at my place of business. If any questions are raised about us meeting, it would be only right that someone like yourself would be interested in olive oil exports and the financial rewards they bring this country.'

Now, at this second meeting at the olive oil exporter's place of business, Bastigna was keen to hear about the solution Legato had come up with.

'You have given it some thought?' asked Bastigna.

'I have,' said Legato. 'And I believe I have a solution. I believe this calls for an assassination.'

CHAPTER FIVE

Friday 10th August

Daniel and Abigail were finishing dressing prior to going down to breakfast, when there was a frantic hammering at the door of their hotel room.

'Something's afoot,' observed Daniel as he strode to the door. He opened it and the portly figure of Giuseppe Saredo rushed in, looking very distressed.

'A tragedy!' he exclaimed.

'What sort of tragedy?' asked Abigail.

'Sarah and Giovanni are dead!'

'Dead?' repeated Abigail and Daniel stared at him, bewildered. 'How? What happened?'

'They were shot. The police believe that Sarah shot Giovanni, then herself.'

'Nonsense!' exploded Abigail angrily.

'I saw the bodies,' said Giuseppe. 'At the Colosseum. There was a pistol in Sarah's hand.' He gestured at the door. 'I have a carriage waiting outside to take us there.'

Inside the carriage, as it hurried along the via Cavour, Giuseppe told them what had happened. 'I arrived early at the site to make sure everything was prepared. I know your talk isn't due to begin until this afternoon, Abigail, but this is the first day of the Festival and it was too important to leave things to chance. Two of the stewards were there already, and they showed me Sarah's and Giovanni's bodies. Two police officers had already arrived – the stewards had gone to find them.

'I told the policemen that Sarah's sister would be at their flat. I gave them the address and one of them went off to find her.'

'Did you see the gunshot wounds?' asked Daniel.

'No,' said Giuseppe. 'To be honest, I was too shaken at the sight of their bodies.' He shook his head, bewildered. 'I don't understand it. What can have happened?'

When they got to the Colosseum, Daniel and Abigail hurried after Giuseppe as he made for three uniformed police officers who were talking to a young woman they recognised as Julia. 'They've removed the bodies,' Giuseppe told them. 'That's where they were when I came for you.'

'Already?' said Daniel in surprise. 'Usually the crime scene remains untouched until a proper examination has been completed.'

'The schoolchildren will be arriving shortly to do their processions,' pointed out Giuseppe. 'They obviously want to clear the area as quickly as possible. And, from what the officer told me when I was here earlier, they don't see it as a crime to investigate. Their belief is that Sarah shot Giovanni and then shot herself.'

He hurried towards where Julia was talking to the three uniformed officers. 'The tall one with all the gold braid is Inspector Volpetti,' said Giuseppe.

'What's he like?' asked Daniel.

'Useless,' groaned Giuseppe.

As they reached the small group, they saw that Julia was in great distress. She kept repeating 'This is all my fault' in Italian.

Abigail translated their Italian conversation for Daniel's benefit.

'It is not your fault, Julia,' said Giuseppe, interrupting the girl and the police officers.

'It is!' insisted Julia. 'Giovanni had been chasing me soon after I arrived in Rome. I resisted him, but a couple of days ago Sarah came in and found us in a compromising situation. It led to a furious row between Sarah and Giovanni, and later between Sarah and me. She accused me of flaunting myself to him. That must be why she shot him, and then herself. Because of me!'

The officer with the gold braid on his uniform, Inspector Volpetti, patted her shoulder sympathetically and reassured her she was not responsible.

'In that case, can I go?' asked Julia. 'I can't stay here, where it happened. I must go home.'

'Of course,' said Volpetti.

'We shall go with you,' said Giuseppe.

'No,' said Julia. 'I have to be alone.'

'It's not a good time to be alone,' said Abigail. 'Please, let me accompany you.'

'No,' snapped Julia. 'I want to be alone!'

With that, she almost ran from the spot.

'She is understandably very distressed,' said Volpetti. He looked at Giuseppe. 'Signor Saredo, I believe you were the one who discovered the bodies.'

'No, two of my stewards were the ones who found them. One of them had gone to find a police officer while the other kept guard. Then I arrived and discovered the tragedy. I left to tell the couple's English friends.' He gestured at Daniel and Abigail. 'Mr and Mrs Wilson. Mrs Wilson is a famous archaeologist who is giving a talk at the Festival.'

'But you saw the bodies, Signor Saredo?'

'I did.'

'The woman had a pistol in her hand?'

'She did.'

'Then what we have just heard from Miss Julia Winstanley confirms what happened. The woman shot her husband, and then herself.'

With that, Volpetti and the two uniformed officers walked off.

'Did she really say that Giovanni was pursuing her?' asked Daniel, surprised.

'Yes,' said Abigail curtly. 'And I don't believe it.'

'But why should she lie?'

'Who knows,' said Abigail.

'I telegraphed Paolo before I came to get you,' said Giuseppe. 'Knowing Paolo, he'll get here as soon as he can.' He shook his head, worn down by the tragedy. 'I can't believe it! Sarah and Giovanni were a perfect couple. They were devoted to one another. There were never any rumours of affairs or either of them being involved with other people. That's why I find it hard to believe this story of Julia's.'

'You and me both,' said Abigail grimly.

Giuseppe looked at them, helplessness on his face. 'I ought to go to the Forum to adjust the programme. Giovanni was due to give a talk tomorrow, but I can't face it at the moment. It's all too much of a shock.' He looked at Abigail and Daniel and asked, 'You are famous for being the Museum Detectives. If Volpetti refuses to investigate their deaths, can you look into this and find out what happened?'

'Us?' said Abigail in surprise. 'Surely that's for the police.'

Giuseppe shook his head. 'You heard what Volpetti said. The police have already made their minds up. Sarah shot Giovanni and then killed herself. There'll be no investigation.'

'But that's just an allegation because of the story that Julia told,' said Abigail. 'Surely they won't just accept it at face value without looking into it.'

'I know Inspector Volpetti. He's the laziest person there is. He'll always find a way to do as little work as possible. He accepts Julia's story because it's easy. But you knew Sarah and Giovanni. Like me, you also have your suspicions about Julia. Please! Sarah did not kill Giovanni. Someone else did it, and we need to find out who.'

'But we're only here for the duration of the Festival, then we return to England,' pointed out Abigail.

'Please!' appealed Giuseppe again. 'I know you have your talk to concentrate on at this moment, but afterwards, at least, please think about it.' He became aware of large groups of children entering the area, accompanied by their teachers and other adults.

'Here are the schoolchildren,' he said. 'I must go and meet them and the priest who'll be doing the blessing. This is a dreadful start to what should have been a truly memorable occasion.'

As Giuseppe hurried off, Daniel turned to Abigail and

asked, 'What do you want to do? Do you want to watch these processions and the blessing, or whatever?'

'No,' said Abigail sadly. 'I'm still in shock at what's happened. Sarah and Giovanni shot dead! I can't believe it.'

'Perhaps we could go to wherever they've taken the bodies and see if we can look at them. See if the wounds fit with what the inspector maintains, especially about Sarah shooting herself.'

'You're thinking of doing what Giuseppe asked and investigating their deaths,' said Abigail.

'It's what we do,' pointed out Daniel.

Abigail looked doubtful. 'Things are done differently here,' she said. 'I'm not sure if the Italian police will be keen on us looking into it.'

'It hasn't stopped us before,' said Daniel. 'Look at the obstructions we've faced from Superintendent Armstrong at Scotland Yard.' He looked towards the children assembling in the middle of the sandy arena. 'The crime scene will be a mess, but it's worth trying to see if we can look at the bodies.'

'Yes,' said Abigail. 'It will give us something positive to do.'

CHAPTER SIX

The first task for Daniel and Abigail was to find out where Sarah and Giovanni's bodies had been taken. They found the local police station and asked for Inspector Volpetti but were informed he was out. When they asked where the bodies of the two victims murdered at the Colosseum that morning had been taken, they were met with a stonewall of bureaucracy: such official information was only available to the next of kin. It was only as the result of extreme pressure from Abigail, insisting she was the official representative for Sarah Maduro's father in England, Brigadier Winstanley, and she needed to pass the information to him, that she was told with great reluctance that the bodies had been taken to the hospital at Isola Tiberena. However, there was even more of a bureaucratic stonewall at the hospital, where despite Abigail's assertions that she was the representative of the next of kin of Sarah Maduro, the hospital authorities resolutely stuck to the line that only the actual next of kin was permitted to view the bodies, and then only once proof of kinship had been produced.

'We need Julia,' said Daniel as they left the hospital.

'She will not help us,' said Abigail.

'It's worth trying,' said Daniel. 'Do you know where their flat is? We can at least ask her.'

'Yes, I know their address because Sarah and I corresponded. It's near the Spanish Steps.' She patted her handbag. 'Luckily, I brought a map of Rome with me.'

Daniel followed Abigail, who walked confidently through the streets as if she knew her way around, just as she had done when they were in Paris. Daniel was impressed, considering how many years it had been since she'd lived in the city. When they reached the Spanish Steps, Daniel saw why they were so well known. It was a series of very wide steps going upwards for some distance, and a large number of people – mainly young – were using them to sit on.

'Is this some kind of meeting place?' asked Daniel.

'It is, unofficially,' said Abigail. 'Many artists live in this area, and a lot of these young people are here to literally show off in the hope they will be picked to model for them.'

'It all sounds a bit precarious,' commented Daniel.

'It is,' agreed Abigail. 'Only one or two will be lucky to be chosen; the rest just hang about and are targets for predators of all sorts.' She pointed to a pair of tall three-storey buildings attached together at one side of the steps.

'That's where John Keats lived and died,' she said.

'John Keats? The English poet?'

'The very same. He had a couple of rooms on the second floor. He had tuberculosis and his doctor advised a change of climate, so he came to Rome. That was in November 1820. Sadly, it didn't help him. He died in February 1821. The traditional way of dealing with any property where there'd been tuberculosis was to scrape the walls and burn everything in the place, and that's what they did.

'I believe some American is trying to raise funds to buy the house and turn it into a museum celebrating Keats. Whether that will happen is another matter.'

She turned away from the Spanish Steps and Daniel followed her a short distance to a narrow street, which she turned into. After a few yards she stopped at a house. She checked the numbers on the wall by the doors.

'This is it,' she said.

She knocked. They waited. There was no answer. Abigail knocked again, louder this time. Still no response from inside.

'Either she's out, or she's hiding from us,' said Daniel. He looked at his watch. 'Anyway, I think we ought to get back to the Colosseum. You don't want to be late for your session.'

When they got back to the Colosseum the event with the schoolchildren had ended, and the children and the audience were vacating the area. Giuseppe was heavily engaged in conversation with the priest who'd carried out the blessing, and some of the teachers.

'He's making sure they're all happy,' commented Daniel. 'He'd make a good politician. Do you want to get something to eat before you start your session?'

Abigail shook her head. 'No. To be honest, after what's happened to Sarah and Giovanni, and not knowing what's to come this afternoon, I couldn't face food. Later, after it's all over. Then I'll feel more up to it. But you go and get something.'

'No,' said Daniel. 'After the running around we've done, I just want to sit and recover. But it's a pity about those tunnels.

I was quite looking forward to going down below and seeing what they're like.'

'There'll be plenty of time for us to do that later, and without attracting attention. When the crowds are at the Forum, for example. Or possibly on Sunday. As you pointed out, nothing's happening on Sunday.'

Inspector Volpetti looked up at the knock on his office door.

'Enter!' he called.

The door opened and Sergeant Lorenzo Capaldi entered, marched to the inspector's desk, stood to attention and saluted smartly.

'You sent for me, sir?'

'I did,' said Volpetti. He looked on his best sergeant with pride. Capaldi had been with Inspector Volpetti's squad for four years. Honest, trustworthy and a firm disciplinarian with the officers under him, Capaldi was indeed a police officer to be proud of and an asset to his squad. With one of the best arrest records in the city, he had helped make this district one of the safest in Rome.

'You heard of the double killing at the Colosseum?' Volpetti asked.

'I did, sir.'

'There's another matter connected with it that I would like looked into. Two English private detectives, a man and a woman, are here and they seem very interested in the case. Very interested. Their names are Mr Daniel and Mrs Abigail Wilson. They are here because Mrs Wilson is also a famous archaeologist, and she is giving some talks at the Colosseum as part of this Classical Rome Festival. It seems she was here on an archaeological dig at the Colosseum some fifteen years ago, working alongside Sarah Maduro, the woman who was shot. Sarah Maduro was English and her former name was Sarah Winstanley.'

'Yes, sir,' nodded Capaldi.

'My concern is that this English couple may interfere with our official investigation. Ideally, I would like to ban them from looking into the case, but that is impossible. Mrs Wilson has a friendship with Giuseppe Saredo, the organiser of the Festival, and she is – as I have said – a famous archaeologist. Her presence here is seen as important to Rome. So, I would like their movements observed and reported on. Discreetly, of course. This is a job for one of your most reliable constables. I would like you to arrange it.'

'Yes, sir. That will be arranged immediately. I would recommend Constable Nuno for the job. He is an efficient officer, and also discreet. I will tell him for this he is to leave aside his uniform and wear plain clothes, if you agree.'

'I do,' said Volpetti. 'I leave it in your capable hands. One more thing – if the couple separate at any time, Constable Nuno is to concentrate on following the woman. Thank you, Sergeant.'

As Lorenzo Capaldi left the inspector's office, his mind was a whirl of thoughts. He'd heard about the killings at the Colosseum but had not been involved in any part of the investigation. What made this English couple so special? And particularly the woman, this Mrs Abigail Wilson?

While Abigail did her talk-cum-guided tour of the Colosseum with a group of attendees, Daniel elected to sit in one of the seats that edged the arena and watch from a distance. Ordinarily, when Abigail gave a talk, he attended, even if it was in a language he didn't understand, such as the time she'd given one in French at the Louvre on her expedition to Egypt. But in this case, it was a mobile session, the crowd following Abigail from place to place, with much talk in Italian, including Abigail giving directions, and Daniel didn't want to cause unnecessary confusion. Instead he sat and watched in admiration as she pointed out various parts of the giant stadium to her group and gave a history of each. He waited until she was finished and approaching him, before he rose to his feet.

'You are wonderful,' he complimented her. 'Considering what you've been through today – after all, Sarah was your friend – you've been nothing short of magnificent.'

'I certainly don't feel it,' she said. 'All I want to do is get to our hotel and collapse in a heap. And then, in an hour or so, I should be able to eat something.'

'The hotel it is,' said Daniel. 'And, for once, we'll take a carriage.'

CHAPTER SEVEN

Saturday 11th August

After a night's sleep, Abigail felt better able to face the world.

'At least I haven't got to do a session today,' she said.

They went down to breakfast, and as they were finishing Giuseppe arrived, accompanied by a young man he introduced as Paolo.

'He's just arrived from Milan,' he told them.

'I recognise you,' smiled Abigail. 'Although the last time I saw you, you were only nine years old.'

'I remember you,' said Paolo. 'The famous Abigail Fenton, that's what my mother and father said about you. The famous archaeologist. You were on your way to Egypt.'

'I was,' said Abigail. 'Now I'm here for this festival Giuseppe is organising. And I'm Abigail Wilson now. This is my husband, Daniel.'

Paolo and Daniel shook hands.

'I'm afraid I don't speak Italian very well,' apologised Daniel.

'That's no problem,' said Paolo in English. 'My mother spoke English at home as well as Italian so my sister and I would have both languages.'

'We're both so very sorry about what's happened,' said Abigail.

'Giuseppe told me what the police believe. That my mother shot my father and then killed herself because of what my mother's sister alleges.' He looked at them with disgust. 'It is lies. All lies.'

'I agree,' said Abigail. 'And so does Giuseppe. What did you make of your mother's sister, Julia?'

'I never really knew her. She arrived to stay with them the day before I left for Milan. I left the next morning. She was still in her room, so I never really saw her.'

'Did your mother or father write to tell you about her?'

'They wrote, but they never mentioned her.' His face took on a grim expression as he said, 'But now I need to talk to her. Is she still at our place?'

'I assume so,' said Giuseppe. 'I'm guessing that's where she went when the police said she could go.'

'Then that's where I'm going,' said Paolo.

'We'll come with you,' said Abigail. 'We'll just finish our coffees.'

Daniel understood immediately: Abigail was concerned that Paolo would get into a big row with Julia, which might turn violent.

Coffees finished, Abigail, Daniel, Paolo and Giuseppe made their way into the street.

'I have to get to the Forum,' said Giuseppe. 'I shall be doing Giovanni's talk about it. I know what he was planning to say, because we used to discuss it.'

'That's no problem,' said Abigail. 'We'll go with Paolo.'

While Giuseppe left for the Forum, Daniel and Abigail stood on the pavement beside Paolo.

'On foot, or shall we get a carriage?' asked Abigail.

'On foot,' answered Paolo firmly. 'I like to walk everywhere, providing it's within distance. And some of the cab drivers double their prices as soon as they hear an English accent.'

Paolo walked at a fast pace, and they could see from the grim expression on his face that he was dead set on confronting his English aunt. Daniel shot a warning look to Abigail, and she nodded and made sure she kept up with Paolo. Just like the previous day, they found themselves close to the Spanish Steps, then heading down the nearby narrow street towards the flat. When they got to the house, Paolo took his key from his pocket and unlocked the front door. He was about to walk in, but Abigail beat him to it, calling out, 'Julia! It's Abigail!'

There was no answer.

'I expect she's hiding,' muttered Paolo darkly, and he hurried upstairs with Abigail and Daniel close behind him. He burst into one of the rooms without knocking, then stopped.

'She's not here,' he said.

'Perhaps she's gone out,' said Abigail.

Paolo stood surveying the small bedroom, then he strode to the wardrobe and pulled it open.

'Her luggage has gone,' he announced.

Daniel and Abigail gathered around him, puzzled. He pointed at the empty wardrobe. 'She had a bag with her, one of those big decorated cloth bags. It had her clothes in. She's gone.'

'But to where?' asked Abigail.

'And why?' added Daniel.

'Perhaps the police suggested she move from here. If so, there's one way to find out,' said Abigail. 'The inspector in charge of the case is Inspector Volpetti. He spoke to Julia at the Colosseum. Do you know him?'

'I've heard his name but I've never met him. Ma and Pa used to talk about him whenever anything happened at the Forum and the police were called. They said he was an idiot.'

'Yes, Giuseppe gave us the same impression,' said Daniel.

A short while later they were entering a large building signposted with the words 'Polizia di Stato', not far from the Colosseum. Paolo and Daniel proposed that Abigail be the one to make the enquiries because she had a good command of Italian, and her manner had authority stamped all over it.

'We are here to see Inspector Volpetti,' Abigail announced. She gave their names, then added, 'It's very urgent.' The tone of her voice sent the officer hurrying to a door just around the corner of a corridor. They heard a knock at the door, a gabble of voices in rapid Italian, and then the figure of Inspector Volpetti appeared.

'We have come to talk to you about the Maduro killings investigation,' said Abigail.

'There is no investigation,' said Volpetti. 'We know what happened: she shot him, then herself. We have the evidence of Signora Maduro's sister.'

'It's about her sister we've come to see you. Have you moved her from their flat?'

Volpetti looked at her, puzzled. 'No. Why would we do that?'

'In that case, she's vanished,' said Abigail.

'Vanished?'

Abigail gestured at Paolo. 'This is Paolo, the Maduros' son.

He's come from Milan after he heard what had happened to his parents. He wanted to talk to Julia, so we went to their flat, but she wasn't there.'

'I expect she'd just gone out for a moment,' said Volpetti.

Abigail shook her head. 'The luggage she'd brought with her had gone.'

Volpetti thought this over, then announced, 'I expect she couldn't cope with staying here any longer after what had happened. I don't doubt she has returned to England.'

'At such short notice? Without telling anyone? Surely she would have felt it right to inform the police of what she was doing?'

'Why?' asked Volpetti. 'As I say, there is no investigation. She is free to go wherever she wants.'

'So you're not going to look for her?' asked Abigail.

'No,' said Volpetti. 'We have enough work to keep us busy without chasing off looking for young English women who may have decided to return home.'

'But say she hasn't?' demanded Paolo angrily.

Volpetti shrugged. 'That is up to her. She's committed no offence.'

'Won't you at least check at the Termini to see if she caught a train?' asked Abigail.

'No,' said Volpetti. 'If she has decided to leave, that's up to her.'

'This is unbelievable,' muttered Abigail as they left the police station.

'Giuseppe said to us he is the laziest person ever,' Daniel reminded her.

'But it's obvious she's run away,' said Abigail. 'We all agree her story about Giovanni chasing her is nonsense. So, she's hiding something. Something about the murder. We need to find her and get her to tell us what it is.'

'Search Rome for some teenage English girl who speaks Italian?' said Paolo scornfully. 'Impossible!'

'There may be a way,' said Abigail thoughtfully. 'Giuseppe seems to know a lot of people. It wouldn't surprise me to find that some of them are policemen, and hopefully ones who aren't as lazy as Inspector Volpetti. There was a photograph of Julia with your mother on a sideboard at your place. We'll ask Giuseppe if he can get copies of it made and for people he knows to show it around. If she's still in Rome, she must be somewhere, and she'll need to go out to eat or buy food.'

'Unless, as the inspector said, she's left for England,' said Daniel.

'In that case, we'll take the photo first of all to the Termini station and show it around, and ask if anyone saw her buying a ticket, or getting on a train.'

'Right,' said Daniel. 'So, it's back to the flat and get the photograph.'

CHAPTER EIGHT

In the 1850s, two friends left Sicily for mainland Italy and arrived in Rome. Federico Alessio and Luca Casimiro, both in their twenties, had been close friends since early childhood. Both were considered trouble by some in the part of Sicily where they lived, but not by everyone. Their families looked after and protected them. Until, that is, a fight involving Federico led to Bartelo Sciacci – the son of the most important local landowner, Benedetto Sciacci – dying.

'It wasn't my fault,' protested Federico. 'His skull must have been as thin as an eggshell.'

But whether that was true or not, it was decided by both families that the two young men had to leave the island. It was expected that members of the Sciacci family would follow them to Italy to exact retribution. But it was felt that Federico and Luca had more chance of survival in a big city like Rome, where the landowner's family would also be strangers. As an added precaution it was decided the young men should change their surnames, so Federico Alessio became Federico Legato and Luca Casimiro became Luca Capaldi.

So the two young men came to Rome, and settled in

a district known as Palatine Hill. As was their habit, they continued in the same line of business they'd been involved with in Sicily, which involved obtaining money by any means possible, often including exerting pressure on certain individuals. It was Federico who selected their targets; he had a nose for vulnerability. As time went by, they gathered a small gang of like-minded young men around them. It was acknowledged by the gang that Federico was the leader and Luca his fierce and trusted lieutenant. As the years passed both men grew to middle age, married and became prosperous and feared. Both had sons who followed them into the family business, learning everything from both Federico and Luca: how to make money, how to keep it and how to defend their territory. They described themselves as belonging to the Cosa Nostra, an organisation to which many of their male relatives had belonged in Sicily. In criminal terms, they were very successful. But by the 1870s, when both men were in their late forties, Federico felt a change was needed if their business was to flourish safely, and he outlined his plan to Luca, who agreed. In turn the two men summoned their sons, Rocco and Lorenzo, both now in their twenties.

'We feel,' Federico told them, 'that we will be more successful if one of you joins the police force.'

The two sons looked at him as if he'd gone mad.

'The police?' repeated Rocco, stunned.

Federico looked at Lorenzo. 'It needs to be you,' he said.

'But why?' asked Rocco, taking the lead just as his grandfather and father had done. Lorenzo nodded in agreement.

'Because if Lorenzo is in the police and he rises to a good

position, it will mean we will know what is going on within the force. Inside intelligence is vital, more so than ever. Lorenzo will be in a position to alert us if any parts of our operations are in danger.'

'But how can I rise to a good position?' asked Lorenzo. 'The police will be aware of who I am. They may even stop me from joining.'

'We have very good contacts within the elected local committee,' Federico assured him. 'You will not be prevented from joining.'

'But how do you think I will rise within the police? They will be suspicious of me.'

'Not if you are very successful at making arrests.'

'But who am I to arrest? Our own people?'

'No,' said Federico. He gestured towards Luca. 'I will let your father explain.'

'There are plenty of petty criminals who are nothing to do with us,' said Luca. 'In fact, they are a nuisance to us and our activities. We will give you their names. Once you have been made a constable, you can start by arresting one or two of them and making sure they are charged. The more of these petty criminals you can remove from the streets, the greater your reputation will be inside the police force, and the easier it will be for us to operate without them getting in the way.'

Rocco thought this over, then he said, 'It is a good plan. If Lorenzo agrees.'

Lorenzo also thought it over, then nodded. 'It is a good plan,' he said. 'If you can get me into the police force, I shall make sure I rise up through the ranks.'

And so it was done. Within two years of Lorenzo becoming

a constable, his arrest rate had made him a hero in the eyes of the police board, and he was promoted to sergeant.

'Sergeant is good,' Luca and Federico told him. 'You do not want to rise any further. Higher than sergeant, you will be subject to greater scrutiny.'

And so, with guidance from his grandfather and father, Rocco Legato built on the group's successes and the Celian Hill Cosa Nostra became one of the most powerful in Rome – not least because of the inside information they received from Police Sergeant Lorenzo Capaldi, who had one of the best arrest records in the city. His superiors often recommended him for higher promotion, but he tactfully told them he preferred remaining a sergeant. 'It keeps me in touch with the ordinary constables,' he said, 'and I can keep an eye on them.'

The two older men, Federico and Luca, faded into the background, happy to let Rocco and Lorenzo run things, assured they were in good hands.

CHAPTER NINE

Fortunately, Paolo knew some of the people who worked at the Termini, including a couple in the ticket office and some of the porters. They showed the photograph of Julia around, but everyone Paolo spoke to told them there had been no sight of this woman at the station.

'So, she's still somewhere in Rome,' said Daniel.

'In that case, we need to get this photograph of her to Giuseppe,' said Abigail.

'Before we do that, I need to see my parents' bodies,' said Paolo. 'This is why I came here, to pay my respects to them.'

'Of course,' said Abigail. 'My apologies, Paolo. We were told which hospital they'd been taken to and we tried to see them yesterday, but we were told only next of kin were permitted. So you should be all right.'

'Not necessarily,' said Paolo ruefully. 'I know how difficult the people in these hospitals can be. They will demand proof that these are my parents before they let me in. How can I do that?'

'Giuseppe,' suggested Daniel. 'He seems to know everything. Let's go to the Forum and ask him.'

'He might be in the middle of his talk,' said Abigail.

'Even if he is, I get the impression he won't mind being interrupted for a few seconds,' said Daniel.

'That's true,' said Abigail.

They made their way to the Forum, where they found Giuseppe delivering his talk very animatedly to a rapt audience who followed him as he moved from ruined section to ruined section, explaining the meaning and importance of each.

'We're very sorry to trouble you, Giuseppe,' apologised Abigail. 'Paolo is here to pay his respects to his parents, but there are problems with him being allowed in. When we went to the hospital where they are yesterday, we were refused entry. Paolo's concerned because they might not believe he's really next of kin.'

'Of course,' said Giuseppe. 'In fact, if you hold on a moment, I'll make arrangements for one of my assistants to take over from me while I come with you. Sometimes the staff at the mortuaries can be difficult. I know some people at the hospital mortuary who owe me favours.'

'May we come with you?' asked Abigail. 'We don't wish to intrude on your grief, Paolo, but we've decided to investigate their murders. None of us believe that your mother killed your father and then shot herself. The more information we can gather about their deaths, the better.'

'They are the famous Museum Detectives from England,' added Giuseppe.

'I know,' said Paolo. 'My mother used to read me stories about you from the English newspapers she had sent here.'

Giuseppe called one of his assistants over and asked him

to continue the session, promising he'd return as soon as he could. Then he led the way to the hospital.

Giuseppe was as good as his word. All four of them were allowed into the mortuary. The bodies of Giovanni and Sarah were on tables, each covered with a cloth. The attendant rolled the cloth down to reveal their faces. Daniel, Abigail and Giuseppe stood back to allow Paolo to bend over his parents' bodies, kiss them gently and then murmur words of farewell.

'Where did Sarah shoot herself?' Abigail murmured to Giuseppe. 'There are no wounds to her head.'

Giuseppe had a quiet word with the attendant, who nodded in understanding and replied.

'In the stomach,' Abigail translated for Daniel's benefit.

The attendant asked if they wanted to see the fatal wound. Giuseppe looked at Abigail, who shook her head when she saw the look of distress on Paolo's face. 'No,' she said. 'We'll take his word for it.' She turned to Paolo and said, 'We'll leave you alone with them now, Paolo. We'll be outside in the corridor when you're ready.'

'*Grazie*,' muttered Paolo.

'What do you think?' asked Giuseppe when he, Abigail and Daniel were in the corridor.

'It's rare for anyone committing suicide to shoot themselves in the stomach,' said Daniel. 'Usually, it's the head. Sometimes, but rarely, in the heart. But in all my years at Scotland Yard, we never had a suicide who shot themselves in the stomach.'

'The lazy and incompetent Inspector Volpetti,' grunted Giuseppe. 'And now I have to return to the Forum.'

Abigail produced the photograph of Julia with Sarah.

'Is it possible for you to get this copied?' she asked. 'We were thinking that you might have contacts who could show this around, in case anyone's seen Julia. We know she didn't catch a train anywhere, so she's still here in Rome.'

'Of course,' said Giuseppe, taking the photograph. 'I know quite a few of the local police – it'll be worth asking them. Good people. Not like that waste of space Inspector Volpetti.'

The sound of approaching footsteps made them turn, and they saw Paolo appear.

'Thank you, Giuseppe,' said Paolo. 'Without you there, I'm not sure they'd have even let me see my parents.'

'No problem at all,' Giuseppe reassured him. 'But now I have to return to the Festival and take over from my assistant. And while I'm there I'll get copies made of this photo of Julia. I'll see you tomorrow, Paolo.'

Paolo shook his head. 'I have to return to Milan today,' he said. 'If I don't work, I don't get paid. I just came to pay my respects to my parents. But, please, let me know once the date for the funeral is set, and I will return.'

'Of course,' said Giuseppe.

He and Paolo shook hands, then Giuseppe left.

'He's a good man,' said Paolo.

'He is,' said Abigail. 'We are lucky to have him on our side. As you've seen, Inspector Volpetti is no help. If we're to find out who killed your parents, we're going to need Giuseppe with his knowledge of people here in Rome, and anything going on that your parents might have been involved with. Now we've discounted the police's theory about the murder, we're starting completely from scratch.'

Paolo looked thoughtful, then he said, 'Would you mind walking with me to the railway station? I've had some thoughts, and we can talk as we walk.'

'Of course,' said Abigail.

'Absolutely,' added Daniel.

CHAPTER TEN

As they made their way to the Termini, Paolo said, 'I wonder if the killings may have been political.'

'Political?' asked Daniel.

'These are dangerous times in Italy. If they can kill the King, they can kill anyone.'

'Kill the King?' echoed Abigail, shocked.

'King Umberto,' said Paolo. 'He was shot dead. Assassinated.'

'Why?' asked Daniel.

'Do you know about the massacre of workers in Milan?' asked Paolo. 'It's known as the Bava Beccaris massacre.'

Daniel directed an enquiring look to Abigail, who shook her head apologetically.

'I'm sorry, no,' she said. 'There was nothing in the British newspapers about it. When was it? Where was it?'

'It was two years ago, in Milan.'

'Where you work. Were you there?'

'No. I only started work there at Pirelli this year, but they still talk about it. It started because of the rising food prices. Wheat prices went from 225 lire a tonne to 330 lire. Workers organised a strike against the huge rise in food prices and when the police tried to quell the demonstration, the son of a deputy from Milan was killed by police. The next day the workers at the Pirelli factory went on strike and leaflets were distributed about the police killing the young man. The ill-feeling led to more riots, and more police being called in. The government declared a state of siege in Milan. A general called Fiorenzo Bava Beccaris, a veteran of many wars, was sent to Milan with orders to quell the riots. Infantry, cavalry and artillery were sent in. I've been told Beccaris's forces had forty-five thousand men. The strikers had set up barricades in the city and Beccaris ordered his troops to remove them. Milan is the industrial heart of Italy, with motor vehicle factories and weapons manufacturers. Some of the demonstrators had got hold of rifles. It became a battle. Figures vary on how many people were killed. I've been told that four hundred were killed and two thousand wounded.

'The key people who'd organised the strike and the demonstrations were arrested and charged with sedition. Around one and a half thousand people were sent to prison.'

'So, the rioting was forcibly stopped.'

'Yes, but the anger of the people was still there. And still is. Not just in Milan but in Florence and Livorno. The anger is widespread, and news about it spread to Italians abroad. Thousands of Italians had migrated to America because of the poverty they suffered in this country, and when the migrants heard about the massacre, they were angry, too. The anger was compounded when General Beccaris was praised by the King, Umberto, for putting down the uprising and awarded a medal. A month ago, an Italian emigrant to America, a man called Gaetano Bresci, came back to Italy and assassinated the

King. Shot him. He said it was in revenge for the massacre.'

'But this massacre had happened two years before.'

'Yes, but it takes a long time for letters to get to America, and for travellers to get to Italy. The thing is, it's still a very dangerous time here in Italy, so when Papa began to get involved in agitating on behalf of the workers and the farmers, I warned him of the danger. This was before Bresci shot and killed the King, but everyone knew these were uncertain and dangerous times.'

'What happened to this Bresci?'

'He was captured and sentenced to life imprisonment.'

'Was your mother involved in Giovanni's political activity too?'

'No. She said she shared his opinions, but I think that was mainly to quieten him down about them.'

'What form did his political activity take?'

'Nothing violent in any way. He didn't join marches or demonstrations. He wrote articles for newspapers, and leaflets.'

'So his name would have been known.'

'Oh yes. He always put his name to the articles he wrote, and his letters to newspapers.'

Julia sat in the small, squalid room that *he* had found for them. *Squalid*, she thought, and her mouth twisted into a smile of satisfaction as she tossed the word around inside her head. It had been her father's favourite term of abuse, especially once she turned fifteen and he began using it to express his loathing of the people she mixed with and the places where they lived. Squalid was his term of disgust for her friend, Marion, who lived in a poor part of the town near the Hertfordshire village where former brigadier Herbert Winstanley lived with his wife and daughter. He did not approve of the poor. He especially did not approve of any poor who got into trouble with the law, as Marion had done when she was caught shoplifting. As a magistrate he was all for having Marion flogged. It was fortunate for Marion that she'd appeared in the town court before a liberal-minded magistrate, rather than in the village magistrate's court, which was Brigadier Winstanley's fiefdom.

The bad feelings between the brigadier and his daughter reached a climax of antagonism when he discovered that she was keeping company with Jason Dickens, a local rogue and poacher who was married with four young children. The brigadier barred her from having anything to do with Dickens, even going as far as locking her in her bedroom when she came home from school. When he discovered that Julia was actually truanting from school during the daytime in order to spend time with Jason, he became apoplectic. He ordered the local constable to arrest Dickens, but the constable pointed out there was no evidence to justify such an arrest.

'But he's a known poacher!' burst out the brigadier.

'We can't prove it,' said the constable. 'We have no evidence. Whoever he sells the animals he captures to are keeping quiet about it.'

'Well, get some evidence!' raged the brigadier. 'I want him flogged and put in prison!'

And, by some means as a result of pressure by the brigadier, evidence surfaced, and Jason Dickens was duly tried in the brigadier's court, found guilty, flogged and sent to prison for a year.

Julia was distraught. She raged at her father and told him

she would be going to live with Jason when he was released from prison.

'I love him!' she declared.

'He's already married with four children,' the brigadier stormed at her.

'I don't care,' said Julia. 'We don't need a marriage licence to prove our love for one another.'

'You're underage,' the brigadier had snapped. 'I won't allow it.'

'You can't stop me,' Julia had retorted. 'We'll run away together and go somewhere you can't find us.'

So it was that the brigadier took definitive action. He wrote to his older daughter, Sarah, and asked her if Julia could come to stay with her and her family in Rome. *She's got into bad company here which she needs to be away from*, he wrote. *Time spent with a responsible and respectable family like yours is what she needs.*

When Julia learnt of his plans, she flatly refused to go. But the brigadier had one major card to play. He told Julia that if she didn't, he would ensure that Jason Dickens would be transferred to another prison and subjected to hard labour, breaking rocks. He'd also use his influence to get Jason's sentence extended by another year.

'The chances are, after an extra year of that treatment, he'll be dead or crippled,' the brigadier told her.

And so Julia agreed to go to Italy to stay with her sister and Sarah's family. But in her heart, she vowed that she'd return when Jason was released from prison and the pair would run away together. All she had to do was wait.

But that was before she met *him* in Italy. Her man. The

true love of her life. When she was with *him*, she realised that what she'd felt for Jason had just been a teenage infatuation. The *man* was in a different league.

Yes, he was married, but that didn't matter. Of course, it meant that she couldn't share the story of her love for him with Sarah, or anyone else. It had to be secret.

The Man had rented this room for them. A squalid room in a poor part of the city, which had suited Julia down to the ground. She wasn't likely to run into any of Sarah's or Giovanni's friends in this place.

And then the worst had happened: Giovanni had been in the area and had seen her and The Man coming out of the house together. She and The Man had hurried away, hoping that Giovanni hadn't seen them, but it was obvious he had from a comment she overheard him making to Sarah later on.

Suddenly everything was at risk. She couldn't lose The Man! She mustn't! She'd die if that happened.

When she'd told The Man, he agreed that something had to be done. And it had been.

It had been The Man who suggested she leave the flat and move into this room. 'You need to be away from there. There will be suspicions about you. We have to avoid that, if we're going to be together.'

'When will we be together?' she'd asked, desperate for him.

'Soon,' he'd promised her. 'Very soon.'

Very soon, she told herself. *Soon we'll be together.*

After Paolo had caught his train, Daniel and Abigail discussed what Paolo had just told them, but Daniel in particular was unsure about its relevance. 'They were both shot. Sarah wasn't so vocal about politics, so why shoot her?'

'I still think it comes back to Julia,' said Abigail. 'Why did she lie about Giovanni? We need to find her.'

'Hopefully Giuseppe will do that,' said Daniel.

'Until then, we can play our part. We'll get a copy of the photo of Julia from Giuseppe when he's printed them and talk to the neighbours near their flat. Ask them if they've seen Julia with anyone. Did she have friends in the area? There must be some neighbours who noticed her. After all, she was a stranger here.'

CHAPTER ELEVEN

Sunday 12th August

Rocco Legato sat with his old friend, Lorenzo Capaldi, atop the Palatine Hill. Today there were no festival events going on, no visitors here, except for five large muscular-looking men who maintained a discreet distance, but at the same time kept a watchful eye on the two men sitting talking. Capaldi was not wearing his police uniform; they were just two middle-aged men chatting on a relaxed Sunday.

'You say Inspector Volpetti wants this English couple watched?' said Legato.

'He seems particularly interested in the woman, Mrs Wilson. She is an archaeologist.'

'Yes, I have seen the programme,' said Legato.

'She was a friend of Sarah Maduro,' added Capaldi.

'The woman who was killed at the Colosseum,' nodded Legato. 'Why does he want her watched?'

'He says he's worried that she might interfere with the official investigation into the killings. She and her husband, Daniel Wilson, have a good reputation as private detectives. They specialise in murders at museums. I'm told they recently solved a series of murders at the Louvre in Paris.' He hesitated, then said, 'I thought you needed to know, in case we have any connection with what happened at the Colosseum.'

Legato thought about his, then said, 'As far as I know, we had nothing to do with it. But perhaps we should have, now, in view of this new development. Who is this officer you've tasked with keeping watch on the Wilsons?'

'Constable Nuno. He is very efficient.'

'It will be interesting to see his report on their activities,' murmured Legato.

Capaldi nodded. 'That will be arranged.'

Julia lay in bed and watched Vito as he dressed.

'Do you have to go out?' she asked coyly, and ran her hand slowly over her body.

'Yes,' said Vito. 'I have to meet Niccolo and Matteo.'

'Again?' she asked with a look of disappointment.

He came to her, bent down and kissed her.

'What we're doing will make me famous,' he said. 'And rich.'

'Rich?' she said.

'Rich,' he repeated, and smiled.

She ran her hand slowly over her body again and whispered, 'Do you have to go just now? Will ten minutes longer be too much?'

Vito looked down at her, so desirable. He'd never known anyone who could inflame his body the way she did. He took off his jacket and undid his trousers.

'We'll make it fifteen,' he said.

Daniel and Abigail decided to go to Sarah and Giovanni's flat to see if the neighbours had any information about Julia.

As it was a Sunday, most people seemed to be out, either at church or watching the various processions that were taking place around the city centre. At each place where there was someone in, Abigail showed the copy of the photograph of Julia that Giuseppe had given them and asked – in her fluent Italian – if they'd seen this woman recently. A couple of the neighbours had seen her coming to and from the flat, but none of them had seen her with anyone other than Sarah and Giovanni.

'If Julia did have a boyfriend or a secret lover, he never came to the flat,' Abigail told Daniel when they'd finished.

'You think she did have?' asked Daniel.

'I'm sure of it,' said Abigail. 'My guess is she used to meet him somewhere away from the flat. The problem is, where?'

'And who was he? An older man, or someone her own age? Is she with him now?' He sighed. 'We're not going to get much further with our search for Julia today, I feel. Shall we go to the Colosseum, and you can show me those tunnels.'

Vito and Niccolo sat in the shade of a tree in the Lungotevere, the boulevard that ran along the banks of the River Tiber.

'Where's Matteo?' demanded Vito. 'He knows we're supposed to meet here at this time.'

Vito was the eldest of the three who made up the group of anarchists. Vito was twenty-four years old, married with two children, and worked for the Polizia Ferroviaria, the railway police who kept order at the main stations. He had been at the Termini when that interfering fool, Paolo Maduro, had turned up with the English couple the day before, showing the photograph of Julia around and asking if anyone had seen her board a train. First they'd gone to the ticket office, then they'd spoken to some of the porters. At that point Vito had intercepted them and asked them what they were doing. They told him they were looking for an English girl and had showed him Julia's photograph. He had shaken his head and told them he hadn't seen her, but assured them he would keep a watch out.

Paolo Maduro and the English couple would have to be dealt with. Things had progressed too far for their plans to change. This was why he'd called this meeting of the group, but Matteo hadn't appeared.

'He had to go to church,' said Niccolo. 'You know what his family are like.'

Yes, thought Vito, he knew what Matteo's family were like. Catholics who loved the Church more than they loved other people, like so many families. Especially here in Rome, where the Pope was seen as Christ's voice on earth.

There was the sound of running footsteps and then Matteo appeared, out of breath from running. Like Niccolo, he was in his late teens; and, like Niccolo, he revered the older Vito.

'You are late,' snapped Vito at him in irritation.

'I had to go to church,' apologised Matteo. 'I couldn't get out of it. It's the month of the Immaculate Heart of Mary and my mother insisted I go with them and my sisters.'

'There's always some festival or other,' complained Vito. 'The Sacred Heart of Jesus. The Immaculate Heart of Mary.'

'My mother would have got suspicious if I hadn't gone,' defended Matteo. 'She would have told the priest, and he would have questioned me about where I was when I should have been in church. There would have been trouble.'

'All right,' said Vito. 'But you are here now.'

'Everything is still on for Friday?' asked Matteo.

'Of course it is,' said Vito.

Friday was the day when the celebrations would be taking place at the Colosseum to celebrate the ending of the Festival. It would be the day when all the important people would be there, including the Prime Minister, Giuseppe Saracco. And it would be the day when Saracco would be shot and killed, just as King Umberto had been. And it was Vito who was supposed to do the shooting. Those were the orders from Rocco Legato, and Rocco Legato was not a man people said no to.

No reason had been given for why the Prime Minister would be shot. Vito thought it had been the assassination of King Umberto that had given Legato the idea. And although Vito had agreed to do it, as far as Vito was concerned, the main thing was that he, Vito, had to get away with it. Although there was no death penalty in Italy, anyone found guilty of killing was sentenced to life imprisonment, as had happened with the assassin who'd shot the King. Well, that wasn't going to happen to Vito – on that, Vito was absolutely determined. Let someone else take the blame. Which meant either Niccolo or Matteo. Vito hadn't decided on which of them yet. All he knew was that he'd been approached by Rocco Legato, a man he knew to be a major figure in Rome's organised crime organisation because he'd been pointed out to Vito by senior officers.

'Watch out for that one,' he'd been warned. 'He's very dangerous.'

But not to me, thought Vito. Ever since he'd joined the Polizia Ferroviaria, he'd made a point of cultivating the criminal fraternity who hung around the railway stations. At first in small ways, turning a blind eye to minor things – pickpocketing, cheating on train fares – for which he'd been rewarded with a few lire. Gradually, the crimes had become bigger, and so had the payments he received. Robberies. Assaults. And then a robbery happened that went wrong. As a passenger was leaving the station, carrying an expensive-looking briefcase, he was followed by two men. One of them had produced a thin, long-bladed knife, which he held out towards the man as he told him to hand over the briefcase. Vito had been tipped off about this robbery and promised a good amount of money if he made sure no one interfered, so he kept himself back; but he kept a discreet eye on it from a hiding place, just in case he was needed. But then it all went wrong. The man refused to hand over his briefcase, and as the two men approached him, he swung the briefcase at them, hitting the one without the knife in the face. He then turned his attention to the armed robber, rushing at him.

The robber with the knife pushed out his hand to defend himself, and the man with the briefcase ran onto the long, thin blade.

It was all over in seconds.

Vito came out from his hiding place and told the men to walk quietly and calmly away and take the briefcase with them. Once the men were well away from the station, Vito blew his police whistle, summoning his colleagues and the station staff. The story he told was that he'd come upon a fight between three men, and two ran off, leaving the third dead on the ground. The description he gave of the two men who'd got away was nothing like the two actual murdering robbers.

That evening, the two robbers turned up at Vito's house

with a paper bag containing a bundle of high-value banknotes. They told him it was from their boss in gratitude for his actions.

A few days later, Vito had another visitor, Rocco Legato, who repeated how grateful he was to Vito for what he'd done, and asked if Vito would consider taking on a task that would be worth a great deal of money to him. A great deal of money.

'We understand that you have volunteered to be one of the police guards for the Prime Minister when he comes to this festival at the Colosseum,' said Legato.

'Yes,' replied Vito. He'd volunteered because it meant more money for an easy job.

'You will be in the ideal place for this task,' said Legato. 'If you agree to undertake it, that is. It'll be up to you. If you don't want to do it, that's no problem. We have others who will be pleased to do it for the money we will be paying, but we were very impressed at the way you dealt with that business at the railway station. You did not panic. That shows clear thinking and courage.'

'What is the task?' asked Vito. 'And how much money is it worth?'

Legato smiled. 'I'll answer your second question first,' he said. And he told Vito the payment that would be due. It really was a great deal of money, more than Vito had ever seen in his life; and more than he could earn in many years as a railway policeman.

'I'm interested,' said Vito, doing his best not to show his excitement.

'The task is shooting the Prime Minister,' said Legato. When Vito did not frown or give him a look of denial at the idea, Legato continued. 'Your role as part of his police guard will be perfect. We have concocted a plan to ensure you will get away. You will need to bring in a friend, someone you can trust, and who trusts you. They will be the one who gets the blame.'

'They will deny it and say it was me,' pointed out Vito.

'Not if they are dead,' said Legato.

Then Legato had produced a large roll of banknotes, which he offered to Vito. 'If you agree, this is the advance payment. The rest will follow after the task is completed.'

Vito had taken the money.

'What is the plan?' he asked.

'Later,' said Legato. 'After you have told us who you have chosen to be in it with you. We need to check them out.'

'Of course,' said Vito.

Afterwards, Vito had told himself, *Like hell am I going to shoot the Prime Minister*. They might not execute murderers in Italy, but his life would be over if he was caught. And he would be caught – something as big as assassinating the Prime Minister would not go without an arrest. Or the death of the assassin. The truth was that Vito did not trust Rocco Legato. The problem was that he had agreed to do the job. The Cosa Nostra did not take kindly to people who agreed to do something and then reneged. A bullet in the head was the usual retribution. He should never have agreed, but faced with the powerful figure of Rocco Legato, it would have been madness to have denied him. And taking the money had been good. The question now was: how was he to get out of this without being killed? The only answer he could come up with was to involve Niccolo or Matteo, get one of them to carry out the shooting. Then shoot him. That way Vito would be seen as a hero, but the Prime Minister would be dead. Job done.

CHAPTER TWELVE

Daniel and Abigail approached the small rough entrance to the underground tunnels of the Colosseum. It had a wooden barrier across the low open doorway, and a steward stood beside the barrier guarding it. A sign in Italian hung from the barrier.

'Entry forbidden?' guessed Daniel.

'Absolutely right,' said Abigail. She said a few words to the steward, one of those she'd been introduced to by Giuseppe on the day of her talk, explaining that she would be taking her companion to view the underground space, for which she had the permission of Signor Saredo. The steward nodded and pointed to some oil lamps on the ground beside the doorway. Abigail thanked him up and picked up two, one of which she handed to Daniel.

'We're going to need these,' she said.

They lit the lamps, then stepped through the low doorway and found a steep staircase going down.

'Be careful,' warned Abigail. 'There's been very little repair work done to the underground section.'

'Perhaps it's a good thing Giuseppe cautioned against taking crowds of people down here,' said Daniel.

'On reflection, I think you're right,' admitted Abigail. 'It's been fifteen years since I was last here and some excavation work had started, but it looks like not much has been done since then.'

She led the way down the long flight of stone steps that ended in a high-ceilinged corridor made of huge blocks of stone.

'This underground area is called the hypogeum,' explained Abigail. 'Not just this corridor, but the whole underground complex. This is just one of many corridors that goes beneath the arena. They criss-cross, like road junctions. When we were excavating here, most of our work was done above ground – the rows of seating and the actual arena – but for me this was the most fascinating part. This was where the gladiators waited before being sent into the arena. And the wild animals many of them would be fighting: lions, tigers, bears. There were also elephants and giraffes, which is why the ceilings are so high.'

'They fought giraffes and elephants?' said Daniel, surprised.

'The elephants and giraffes were hunted around the arena and badly wounded before being killed. The other wild animals were kept starved so that when they entered the arena, they would tear their victims apart. And their victims weren't always gladiators – many were prisoners who'd been put into the arena to be torn to pieces and eaten for the delight of the spectators.'

'I thought the ancient Romans were supposed to be civilised,' said Daniel.

'They believed they were,' said Abigail. 'Just because their senators debated at the Forum, but in truth they were the most bloodthirsty of people. Especially the emperors. The emperor Diocletian had seventeen thousand slaughtered in one month alone.'

Abigail pointed to where a thick round piece of wood had collapsed in the tunnel, then she pointed upwards.

'You can just see where there was a trapdoor in the ceiling. That opened in the arena. That piece of wood there would have been part of the mechanics to bring the animals up and through the trapdoor into the arena. The animals would be in cages on a platform. It was a clever system, using pulleys and winches, and also water for some of the larger animals.'

'Water?'

'Hydraulics,' said Abigail. 'Water power to lift the platform. They used the platforms and hoists to bring the gladiators up, too. The trapdoors were located all over the arena, so that the audience didn't know where the next combatants were coming from. They loved the element of surprise. It all added to the drama.'

'You almost sound as if you approve of what happened here,' said Daniel disapprovingly. 'It was bloodthirsty, sadistic, appalling.'

'All of those things,' agreed Abigail. 'But you have to admire the technology, the ingenuity of the mechanical workings.'

'Perhaps, but I don't admire what it was used for.' He looked ahead to where it seemed that part of the stone wall at one side had collapsed. 'How much further can we go?' he asked.

'I think we ought to stop here,' said Abigail. 'I was curious to see how much work had been done since I was here last. The truth is not a lot, but a proper excavation of the whole tunnel system, the hypogeum, will take an awful lot of money, which Italy doesn't have right now. But at least you get an idea of what it's like underneath the arena.'

As they made their way back along the corridor, Abigail

pointed out various doors. 'These rooms are where the gladiators waited to go into the arena.'

'Fully aware they were likely to die,' grunted Daniel.

'Most of them would have died anyway. Gladiators were drawn from slaves, prisoners of war, condemned criminals. This way they did have a chance.'

'Not much of one against wild animals.'

'They did have a chance if they were fighting one against one. The Romans did their best to make the contests equal. Different gladiatorial styles were given different weapons. The secutor was heavily armoured, including a protective helmet. The retiarius wore armour only on his left arm, and used a net, a trident and a dagger against his opponent. Enemy soldiers who'd been captured by the Romans – and you have to remember that the Roman state was in a constant war with various enemy nations – were given the opportunity of becoming gladiators. It was supposed to give them a chance to redeem their honour. The other choice was death. Interestingly, there were some women gladiators.'

'Women?' said Daniel, surprised.

'Not many, but they are mentioned in some of the historical documents I've seen, where women were pitched against other women, armed with swords and spears. Usually, again, they were prisoners taken during the various wars the Romans fought.'

They reached the long staircase they'd come into the underground tunnels by, and began to climb.

'Fascinating, isn't it,' said Abigail.

'Hideous,' said Daniel.

'True,' said Abigail. 'But then that's the reality of history.'

* * *

Niccolo and Matteo listened intently as Vito outlined how the assassination of the Prime Minister was to happen.

'We will wait until the celebration is over and the dignitaries are leaving. We will find a way to get the Prime Minister on his own, and then we will shoot him. I will have my gun and one of you will also have one.'

'Neither of us own a gun,' pointed out Matteo.

'I will bring along a spare,' said Vito. 'I will sign one out from the police station. Which of you wants to do it?'

Matteo looked troubled at this and lowered his face, unable to look Vito in the eyes.

'I will!' announced Niccolo.

'You are having doubts, Matteo?' asked Vito.

'No,' said Matteo quickly. 'But I have never fired a gun. I worry I might get it wrong.'

'I've fired a gun,' said Niccolo proudly. 'It was at a sideshow at a fair. I won a prize.'

Vito nodded. 'There is nothing to fear,' said Vito. 'There is no death penalty. Because you are young you won't go to prison. Only I will go to prison, but I will do that because I will be a martyr for Italy's freedom.'

And because I will have a great deal of money hidden away, Vito thought, but he did not tell the other two about being paid. That was his secret. As was his plan for Niccolo to take the blame, while he, Vito, would be a hero. It was fortunate that both boys were idealistic fools. They'd believed all the claptrap that had been spoken about Italy's freedom.

As Niccolo walked home, it struck him that Vito had really meant what he said, about shooting the Prime Minister. Why?

Vito had never explained why it was so important, just that it was needed 'for Italy'. At first Niccolo had thought it was Vito being deliberately provocative, saying outrageous things just to shock, but he now realised that Vito it was serious. And it would happen this Friday, at the big celebration to mark the ending of the Classical Rome Festival, which the Prime Minister, Giuseppe Saracco, would be attending.

I cannot let Vito do this, thought Niccolo. *But how do I stop him? If I try to talk him out of it, he will just get angry with me. But if I do nothing, the Prime Minister will die and I will be partly to blame because I knew it was going to happen, but I did nothing to stop it.*

If only there was someone he could tell.

And then it struck him: Sergeant Capaldi. Everyone knew Sergeant Capaldi. He was a good, friendly local police officer, with a great record for arresting villains. And he did it peacefully. And he was also detailed to be part of the local police force who would be guarding the Prime Minister on the final day of the Festival; he'd proudly made a point of letting local people know. Sergeant Capaldi could stop Vito, and in a peaceful way. And once it was done, Niccolo would let his family know that he'd been the one who'd saved the life of the Prime Minister. That would stop them telling him he was useless.

Vito stood in the room in a daze and looked down at Julia's body lying on the floor, the cord with which she'd been killed still around her neck. Who had done this? He'd only been out for two hours at the most. In that time someone had come into this room and strangled her. Who? And why?

He'd warned her about keeping the door secure, but she

had this habit of leaving it unlocked. 'I want you to be able to wander in whenever you come round,' she'd told him. 'Because I'll always be ready for you.'

And she always had been. His eyes filled with tears as he remembered their time together, which had been brief but the most passionate he'd ever known. She had unleashed feelings in him he'd never known he had. There'd been other women before, too many of them perhaps, but they'd been disposable sideshows that had helped to keep his marriage afloat. Until Julia entered his life. He'd never known the real ecstasy of love-making before her, her body tearing at him like a rapacious demon, ripping his emotions to pieces. And now, she was gone. Dead.

After the feeling of black despair came the overwhelming need for self-preservation. He had to get rid of her body. It mustn't be discovered here – that would bring the inquiry to him, and there'd be no way for him to talk himself out of this. She was dressed, which mean she'd possibly been thinking of going out. Had she gone out and met someone and brought them back to this room? Maybe? She had an insatiable appetite.

A lump came into his throat, and more tears to his eyes, as he began to roll Julia's body up in the rug. He wouldn't be able to carry her far, but it would be enough that she was gone from here.

CHAPTER THIRTEEN

When Matteo got home, he found his angry mother waiting for him.

'Where have you been?' she demanded.

'With Niccolo and Vito,' he said.

'You should have been at the church.'

'I was at the church,' protested Matteo. 'You saw me. I was with you and Papa and Marissa.'

'And then you sneaked off.'

'I did not sneak off. The service had ended so I left.'

'I promised Father Borelli you'd help gather up the missals, but when I looked for you, you'd gone to join your loutish friends.'

'They're not loutish,' said Matteo defensively. 'Vito is a policeman with the railway police.'

'And he cheats on his wife. Everyone knows that. He is despicable. And as for that Niccolo . . .'

'What's wrong with Niccolo?'

'What does he do? He doesn't work.'

'He helps his uncle at his clothes shop.'

'That's not a proper job.'

'He wants to start his own business.'

'Doing what?'

'Selling clothes from a stall at the market. He's learning the trade from his uncle. He says he can make good money at it.'

'And when will you make good money?' demanded his mother.

'Signor Tortelli has promised me a raise,' said Matteo.

Matteo worked for Luigi Tortelli, who owned a general store. Matteo delivered newspapers, kept the stock room tidy, and did whatever else Signor Tortelli wanted him to do.

His mother shook her head.

'You and Niccolo and Vito are just useless. You hang about in the park, wasting time, doing nothing.'

'We are doing something,' said Matteo. 'We are talking about what we're going to do with our lives. To make them better.'

'Talk is all you can do,' snapped his mother. 'Talk is cheap. Which is what you and your friends are. Cheap and useless.'

Maria Rossellini was doing what she did every Sunday. While others spent their time going to church, or taking part in church processions, Maria walked through the narrow alleyways at the back of the Campo de' Fiori, the main market, her eyes on the ground for any fallen fruit or vegetables. Some of it was rotten, but plenty of what she found was only slightly damaged, with bits that could be cut out. When it was cooked or sliced up, no one would notice. With seven children to feed she had little choice other than to forage, especially with a husband who earned very little. It wasn't his fault, Tomasso did his best, but with things the way they were, with workers being laid off, and prices rising all the time, they were lucky they had a roof over their heads. Her heart gave a leap as she saw three oranges lying close to a doorway. They'd obviously fallen unnoticed from a cart as the stallholder pushed it along this alley on his way home from the market. She moved forward and snatched them up, fearful that someone else might come along and take them. It was only then that she became aware of the women's clothes spilling out from a rolled-up rug propped up in the doorway in an untidy heap. This was treasure indeed! The material looked good – it could be cut down and turned into clothes for both her girls and her boys. As she began to sort through it, she became aware that this wasn't just clothes; there was something solid beneath them. She peeled back the top layer, and saw the head of a young woman. Her first thought was that she was asleep, possibly drunk, but when she looked closer, she saw that she was dead.

CHAPTER FOURTEEN

Monday 13th August

Vito, resplendent in his railway police uniform, sat in the cosy office at the back of the olive oil exporter's, Legato and Company. It was Rocco Legato's front, justifying his obvious wealth, but it was also a successful company in its own right.

'You have chosen the one who will be with you?' asked Legato.

'I have,' said Vito. 'It is my friend Niccolo.'

Although he was doing his best to appear self-controlled and calm, Vito could not get the image of Julia lying dead on the floor of the room out of his head. He did his best to force the memory away; he could not afford to show how badly he'd been affected by her death in front of Rocco Legato. He needed Legato to trust him.

'Why him and not the other, Matteo?'

'Matteo is too close to his very religious family. Especially his mother. If his mother asked him to do something on the day, he might well do that. Niccolo is eager to please.'

'Good,' said Legato. 'This is the plan. One of my people will be with you. His name is Lorenzo and he is a police sergeant. He will be part of the official guard to protect the

Prime Minister. Your friend, Niccolo, will be standing with the crowd of onlookers. At some point Lorenzo will tell you to summon Niccolo to you. He will appear to whisper something to you. Can he do that?'

'He can,' said Vito. 'He will.'

'You, in your turn, will appear to whisper to Lorenzo. Lorenzo will approach the Prime Minister and inform him that, for security reasons, he needs to be escorted to a waiting vehicle. You, Lorenzo and Niccolo will then escort the Prime Minister towards where a carriage will be waiting. Lorenzo will hand you a pistol. The one you will be using to shoot the Prime Minister needs to be different from your own regular sidearm. When Lorenzo gives you the signal, you will shoot the Prime Minister, and immediately throw the pistol at the feet of your friend, Niccolo. You will then shoot Niccolo with your regular firearm.

'When the other officers hurry to you, as they will, Lorenzo will tell them that you and he saw Niccolo pull out a pistol and aim it at the Prime Minister. Unfortunately, it was too late to save the life of the Prime Minister, but your quick thinking led to the assassin being killed. The important thing is that your two friends, Niccolo and Matteo, must know absolutely nothing about Lorenzo's part in this. You will have told them that you plan to kill the Prime Minister with their assistance, but you must not under any circumstances mention the part that my man, Lorenzo, will be playing. Can you remember all that?'

'I can,' Vito assured him.

Even as he gave this assurance, it struck Vito that there was a lot more going on with this plan. He was sure he was being set up. For one thing, this other policeman, the sergeant whom Legato casually referred to as Lorenzo – Vito knew his name was Lorenzo Capaldi, and Vito had heard stories on the street of how Legato and Lorenzo had been very close friends since they were small children. But this plan would put Lorenzo Capaldi in a risky situation, and Vito did not believe that Legato would do that. Yes, Legato was ruthless, everyone knew that. A cold-hearted killer. Which was why Vito hadn't turned him down face to face when Legato had first proposed the idea, worried he would be risking his life by doing so. But Legato wasn't going to put Lorenzo Capaldi there to protect Vito. Which meant that Capaldi would be there to kill Vito. The Prime Minister would die, and Vito would get the blame.

Oh no, thought Vito. *That's not the way it's going to happen. I'm coming out of this alive.*

Daniel followed Abigail as they walked past the Colosseum and through a huge arch, which Abigail informed him was the Arch of Constantine, and then began their ascent up a hill which brought them into a vast area of greenery, dotted with the ruins of what had once been large buildings.

'This is the Palatine Hill,' Abigail told him. 'One of the most ancient parts of the city. It was once the most desirable place to live in Rome, the height of luxurious building. The word "palace" comes from the Latin *palatine*. Imperial palaces were built on the Palatine, although there are very few relics these days of that time.'

Daniel looked down upon the large complex of ruins that was the Roman Forum below them.

'Incredible,' he murmured. 'I can see why you became so

enamoured of Roman archaeology. Even though much of it's in ruins, you can get the feeling of how it must have looked thousands of years ago.'

'Ah, there's Giuseppe,' said Abigail, pointing to where Giuseppe was engaged in a deep conversation with a young uniformed police officer. The officer shook Giuseppe's hand, then departed, and Abigail and Daniel hurried to join him.

'We're early for today's talk on the Palatine,' said Abigail. 'I wanted to give Daniel a chance to get the feel of the place. Who was that you were talking to just now?'

'A friend of mine, one of my contacts in the police force,' said Giuseppe unhappily. 'He was telling me that Julia's been found.'

'Where?' asked Daniel.

'In a doorway in an alley off the Campo de' Fiori.'

'That's the main fruit and vegetable market,' Abigail explained to Daniel. Then she asked Giuseppe, 'What was she doing there? Where is she now?'

'She's at the mortuary,' said Giuseppe. 'She'd been strangled. My contact told me one of his comrades who patrols in that area was told about it by the woman who found her body. He showed him the photograph of Julia, and he confirmed it was her.'

'It's obviously connected with the deaths of Sarah and Giovanni,' said Abigail. 'We need to find details of what happened. The doorway where she was found. Speak to the woman who found her. How was she strangled, with hands or by a cord of something?'

'My friend didn't know,' said Giuseppe.

'Has her death been reported to Inspector Volpetti?' asked Abigail.

'I don't know,' admitted Giuseppe. 'Her body was found yesterday, but whether the officer who found her passed her identity on to the inspector . . . ?' He shrugged. 'Communications between street officers and the people at headquarters are not often the best.'

'In that case, I suggest we call on Inspector Volpetti and tell him,' said Daniel. 'We'll soon find out if he knew.'

'But please, don't tell him that you got this information from an officer who I'd given the picture of Julia to. It will get him in trouble and stop people helping me in any future issues.' He looked at them apologetically as he added, 'I'd go with you to see the inspector, but I need to be here. After all, I'm supposed to be co-ordinating this festival.'

'Don't worry,' Abigail reassured him. 'We'll let you know how we get on.'

Inspector Volpetti was in his office, and didn't seem very pleased to see them.

'We're here about Julia Winstanley, Sarah Maduro's sister,' said Abigail. 'We understand her body was found, strangled, near to the Campo de' Fiori yesterday.'

'How do you know?' demanded Volpetti.

'We've been keeping our ears open. We also distributed a photograph of Julia to find out if anyone had seen her. That's how we learnt her body had been found at the Campo de' Fiori.'

'Who told you?' demanded Volpetti again.

'Does it matter?' asked Abigail.

'It does,' said Volpetti. 'It means someone is betraying official police business to outsiders.'

'Is her murder supposed to be a secret?' asked Abigail.

At this, Volpetti looked uncomfortable.

'May we ask why we weren't informed about Julia's murder?' pressed Abigail.

'We only inform the next of kin in cases like this,' replied Volpetti. 'This young woman was a stranger here in Rome. She had no next of kin except her sister, who is dead.'

'Wrong,' said Abigail. 'Sarah had a son, Paolo. Paolo was therefore Julia's nephew. Julia also has next of kin in England, her father and mother. They need to be informed.'

'We do not have an address for them,' said Volpetti.

'Their details will be at the flat where Sarah and Giovanni lived,' said Abigail.

'That may be,' said Volpetti, 'but it will not be a simple matter to find the address of Sarah's parents in England. We do not know where to look, and it is not our job to go through their possessions searching for them. It will take time.'

'I will get the address for you,' said Abigail.

Volpetti studied Abigail for a moment, then asked, 'Do you have keys to their flat?'

'Giuseppe Saredo has them. Paolo left him his keys when he returned to Milan. We will also give you Paolo's address in Milan in order that you can inform him officially, as he is Julia's next of kin living in Italy.'

Volpetti glowered at her, before he said resignedly, 'Very well. If you give me those addresses, I will see that they are formally notified.'

'And what have you discovered about the person who murdered Julia?' asked Abigail.

Volpetti looked at Abigail, puzzled by the question. 'We have discovered nothing except that she was strangled. We expect it was just some drifter or tramp. There are plenty of that type who hang about the Campo de' Fiori, looking for vulnerable people to prey on and rob.'

'Do you know where she had been staying?' asked Abigail.

'No,' said Volpetti. 'Why do you need to know?'

'Because she didn't seem to have her luggage with her. There could be things in her luggage that need to be returned to her next of kin.'

'We do not know where she was staying,' repeated Volpetti stubbornly.

'Will you make efforts to find out?' asked Abigail. 'If not, we will.'

CHAPTER FIFTEEN

'You've made an enemy of Inspector Volpetti,' grinned Daniel as they left the police station.

'An enemy, perhaps, but not someone who seems able to do anything about it. As Giuseppe says, he is lazy.'

'He was more than just lazy – I thought he was being deliberately obstructive,' said Daniel.

'I expect he doesn't like complications,' said Abigail. 'A foreigner being strangled in Rome creates problems for him. Lots of paperwork.'

Daniel smiled at Abigail. 'That was a brilliant touch, reminding him that Paolo was Julia's nephew.'

'He should have known it,' said Abigail. 'We have to find out where Julia was staying before she was killed,' she added suddenly. 'We need to ask Giuseppe to talk to the people he gave the photograph to, and ask him to spread the word among them that we're looking for where she was staying.'

'So, we're staying on after the Festival?' asked Daniel.

'We are,' said Abigail. 'Three murders, and the police are going to do nothing about it. Two of them were old friends of mine. I can't just walk away from this.'

'*We* can't walk away from it,' said Daniel firmly.

They returned to the Palatine Hill, where the session was in full swing. A crowd was being led around by a young man, who was pointing out various places on the site where famous palaces had once stood. Daniel heard him say the names Augustus, Tiberius and Domitian, recognising them from his conversations with Abigail as the names of Roman emperors. He turned to Abigail to comment on this and saw that she was staring at the young man.

'Good Lord!' said Abigail. 'I believe that's Antonio!'

'Who?' asked Daniel.

'Antonio Perucci. He was just a child when I was here fifteen years ago. His father brought him to the site to help in the excavations. We gave him a bucket and spade.'

'How old was he?'

'About six.'

Daniel looked at the young man. 'He looks about twenty-one, so it could well be the same boy.'

Giuseppe appeared and joined them.

'Did you see Inspector Volpetti?' he asked.

'We did,' said Daniel.

Abigail pointed at the young man, who had now moved to another spot on the hill, with more pointing and voluble information.

'Is that Antonio Perucci?' she asked Giuseppe.

'It is,' he said. 'That very first dig when he was just small obviously inspired him, because he went on to study archaeology, specialising in classical Roman remains.' He smiled. 'I wondered if you might remember him when you saw his name on the programme.'

'To be honest, it didn't really register,' admitted Abigail.

'When he's finished, I'll introduce you to him,' said Giuseppe. 'He'll be thrilled to talk to you. He still talks about the original dig here all those years ago. He said you and Sarah gave him a bucket and spade.'

'How astonishing he should remember that.'

'Not really. You had a great impact on him. He's kept track of your career, reading the reports in the archaeology journals about you. You're really quite famous. Antonio has followed in your footsteps. He's in the final year of an archaeology degree at the university.' Then he repeated his original question with a touch of impatience. 'But how did you get on with Inspector Volpetti?'

They told him of their disappointment at the inspector's negative reactions, and how they'd had to force him to agree to let Paolo and Julia's parents know about Julia's death.

'He seemed most upset at the fact that we knew about her death. He demanded to know who'd told us. But, to reassure you, we didn't tell him. Just that we'd kept our ears to the ground. We've also decided to stay on after the Festival and try and find out who killed Sarah and Giovanni, and now Julia.'

'That is wonderful news!' exulted Giuseppe. 'If there is anything I can do, with the people I have contacts with, you shall have every co-operation.'

'Thank you,' said Abigail. 'It occurred to us that perhaps the best way for us to continue our investigation is to move out of the hotel and stay at their flat. We can go through any paperwork at the place. Something there might give us clues as to what they were doing recently, who they were in contact with, that sort of thing. I think we all agree that the business of Sarah shooting Giovanni because he was pursuing Julia and then killing herself is rubbish. Hopefully there'll be some clues as to who may have wanted to kill them in their papers.'

'Paolo suggested their deaths may have been political,' said Daniel. 'He said Giovanni wrote articles in the papers and magazines in support of the workers.'

'He did,' said Giuseppe, 'but not the rabble-rousing sort of articles some produce. His were thoughtful, clever.' Then he sighed and admitted, 'But, sadly, there is no reasoning to some people and why they take the actions they do.'

'Paolo told us about the King being assassinated,' added Daniel.

Giuseppe shook his head in despair. 'That's the sort of thing I mean. There is no real sense to things like that.' He produced a bunch of keys and handed them to Abigail. 'Here are the keys to their flat. Do you remember where it is?'

'Yes,' said Abigail, pocketing the keys. 'We were there talking to the neighbours, asking questions about Julia. We'll go there first, then later we'll bring our luggage from the hotel. We'll let them know we're checking out early.'

'Will it be possible for us to talk to the policeman who found Julia's body?' asked Daniel. 'It would be good if he could tell us where we can get hold of the woman who actually discovered her, so we can talk to her.'

'I'll see what I can do,' said Giuseppe. 'But he has to know that it will be a secret meeting with him. That none of his superior officers will know that he's talked to you.'

'You can assure him of that,' promised Abigail.

'Ah-ha!' said Giuseppe. 'Antonio has finished. Come, let us go and you can say hello to him.'

They walked to where Antonio Perucci was talking to a couple of people who had more questions to ask him, and waited until he'd finished with them. It became obvious that Antonio was aware of them because he turned to them and bowed.

'Signora Wilson, this is an honour,' he said.

'I was Abigail Fenton when we last met,' smiled Abigail.

'I know,' said Antonio, returning the smile. 'You were here with Signora Maduro, Miss Winstanley as she was then, and it's true to say you both changed my life. My father had brought me to the dig because he was a proud Roman and wanted me to learn about our history, but watching the way you worked, such dedication, such finesse, I knew then that I wanted to do what you did.'

'And you have!' Abigail congratulated him. 'Giuseppe told me you are excelling at the university.'

'Giuseppe exaggerates,' said Antonio. 'But I don't mind. It helps me build my reputation. Although I still have a way to go to reach your level. I have followed your career, which has been truly remarkable. With Flinders Petrie in Egypt. The first woman to lead an exhibition to the pyramids. And yet you are still young!'

'Not as young as I'd like to be. I must congratulate you on your command of English, Antonio. It's really excellent.'

'That is very much thanks to Signora Maduro. She gave me English archaeology magazines and would read them to me as I was growing up. English became a second language for me.' He looked at the pair earnestly. 'I do not understand why anyone would kill her and Giovanni. I know you are the famous Museum Detectives, as well as being an archaeologist. Do you know why they were killed?'

'Not yet, but we are working on it,' said Abigail.

'In that case, if there is any way I can help, don't hesitate to call on me.' He turned to Daniel. 'But I have been rude. Mr Wilson, this is a great honour to meet you.'

Daniel shook the young man by the hand. 'And for me to meet you,' he said warmly.

Antonio produced a small visiting card which he handed to Daniel. 'This is my address,' he said. 'I meant it when I said, if there is anything I can do, to call on me. Signora Maduro was very special to me, as was Giovanni.'

'What a nice young man,' said Daniel as he and Abigail walked away.

'He is indeed,' agreed Abigail. 'And, with his offer of help, we're building up our own Italian version of Sherlock Holmes's Baker Street Irregulars, albeit a more upmarket version. Giuseppe and Antonio. Both with what could be vital contacts and local knowledge, particularly Giuseppe's contacts with ordinary street-level police officers.' She produced the keys Giuseppe had given her. 'I suggest we go to the flat and start to take up residency there. See what clues we can find.'

'Good idea,' said Daniel. 'While you do that, I'll go and get our luggage and check out of the hotel.'

'Can I suggest you take Giuseppe with you, if he's free,' said Abigail. 'For one thing, the booking will be in the Festival's name and they'll be picking up the bill, all of which will be easier for Giuseppe to explain to the hotel staff. Somehow I don't think *arrivederci*, *buongiorno* and *grazie* will suffice.'

Daniel smiled. 'Yes. Good thinking. He can also give me a hand with the luggage and show me the way to the flat. I'm sure I'll get lost on my own with all these similar-looking narrow streets.'

'In the meantime, I'll start going through any letters,' said Abigail. 'I'll see you at the flat.'

CHAPTER SIXTEEN

Francesco Bastigna walked slowly along the wide via Sacra, through the remains of the Forum. As he did so he reflected on what this road had represented in the great days of the Republic. Via Sacra meant Sacred Street, and that was exactly what it had been. It had formed part of the traditional route for all Roman triumphs – the victorious generals returning to be honoured at the Forum following a major battle at which the enemy had been routed; the celebration of the recently deceased emperors, when the body of the late emperor was carried on a pall from the Palatine Hill down the via Sacra into the Forum. Whatever the occasion, there would be crowds of hundreds of thousands celebrating the wonders of Rome and its power. Now, in these times of degradation and social strife, all that remained as a reminder of those great far-off days were these ruins. Society had collapsed, the rabble was in charge, and unless something could be done Rome would never again be a power in the world.

He stopped and sat down on one of the ancient seats that had once borne senators as they debated the futures of choice that lay in store for the Republic. What choice was there now?

He saw the figure of Rocco Legato, strolling along the via Sacra from the opposite direction. He was accompanied by his own small army of protectors, men of bulk, many of them discreetly armed. Was this to be the new face of the Republic? Criminals. Men without honour. Yet they claimed to be men of honour, loyal to their cause, just as the republican senators and politicians had been all those thousands of years ago. But their god was money and power. But hadn't that been the same for the emperors all those years ago? Money and power?

Legato strolled casually over to where Bastigna sat and lowered himself down on a stone seat beside the politician. His men, his protectors, fanned out, taking up watchful positions along the via Sacra and among the ancient ruins. This had been the agreed place for this meeting: nothing to raise any suspicions, just two gentlemen out for a gentle stroll, taking a short respite from their exertions.

'Do things progress?' asked Bastigna.

'They do,' replied Legato.

'Is there anything I need to know?'

'Just that when your distinguished friend arrives at the Colosseum on Friday, make sure you accompany him. One of his police guards will advise you that there is a security issue, and they need to escort him to a vehicle. Dismiss all but the police guard, who will accompany your distinguished friend.'

'And me?'

'There will be no need for you to accompany him. In fact, it is desirous that you do not. You will leave and rejoin the other dignitaries.'

'And then?'

Legato shrugged. 'And then, things may happen. But

you do not need to know about them at this stage. But the outcome will be what you desire.' Legato stood up. 'We shall be in touch again after Friday.'

With that, he moved away from Bastigna and continued along the via Sacra, his men moving to rejoin him, and they walked watchfully together through the site that had once been the glory that was Rome.

Giuseppe was in his office at the Forum when Daniel arrived.

'Ah, Daniel,' Giuseppe greeted him. 'I was coming to the flat to see you and Abigail. I've just been informed we have permission for the funerals of Giovanni and Sarah. They will be on Wednesday morning. I've sent a telegram to Paolo to tell him. I expect he will arrive late on Tuesday, after he's finished work.'

'What about Julia?' asked Daniel. 'Could her funeral be at the same time? She was Sarah's sister.'

'No,' said Giuseppe. 'The authorities say they need to get permission from Brigadier Winstanley. He may wish for her body to be returned to England. So, at the moment, it's just Giovanni and Sarah. The funeral will be at St Ignatius, then things will proceed to the cemetery for the burial.'

'What time?' asked Daniel.

'The service will be at half past nine, the burials at about ten. Do you think Abigail would like to say anything at the service?'

'I'll ask her, but my guess is she'll leave that to Paolo and those who knew the couple better. Yourself, for example.'

Giuseppe nodded. 'I have drafted a few words. Just a few, I stress. This will be painful enough for Paolo, without making it worse by long speeches.' He looked at Daniel enquiringly. 'But you came to see me?'

'Yes. As you know, Abigail and I have decided to stay at the flat. Abigail is currently going through their papers and other things there, looking for clues as to why they were murdered.'

'That's a good idea,' said Giuseppe.

'Would you do me the favour of coming with me to the hotel to settle the bill and collect our luggage for the flat? My lack of Italian is more problematic than I thought it would be.'

'Of course,' said Giuseppe, getting up and reaching for his coat.

Daniel gestured at the papers strewn about his desk. 'I won't be taking you away from anything important?'

'At the moment, everything to do with the Festival is important. And that includes transferring you and Abigail to the flat.'

Giuseppe elected to walk to the hotel, which pleased Daniel. 'Although, with luggage to carry, we'll take a cab back.'

As they walked, Daniel asked Giuseppe what the reaction had been so far to the Festival.

'Excellent!' beamed Giuseppe. 'The talks have gone down very well, and the attendances have been good. Abigail's talk at the Colosseum was very well received. The visit to the Festival on Friday by the Prime Minister is a major coup – it shows the Festival has support at the highest levels of government. With luck, as a result of this, we may get support from different sponsors so we can hold the Festival again, possibly in two years' time.'

Daniel was grateful that Giuseppe had accompanied him to the hotel. Although the staff at reception spoke English, Giuseppe had been able to handle the intricacies of settling the bill, including tips for the hotel staff, and their luggage being packed and taken downstairs.

Giuseppe had decided on a carriage to take them and the luggage to the flat close by the Spanish Steps, where they found Abigail sitting at a table covered with pieces of handwritten pages.

'I've found some things,' said Abigail. She pointed to some papers she'd put on the table. 'Letters to Sarah from her father asking if Julia can come and stay with them – with hints about her getting in bad company in England. But also these.'

She handed Giuseppe some pages with scrawled untidy writing in Italian on them. Giuseppe read them, then looked at her, frowning.

'Threatening letters,' he said.

'That's how I read them,' said Abigail.

'In what way?' asked Daniel.

Abigail picked up one of the letters and handed it to Daniel, translating the badly scrawled writing for him: '"Keep your mouth shut – or else." There are two more, with further threats.' She picked up two other letters, with the same scrawled writing. 'This one says, "You've been warned." The other says, "We mean business."' She showed the second letter to Giuseppe. 'There's something scribbled in Giovanni's handwriting on it. It looks like "Fuschetti" with a question mark.'

Giuseppe looked worried as he took it from her.

'Salvatore Fuschetti,' he said unhappily.

'You know him?' asked Abigail.

'Most people know him. He's a businessman, with criminal connections.'

'What sort of criminal connections?'

'Have you heard of the Cosa Nostra?' asked Giuseppe.

'No,' said Daniel. He looked at Abigail, who shook her head.

'It is a society of criminals. It is said that Fuschetti is one of them.'

'Is he under arrest, or anything?' asked Abigail.

'No,' said Giuseppe.

'Why not?'

'That is not the way things operate here.'

When they looked at him, puzzled, he said, 'You need to know who and what the Cosa Nostra is, and how it has spread. It began in Sicily some fifty years or so ago as a loose federation of peasant gangs who were hired by farmers to protect their crops and animals. Cattle were often stolen and the police seemed unable to do anything about it. The peasant gangs knew who had stolen the cattle, and recovered them, and were rewarded. Ordinary criminals began to fear them because their methods in recovering the cattle or fruit crops that had been stolen were harsh.'

'Killing the thieves?'

'Often. I'm not sure where the term Cosa Nostra – which simply means "our thing" – started, but it became known as the name these gangs used to show they were one organisation. In fact, they were much more fragmented than that, composed of different families. But they became powerful. So much so that the authorities in Sicily didn't try to confront them – to do so meant risking death. Over time, emboldened by their apparent invincibility, the Cosa Nostra expanded from Sicily into other parts of Italy. Their reputation preceded them and now you will find them in every major city, involved in all sorts of crime. Recovering stolen cattle is far behind them now; if there is any form of criminal activity that is profitable, you will find the Cosa Nostra at the heart of it. And, just as was the case in Sicily, the authorities are scared to confront them. The Cosa Nostra have also made a point of controlling locally elected boards, mayors, even government ministers, with large bribes.'

'The carrot and the stick,' murmured Daniel. Giuseppe looked at him with a frown.

'I don't know this phrase,' he said.

'We will give you gifts if you do what we want – the carrot. If you don't, we will beat you. The stick.'

Giuseppe nodded. 'That is exactly so. The Cosa Nostra are involved in everything that happens in Italy: robberies, even industrial disputes.'

'On which side?' asked Abigail.

'On whichever side offers the most money.' He looked at the papers Abigail had shown him. 'They have one overriding rule: *omertà*. Silence. No one talks about the Cosa Nostra's activities to the authorities. To break this rule means death. If this message was sent to Giovanni by the Cosa Nostra, it was warning him what would happen if he spoke about them to the authorities. Although I can't believe that would have happened. There are many in the authorities who are in the pay of the Cosa Nostra, but no one knows who. So the wise man keeps his silence.'

'And would you say that Giovanni was a wise man?' asked Abigail.

'Yes, and no,' said Giuseppe awkwardly. 'If there was anything that he was seriously concerned about, he wouldn't keep quiet about it.'

'Like his letters and articles about the political issues?'

'Exactly. Politics here is about money, and money needs protecting.'

'It's the same in England,' said Daniel. 'But so far it hasn't got to the lengths of criminals murdering people to protect someone's interests.' Then he thought over what he'd said, and added thoughtfully, 'Although I can think of a few occasions when it might have been the case. But nothing on the scale you're talking about.'

'So it's possible that Giovanni was killed by this Cosa Nostra,' said Abigail. 'But why Sarah?'

'They are quite ruthless. They have been known to kill entire families to ensure their security.'

Abigail looked at the notes and said, 'We need to inform the police about this.'

Giuseppe looked at her in bewilderment. 'Didn't you hear what I've just said? The police, especially, are as frightened of them as anyone else. More so. Those poorly paid police officers walking around the streets are potential targets, every one of them.'

'What about the senior officers? Inspectors? Superintendents?'

'And if they are being paid by the Cosa Nostra?'

'Is that possible?'

'It's highly possible. The only way to find out is to report your suspicion that the Cosa Nostra are involved. If the officer you report it to is in the pay of the Cosa Nostra, the first thing he'll do is deny there is any such organisation as the Cosa Nostra. The second thing he'll do is tell the Cosa Nostra you are asking questions about them. At which point your lives become under threat.'

'That's if he's in their pay. What if he isn't?'

'He'll report it to a more senior officer, who'll either pass it on upwards, or do the same as just outlined to you. Deny the Cosa Nostra even exists, and then pass on your details to them.'

'So what do we do?'

'That's a very good question. Of course, their deaths may be nothing to do with the Cosa Nostra but something connected with Julia and what happened to her.'

'So, we're back to square one.'

Giuseppe sighed. 'It's not satisfactory, but I'm telling you how things are.'

Abigail then produced some more letters written in Italian.

'Then there's these,' she said. 'I found them in the bedside drawer on the side I guess was Sarah's, from the decorated pillowcase.'

She handed them to Giuseppe, who read them, then looked at Abigail, concern on his face.

'What are they about?' asked Daniel.

'They are from a woman whose name is Angelina,' said Giuseppe.

'How do you know?' asked Abigail. 'There's no signature on them.'

'Sarah showed one of them to me, but she didn't tell

Giovanni about them and she begged me not to tell him.'

'But she told you who they were from?'

Giuseppe nodded.

'What do they say?' asked Daniel impatiently.

'This one says, "Leave him. He's mine." The other one says, "You have taken my life. I want it back." That's all.'

'Which suggests this Angelina had a fixation on Giovanni.'

'That's how Sarah saw it,' said Giuseppe.

'Who is this woman?'

'She's an archaeology student. She worked with Giovanni at the Forum about three months ago.'

'Did Giovanni ever mention her?' asked Abigail.

'No,' said Giuseppe. 'To be honest, I don't think he was really aware of her. He was all about the work, and Sarah and Paolo. Possibly the best person to talk about her to is Antonio. He worked with Giovanni and this Angelina at the Forum, and once said to me that he was concerned about Angelina.'

'In what way?'

'He said he thought she might be a disturbed person. He said she was always following Giovanni everywhere and she'd get upset and hostile when Antonio appeared.'

'Just the same way Julia acted when we appeared on the scene,' commented Daniel. 'Another disturbed person.'

'So, we have a word with Antonio,' said Abigail.

'That's my suggestion,' said Giuseppe. He looked at the letters that Abigail had found. 'It was a good idea of yours to move into their flat. These are the first concrete proof that they were under threat. Sarah from Angelina, and Giovanni from the Cosa Nostra.' He looked at them, concerned. 'And both are dangerous.'

'By the way,' said Daniel to Abigail, 'Giuseppe's told me the funerals of Giovanni and Sarah will be this Wednesday morning. He's telegraphed Paolo.'

'I expect Paolo will arrive late on Tuesday, after he's finished work.'

'We need to let him know we've moved into the flat,' said Abigail.

'I put that in my telegram,' said Giuseppe. 'It will be good for him to be with friends the night before, and when he wakes in the morning. It will be a tough time for him.'

'Don't worry, we'll be with him,' Abigail reassured him. 'Where is the funeral?'

'St Ignatius.'

'I remember where that is,' said Abigail. 'What about letting people know? It's short notice.'

'I have sent messages out, and word of mouth will spread it. They were a very popular couple.'

CHAPTER SEVENTEEN

After Giuseppe had gone, Daniel and Abigail discussed the latest developments in the case.

'So, we have two sets of threats. One from this Angelina directed at Sarah. And threats to Giovanni from what appears to be this Cosa Nostra,' said Abigail.

'Who sound as if they work as political assassins,' mused Daniel. 'And Paolo suggested the murders were in some way political. So politics and this crime organisation could both be part of it.' He frowned. 'I must admit I'm not overjoyed at the idea of confronting this Cosa Nostra lot, especially as we're told that if anything happens to us, the police won't be looking into it.'

'But I feel we owe it to Sarah to find out who killed her and Giovanni,' said Abigail. Then after a moment's thought she clarified, 'What I mean is *I* owe it to Sarah.'

'Oh no you don't,' said Daniel firmly. 'If we're in this, we're in it together.'

'But are we in it?' asked Abigail. 'In view of what Giuseppe told us, if it is the Cosa Nostra who were behind the killings, I'm not ready to die yet, especially at the hands of some mysterious outfit who won't get caught. And I don't want to lose you.'

'Or it may be this Angelina,' said Daniel. 'Which might be safer in one way, but it depends on whether she is a disturbed person, as Antonio seems to think.'

'We need to talk to Antonio,' said Abigail.

Giuseppe Saracco, the seventy-eight-year-old Prime Minister of Italy, sat at the large ornate desk in his office in the Palazzo Chigi, the heart of the Italian government, watching as Francesco Bastigna, his most trusted adviser, paced in front of the large window overlooking via Del Corso. The Chigi Palace wasn't just the seat of government – it was also the official residence of the Prime Minister, as long as he was in power.

Saracco had come to power on 24th June, just two months earlier, following the downfall of General Luigi Pelloux's government. Pelloux had been a military man, one intent on bringing tough military discipline to Italy. He'd first been made Prime Minister in 1898 after the fall of the Rudini government following the outcry over the Bava Beccaris massacre. Within a year Pelloux had been forced to resign as Prime Minister over his Chinese foreign policy, which had resulted in Italy being forced to back down from its demands to China for a lease to a coaling station at China's Sanmen Bay. Italy became the only Western power to fail to achieve its territorial goals in China, which was seen as a humiliation. However, almost immediately, King Umberto reinstated Pelloux to Prime Minister. Pelloux's first step was to take action against what he saw as dangerous revolutionaries in Italy. His Public Safety Bill made strikes by state employees illegal, banned certain public meetings, dissolved organisations seen as subversive, brought in banishment and preventative arrests for political offences, and tightened control of the press, declaring incitement to violence a crime. The opposition to his bill from the radicals and socialists was fierce, and with more moderate politicians joining the opposition, in May 1990, General Pelloux had been forced to dissolve the government and resign.

'What worries you so much about this event on Friday?' asked Saracco. 'It is a celebration of classical Rome. It is literally just along the road from here, so there will not be the risks that there could be on a long journey.. We will have our protection forces with us. The crowd will be the intelligentsia, archaeologists, historians, students . . .'

'There you have it,' said Bastigna, suddenly spinning round to face Saracco. 'Students! Dangerous radicals.'

'Be careful,' cautioned Saracco, 'you are sounding like Pelloux, and look what happened to him. My attendance at this festival is important. We have to bring this country, which is so disunited, together. Faction fighting against faction. All Pelloux's hardline, iron-first approach did was to make the divisions even worse. This festival celebrates the history and the glory that was Rome. It's to make the people feel proud of their heritage. Without the wonder of ancient Rome, democracy would not have spread across the world as it has. We have to protect that reputation. Bring people together.'

'And the danger?' demanded Bastigna. 'Look what happened to the King, for God's sake! No one was better protected than he. Yet some radical lunatic decided to kill him.'

'The King's position was tainted by the massacre in Milan and the repressive policies of General Pelloux. I was never associated with either. As well as our usual protection guards, I have asked for a force made up of local police officers, all volunteers and therefore loyal to me, to be at the site. They will be sure to recognise any troublemakers and move in swiftly before they can cause any problems. It will be fine, Francesco. You have no need to worry.'

'I always have need to worry,' retorted Bastigna. 'So do all politicians in this country. Remember that.'

Massimo Cassani was considered by some in his area to be the Capo dei Capi, the boss of the bosses of the Cosa Nostra in the district known as Celian Hill. Cassani himself did not like to be described in this way. As far as he was concerned, he was a businessman who had good relationships with other businessmen in the district. If these other businessmen chose to consult him over matters such as territorial disputes, or for advice on how to deal with a certain problem, he was gratified to be considered useful. He prided himself on giving sound – and cautious – advice. Caution was an important word in his vocabulary. Other *capos* in other districts had been incautious, throwing their weight around unnecessarily, doing their best to show how important they were. *But we are personally not that important* was Cassani's creed. *We are bound to one another through brotherhood. We are responsible for our families – both our personal families and our families within the organisation.*

Some of those other more egocentric and forceful *capos* had soon learnt that their way was folly, especially if it meant provoking the true *capi dei capi*, those with the larger organisations which were virtually small armies.

Know your place in the order of things was another of Cassani's creeds. People in Celian Hill knew their place, as did Cassani. Which was why Salvatore Fuschetti had come to seek Cassani's wisdom on a certain matter.

'A problem has surfaced,' said Fuschetti.

'What sort of problem?' asked Cassani.

'There was a shooting at the Colosseum a few days ago.'

Cassani nodded. 'Giovanni Maduro.'

'And his wife, Sarah. An English woman who has lived here for many years.'

Cassani waited attentively.

'Another English woman is at the Colosseum. She has been giving a talk at this festival they are holding. Her name is Abigail Wilson and she is an archaeologist. She worked at the Colosseum with Sarah Maduro some years ago and was a friend of hers, I'm told.'

'And the problem?' prompted Cassani.

'This Abigail Wilson is also a detective. She and her husband, Daniel Wilson, have made a reputation for themselves in solving crimes, particularly murders at museums. Recently they solved a murder at the Louvre, in Paris. Daniel Wilson used to be an inspector with Scotland Yard. He was part of the team that looked into the Jack the Ripper killings in London.'

'Which were never solved,' pointed out Cassani.

'I have heard that he did solve them, but the results were squashed from being made public for political reasons.'

'The same as happens here,' said Cassani.

'Yes, but they do not know how things work here,' said Fuschetti.

'And you think they will investigate the shootings?'

'The police have told them there is no case to investigate,' said Fuschetti. 'The English couple have been informed that the woman shot her husband, and then herself. But I'm told they don't believe this.'

Cassani fell silent, thinking this over. Then he asked, 'Are we involved in any way?'

Fuschetti hesitated, before replying awkwardly, 'I had occasion to warn Maduro over things he was saying.'

'Yes, I read some of his comments in the newspapers.'

'Some very important people in industry requested that he be asked to stop such talk, for which they paid well.'

Again, Cassani fell silent and studied Fuschetti with sharp eyes.

'We did not shoot him,' insisted Fuschetti. 'Merely warned him. That was all. But if it comes out . . .'

'It must not come out,' said Cassani in firm tones. 'This English couple must be . . . dissuaded from their investigations.'

'We understand they are also investigating the death of Sarah Maduro's sister, who had been staying with the Maduros. Her body was found strangled at Campo de' Fiori.'

'Are we involved?' asked Cassani.

'No,' said Fuschetti. 'Not as far as I know.'

'But their looking into this other murder may lead them into areas that we'd prefer not to be looked into.'

Fuschetti nodded.

Cassani thought it over. 'There is a larger problem here,' he said. 'The Colosseum comes under the Palatine Hill district and Signor Legato does not take kindly to intrusions on his territory. Was any action taken to consult Signor Legato before the warnings were issued?'

Fuschetti hesitated, then admitted, 'There was a possible

oversight, which came about because there was no intent on carrying out any attack on Maduro in the Palatine Hill district, so we did not think it would contravene any territorial boundaries.'

'You say "we",' said Cassani thoughtfully. 'Who else was involved?'

'Mario Torriano.'

Mario Torriano was Fuschetti's right-hand man.

'Very well,' announced Cassani. 'Leave it with me. This needs to be handled with thought and precision.'

CHAPTER EIGHTEEN

Inspector Volpetti sat at his desk in his office reading the report from Officer Salvatore Nuno, to whom he'd given the task of following the Wilson couple. 'If they separate, follow the woman,' he'd told him. To Volpetti, Abigail Wilson was the most dangerous. She spoke fluent Italian, for one thing, and seemed to have no inhibitions about talking to anyone.

The report by Officer Nuno began with the couple's visit to the Termini railway station, accompanied by a young man. They'd had a photograph of a young woman which they'd shown around to railway staff.

Later, they'd accompanied this young man to the Termini, where he'd caught a train to Milan.

On the Sunday, the Wilsons had gone to the Colosseum, where they'd explored the tunnels.

On the Monday, they'd gone to Palatine Hill to listen to a tour that was being given. They'd talked to Giuseppe Saredo. Afterwards they had gone to the police station to talk to Inspector Volpetti. They then returned to the Palatine Hill, where they talked to the young man who'd been giving the tour. They also talked again to Signor Saredo.

After this, Daniel Wilson and Signor Saredo had gone somewhere unknown, while Mrs Wilson had gone to the flat where the Maduros had lived. Officer Nuno reported that he'd waited outside the flat, but Mrs Wilson did not reappear. Instead, Mr Wilson and Signor Saredo arrived carrying the couple's luggage. After some time, Signor Saredo left, leaving the Wilsons at the flat.

What were their plans? Volpetti wondered. Had they moved from their hotel into the Maduros' flat? If so, for how long? He'd assumed they would be returning to England once the Festival had finished, but did this mean they would be staying on and looking into the deaths? If so, he had to do something about them.

How had it come to this? he thought despairingly. It was the fault of that damned English girl, Julia. There had been other women before her, but none who had created such intensity. Caused such havoc.

At all costs he had to stop the English detectives from getting to the truth. The woman, especially. He was sure she was closing in on it. But how to stop her? If she hadn't been such a high-profile person, a famous archaeologist and a major factor in this Classical Rome Festival, he'd have been able to fix up an allegation of some minor crime against her and order her deportation. Get her out of the country. But that was out of the question. And he couldn't make a move against her without raising questions about his motives.

Antonio Perucci lived in a small, pleasant flat not far from the Colosseum. Perucci was a bachelor and was delighted to see Abigail and Daniel, although his face clouded over when he heard what they were after.

'Angelina,' he said unhappily. 'Yes, I remember her. Her full name's Angelina Condotti. She volunteered to work with Giovanni in the excavations being carried out at the Forum. I was working occasionally with him, along with my own work at the Palatine.'

'Giuseppe says you described her as disturbed.'

'Yes,' said Antonio. 'It became obvious to me that she was obsessed with Giovanni, although Giovanni didn't appear to notice.'

'How did her obsession manifest itself?' asked Abigail.

'She always made sure she was close to him when the work at the Forum was going on, and she had this habit of glaring at other people who worked with Giovanni. And one evening I was at Giovanni and Sarah's flat for a social engagement – they'd invited me to dinner – and I noticed Angelina hovering about in the street outside their flat. I mentioned this to Giovanni because I wondered if she had come to talk to him about something, but he said there had been no arrangement for her to call at the flat. I went with him to the door to find out what she wanted, but as soon as she saw me, she ran off. And I mean that literally – she ran away. Sarah asked me what was going on, and I told her about Angelina hovering outside, and then disappearing. Sarah laughed and said, "Yes, she's done that before a couple of times. I suppose she's too shy to knock."'

'Sarah wasn't worried?'

'No, she just thought she had a teenage crush on Giovanni. You know, like some school pupils do with their teacher. I mentioned it to Giovanni and suggested it might be worth having a gentle word with her in case she was chasing after him, kind of let her down gently. He said he would, but I'm not sure if he did. He didn't like to hurt people's feelings.'

'Is she still working at the Forum?'

'No. She suddenly stopped coming about three weeks ago. As she was a volunteer, it was thought that she'd just decided to do something else with her time. To be honest, I was relieved when I realised she'd left. I thought her actions were embarrassing.'

'Do you have an address for her?' asked Abigail.

'No, but I'm sure it'll be somewhere in Giovanni's records in his desk at the Forum. He was meticulous about keeping record of everyone who was involved in the work, so that when anything was published about the dig, everyone would receive credit.'

Benedetto Sciacci sat in his kitchen in his mansion in Sicily and looked at his visitor, his nephew, Carlo, his brother's eldest son. Benedetto had the whole of his huge house to choose from, but the kitchen was his favourite place. There was usually something simmering in the cast-iron range, filling the room with the immensely satisfying aroma of the succulent tomatoes grown and picked in the estate's vegetable garden. Benedetto's piercing stare watched Carlo intently as he asked, 'You have really found them? After all this time?'

Carlo nodded. 'We have,' he said. 'It took so long because they changed their names. Alessio became Federico Legato. Casimiro changed his name to Capaldi.'

'How did you find them?'

'A man who helped them when they first arrived in Rome was dying, and he wanted to unburden himself of something he'd done all those years ago.'

'Who was this man?' asked Benedetto.

'Alberto Chiesa. He'd given Alessio and Casimiro shelter when they first arrived in Rome. He knew they were fugitives.'

'They paid him,' said Benedetto.

Carlo nodded. 'And paid him well. But Chiesa wanted to confess what he'd done before he died, so he asked his nephew to bring him a priest. His nephew is a non-believer, but he wanted to keep in his uncle's good books because the old man was wealthy. So he arranged for a friend of his to pose as a priest to take the old man's confession. That was how he learnt what had happened, about Alessio and Casimiro changing their names when they came to Rome.

'The nephew remembered that the Sciacci family had been hunting for Alessio and Casimiro, so he came to Sicily to sell the information to us.'

'Who saw him?'

'I did,' said Carlo.

'Did you pay him?'

'I did, but only after I'd checked his information. I made contact with a friend in Rome and asked him to check on Federico Legato and Luca Capaldi. He told me that both men had had sons of their own who were known citizens. Rocco Legato and Lorenzo Capaldi. I have managed to get photographs of all four men. I have checked them with photographs we had of Federico Alessio and Luca Casimiro. They are the same, Federico Legato and Luca Capaldi, and their sons, Rocco Legato and Lorenzo Capaldi.' He handed the old man an envelope. 'The photographs are in there, as are their details: where they live, their families, where they work. Everything.'

Benedetto nodded. 'You have done well. But we now have to carry out what needs to be done.'

Carlo nodded. 'Yes,' he said. 'And I would like to offer my son, Santola, to carry out this mission. He would be honoured to undertake it.'

'Is he up to it?' asked Benedetto.

'More than up to it. He has shown himself to be a hunter, with great patience, and nerves of iron.'

Benedetto nodded.

'In that case, send him to me.'

CHAPTER NINETEEN

Abigail and Daniel returned to the Forum and found Giuseppe in his office going through paperwork.

'We saw Antonio,' said Abigail. 'He told us Angelina's full name, Angelina Condotti, and said he was sure that Giovanni would have an address for her in his records of the work they did at the Forum.'

'I shall look,' said Giuseppe, and he began to go through a pile of exercise books on one of the shelves. As he searched, he told them, 'I was coming to see you, anyway. I have the information about the woman who found Julia's body, and the policeman who attended and dealt with it.'

'Thank you,' said Abigail. 'We'll talk to them, but discreetly, of course, and see if they have any information that might show us where Julia was staying before she was killed.'

'Abigail feels she could have been involved with some man,' said Daniel.

'That sounds highly likely,' said Giuseppe. 'She was obviously a very passionate person, from what you told me about her father's letters to Sarah expressing his concerns over some young man in England. I can well imagine her getting involved with some man here in Rome.' He smiled. 'Ah, here it is – Angelina's address.'

He wrote it down on a piece of paper, then added two other addresses. 'Maria Rossellini, the woman who found Julia's body. She lives close to the Campo de' Fiori. And Constable Luca Ferrovi, the one who attended. I've written down the station he's based at, but it might be better to call on him at his home, away from the prying eyes of his fellow officers.'

Matteo sat on the doorstep in front of his house and worried about Vito and his plan to shoot the Prime Minister. It was madness! How had he, Matteo, got himself caught up in this lunatic and dangerous scheme? It was Niccolo's fault. Matteo and Niccolo had been friends for years. About a year ago Niccolo had come to Matteo and said, 'There's this man I've met. He's a railway policeman and he's got some fantastic ideas. He's so exciting! You have to meet him.'

So Matteo had. It was true that Vito had a quality about him, a swagger that exuded charisma. He was not at all surprised to learn that Vito was married with two children, but at the same time had various girlfriends. He seemed to take pleasure in telling his new friends the graphic details of his sexual experiences, which Matteo found uncomfortable, but Niccolo seemed to delight in. He also seemed to have strong opinions about the current state of Italian politics, but he talked in such a jumbled fashion that he sounded to Matteo like he was repeating things he'd heard others say but hadn't properly understood. He seemed to have the idea that anarchy was the answer to all of Italy's problems, but exactly how he never said, and Matteo didn't like to ask him. In fact, there was a lot about Vito that Matteo was unsure of, but he didn't like to ask because he would have made fun of him and made him look stupid. He also saw how Niccolo lapped it all up, as if Vito were some kind of all-knowing messiah.

When Vito had first come up with the idea of shooting the Prime Minister, Matteo had thought he was joking. Then he thought Vito was just saying it to sound big. But when he realised that Vito actually meant it, he got scared, especially when he saw that Niccolo seemed to take on the idea so enthusiastically.

I have to get out of this, he thought. *But how?* Vito and Niccolo knew that he, Matteo, knew everything they'd talked about. If he tried to back out, what would they do? Vito had a gun from his job as a railway policeman. He knew how to use it. He'd shot at targets in the park. Niccolo had been impressed by his accuracy, while Matteo had been frightened. If he told the other two he didn't want any part of what was planned, he felt it was quite likely that Vito would shoot him to stop him telling anyone else about the plot. Often, Vito had that mad look in his eyes.

I'm trapped, thought Matteo desperately. *I have to get out of this.*

'So let's recap,' said Daniel as they made their way to the address they'd been given by Giovanni for Maria Rossellini. 'We have Angelina Condotti, obsessed with Giovanni and jealous of Sarah. We have the Cosa Nostra, in the form of Salvatore Fuschetti, who may be the ones who warned Giovanni off from interfering in things politically. Then we have Julia. Was her death connected with the murders of Giovanni and Sarah?'

'I'm pretty sure that's what we'll find,' said Abigail. 'We really need to find out where she was staying after Giovanni and Sarah were killed.'

Maria Rossellini opened her street door to the knock and looked with suspicion at the couple who stood there. She wasn't used to opening the door and finding middle-aged people dressed so very respectably, not unless they were officials of some sort, and officials usually meant trouble. The man doffed his hat politely to her and said '*Buongiorno*,' but his accent showed he wasn't Italian. English, possibly, Maria thought, looking at their clothes. And not poor English, either. Well-to-do. She gave a call which summoned her seven children, and they all gathered around her, hanging onto her skirt and looking out at the couple, their eyes wide with interest at these two unusual-looking people. It was the woman who spoke, and although she did not have the dark pallor of Italian women, she was not milky pale, either. She spoke in fluent Italian with a Roman accent, but the Italian of the educated, not of the streets.

She wanted to know if she was talking to the Maria Rossellini who'd discovered a dead woman in the Campo de' Fiori recently. Maria wanted to know why, her wariness suggesting she sensed trouble. The woman was quick to allay her fears, telling her she was not in trouble of any sort. It was just that the dead woman was a relative of theirs, from England, and they were curious to discover what had happened to her.

'*Inglese?*' asked Maria.

The woman confirmed the dead woman was indeed English and asked when and where Maria had found her, and what had happened after her tragic discovery.

At this, Maria launched into a tale of misery and how she had been taken advantage of by the police. She had been out gathering waste food she could forage for her family – and she put out a hand towards her *bambini*, emphasising the fact they'd had no food that day because the police had prevented her from going about her business. Just because she had been the one who found the dead woman. She expressed her disgust at the police's attitude towards a poor woman such as herself, the mother of seven children and with an invalid husband to care for who was just out trying to scrape together food for them. It was at this point that Abigail suggested that if Maria could show them where she'd discovered the dead woman, there might be some recompense for her time and trouble.

Maria responded positively to this idea. She ordered the children back into the house, with a warning to behave, and told them she would not be gone for long.

She then took Abigail and Daniel on a tortuous route through the narrow streets that led to the market, stopping at the doorway where she'd discovered Julia's body. There then followed a graphic description of Maria unwrapping the cloth and finding the body of a young woman, and how she'd gone in search of a policeman in order to do her proper duty. And how her doing this had led to Maria not being able to find food for that day for her poor children.

Abigail listened to her tale attentively, then opened her purse and handed her some lira notes, with many thanks for her assistance, and the wish that her husband would soon be better.

As Daniel and Abigail walked away from the scene, Daniel asked, 'How much did that cost us?'

'In English terms, hardly anything,' said Abigail. 'You don't begrudge it, surely? A woman who's having difficulty scraping things together, with seven children and an invalid husband?'

'Not at all,' said Daniel, 'I was just curious. In fact, I thought the whole thing was worth every penny, considering she put her heart and soul into the performance. I've rarely seen better on the London stage.'

CHAPTER TWENTY

Daniel and Abigail's next call was to the home of Constable Luca Ferrovi. As they'd promised Giovanni, they were making a point of seeing him away from the police station to avoid questions being asked as to who had given them his name. Fortunately, Luca Ferrovi was off duty and at home, having finished his shift. They told him they were acting on behalf of the Winstanley family, who were in England, and looking into the death of Julia Winstanley. They understood that Constable Ferrovi had been the one who first examined the body after Maria Rosellini had reported finding it.

Luca Ferrovi agreed that this was right. The young woman had been strangled. From the marks on her body, it looked as if it had been done by a thin cord being tightened around her neck. Constable Ferrovi told them he'd never seen the woman before. The body had been taken to the Isola Tiberena, the same hospital where Giovanni's and Sarah's bodies had been taken. He guessed the woman had been dead for about five hours when he examined her, but he was sure doctors at the hospital would know more about that. There had been no blood or anything under her fingernails, which suggested she hadn't struggled against her attacker.

Abigail thanked him and slipped him a banknote in gratitude for his assistance.

As Daniel and Abigail walked away, she said, 'So, she didn't scratch her killer, which makes me think he strangled her from behind.'

'But she knew him,' commented Daniel. 'To allow him to get that close to her suggests intimacy.'

'Unless he crept up on her,' said Abigail.

They then went to the address they'd been given for Angelina Condotti.

'Angelina's not here,' they were told by a young woman. It seemed five women had shared the small house, but Angelina had moved out two weeks earlier. 'We think she's moved in with her boyfriend.'

'Do you know his name?' asked Abigail.

'Alessandro Dubek,' said the young woman.

'Do you have an address for him?'

'No, but you can get hold of him at the Shooting Gallery. It's a gun club.' And she made a gun with her fist, her forefinger pointed, which made Daniel look quizzically at Abigail.

'Where do we find this gun club?' asked Abigail.

The woman gave her an address off the via Cavour.

As they walked away from the house, Abigail translated the conversation for Daniel's benefit.

'So that's why she made the sign of a gun,' mused Daniel thoughtfully. 'This opens up a whole new aspect to the case. But are we looking at Angelina, or her boyfriend?'

'Maybe both,' said Abigail.

The Shooting Gallery was in a basement under a shop in

one of the side streets off via Cavour. As Daniel and Abigail neared it, Abigail suddenly stopped.

'Stay back,' she whispered urgently.

Puzzled, Daniel did as she said, and the two sought refuge in a nearby shop doorway. It was then that Daniel saw what had caught Abigail's eye. The tall figure of Inspector Volpetti, wearing his police uniform, was coming up the steps that led down to the Shooting Gallery. He was carrying a long case that appeared to contain a rifle. They waited until he had disappeared, before heading for the entrance to the gun club.

'Interesting,' commented Daniel.

Daniel and Abigail walked down the stairs and found themselves in a small reception room where a counter barred the access to the actual shooting area, which was behind a closed door. They could hear the sounds of explosions and the thwack of bullets finding the targets.

'Definitely the right place,' murmured Daniel.

As before, Abigail did the talking to the tall, thin young man behind the counter.

'We're sorry to trouble you,' she said, with a friendly smile, 'but we're looking for Alessandro Dubek.'

The young man looked at her, then at Daniel, suspiciously.

'What do you want with him?' he asked.

'We just want to ask him to pass on some information to a friend of his.'

'Which friend would that be?' he asked warily.

'Angelina Condotti,' said Abigail. She put on her most appealing smile as she asked him, 'I believe in fact that I might be talking to Alessandro Dubek?'

He hesitated, then said reluctantly, 'You might be. But I have no contact with Miss Condotti.'

'You have broken off your friendship?' asked Abigail, sympathetically.

'She broke it off,' he said sullenly.

'I'm so sorry to hear that,' said Abigail. 'Do you know where we can get in touch with her?'

'No,' said Dubek. 'I thought she might have gone back to the house she lived in with those women.'

'Alas, no,' said Abigail. 'It was they who suggested we enquire here. Out of curiosity, was she interested in learning how to use a gun?'

'Yes,' said Dubek. 'That was how we met. She was standing outside the entrance looking at the pictures of guns and shooting one day when I left the Gallery. I asked her if she wanted anything, and she said she wanted to learn how to use a gun. I asked her why, and she said for hunting. I told her she needed to learn how to handle a rifle, but she said a rifle would be too bulky for her. She wanted to use a pistol. I told her I worked here and I could teach her, if she liked. She asked me how much it would cost for lessons, and I told her I'd give them to her free, if she bought a gun.'

'And did she?'

'She did. She tried various pistols that I recommended to her, and she settled on a Pistola Rotazione modello 89. It is a good pistol. It fires six rounds and is very reliable.'

'If you don't mind me asking, why did you and she break up?' asked Abigail.

'I don't know,' said Dubek. 'Perhaps she thought I'd taught her all I could.' He laughed bitterly. 'It struck me that she was

129

only interested in me for what I could teach her.' He looked enquiringly at Abigail. 'But you said you had some information for her?'

'Yes,' said Abigail. 'We wanted to let her know that two friends of hers, Giovanni Saredo and his wife Sarah, are dead. They were shot dead at the Colosseum. Sarah and Giovanni were old friends of mine and we're trying to find out what happened.'

'Why?' asked Dubek. 'That is a job for the police.'

'We're just trying to help the police,' said Abigail. 'As I said, the Saredos were old friends.'

Dubek fell into a thoughtful silence, then he said, 'She liked to go to the coffee stall in the Termini station. It's called DeLuca's. You could ask there. There's a young woman who works there called Lucia. She and Angelina used to often talk together. Lucia might know where she is.'

'Thank you,' said Abigail. 'One last thing. As we were coming in, we passed someone we know, Inspector Volpetti of the police. He was just leaving, and carrying what looked like a rifle.'

Dubek nodded. 'Yes, he comes here often to practise with it. He is a great hunter. Boars are his speciality.'

'Is he a good shot?' asked Abigail.

'Very good,' said Dubek. 'He rarely misses the centre of the target.'

CHAPTER TWENTY-ONE

Vito was doing his regular round at the Termini railway station, watching out for suspicious-looking characters. As he strolled from platform gate to platform gate, he thought about his plan for Friday. His plan, not Rocco Legato's. Niccolo would be the scapegoat, of course, as Legato had planned. The addition of this renegade police officer, Lorenzo, would now be a positive for him. When Lorenzo handed him the pistol he was to use, he would shoot Lorenzo. Then Niccolo. Then, finally, the Prime Minister. His story would be that Niccolo had shot the Prime Minister and Lorenzo. Vito had shot Niccolo. All done. The Prime Minister dead, as Rocco Legato had ordered. The only two people who could implicate him, Lorenzo and Niccolo, also dead. Vito would be in the clear.

Suddenly Vito spotted the English couple, the Wilsons, walking through the Termini, making for the coffee stall. They went to the counter and ordered drinks from Lucia, who was serving. *What are they up to?* he wondered.

He watched from a distance as the English couple walked to a table, Lucia accompanying them, carrying two cups of coffee, which she set down. Lucia then sat down at the table with the couple. Vito could see they were asking Lucia questions, and Lucia was responding, nodding her head as she spoke. The woman then handed what looked like money to Lucia, who then returned to the counter.

Vito waited until the English couple had left before strolling over to the coffee stall.

'Hi, Lucia,' he said, with a friendly smile.

'Hello to you,' said Lucia, returning his smile.

'That couple you were talking to just now,' he said. 'The English pair.'

'English?' said Lucia, surprised. 'Only the woman talked, and she spoke perfect Italian.'

'What were they after?'

'They wanted to know where they could find Angelina. You know, my friend Angelina Condotti who pops in for coffee and a chat now and then.'

'Oh yes, I know her,' said Vito. 'Why did they want to get hold of her?'

'They didn't say. Just said they had some information about a friend of Angelina's they wanted to pass on to her.'

'They didn't say what?'

'No. In the end they gave me the address they're staying at in Rome, and asked me if I'd ask Angelina to get in touch with them.' She gave a wink and added, 'They paid me a tip and told me to tell her there'd be one for her if she called on them.'

'It must be important,' said Vito.

Lucia shrugged. 'I don't know,' she said.

This is disturbing, thought Vito as he walked away. Angelina had been close to Giovanni Maduro, Vito remembered. Had the Maduros said anything to her about Julia that could lead to him?

Paolo arrived early that evening. Abigail had already gone out to a nearby restaurant and chosen three pizzas, which were currently in the oven. Paolo was hungry after his long train journey, so they waited until the meal was on the table before they began to exchange recent events with one another.

'Julia's dead,' Abigail told him as they ate.

Paolo nodded. 'Yes, Giovanni mentioned that in his telegram to me about the funerals. He didn't give any details, just "Julia dead". But it was a telegram.'

'She was murdered,' said Daniel. 'Someone strangled her.'

'Her body was found in a doorway in Campo de' Fiori,' added Abigail.

'When was she killed?'

'Sunday, but we didn't hear about it from Giuseppe until Monday, yesterday.'

'So it's unlikely Inspector Volpetti will be sending me a letter any time soon,' said Paolo sourly. 'With the police I expect it'll be weeks before he writes to me, if he does it at all.' He looked at them, curious. 'Do you think it's connected with the murder of my parents?'

'Yes,' said Abigail. 'But, at the moment, we can't see what the connection is.'

'Have you got any thoughts about who may have killed them, and why?'

'Lots of names have come up. Do you know a woman called Angelina Condotti?'

Paolo shook his head. 'No.'

'Apparently she was besotted with your father, but he showed no interest in her. Angelina wrote threatening letters to your mother telling her to leave Giovanni to her.'

'She never said anything about this to me.'

'Nor to your father, apparently,' said Abigail. 'I think she thought she was like how some obsessed teenagers get with a teacher at school.'

'Who is she, this Angelina?'

'An archaeology student who volunteered to work with Giovanni at the dig at the Forum.'

'Have you spoken to her?'

'No. We're trying to find her, but so far she seems to have disappeared. She left the dig at the Forum some weeks ago. The Cosa Nostra have also popped up in our investigations. We found threatening messages to your father to stop interfering in politics.'

'I told you I thought politics might play a part in this!' said Paolo. He looked worried. 'If the Cosa Nostra are involved, this is serious. How did you find out about them?'

'We found letters to your father warning him to stop writing newspaper articles. Your father had written "Fuschetti" on one of them, with a question mark.'

'Salvatore Fuschetti,' said Paolo.

'You know him?'

'I know of him,' said Paolo. 'He's a dangerous individual by all accounts. Do you think he had my parents shot?'

'We don't know,' admitted Daniel.

'At the moment we're thinking that either this Angelina Condotti or the Cosa Nostra may have been behind it,' said

Abigail. 'But we still have a lot to find out.'

'Our investigation isn't helped by Inspector Volpetti, who seems determined not to help us,' added Daniel.

'How are things in Milan?' asked Abigail.

Paolo shrugged. 'As always, unsettled. The people are unhappy. The unions are unhappy. The politicians squabble instead of sorting things out. This country's in a mess.' He looked thoughtful and said, 'I'm seriously thinking of emigrating to America.'

'Why?' asked Abigail.

'There are more opportunities there. Also, there's already a very large Italian community there all over America, and Italians always take care of their own. There's this man called Henry Ford in Detroit who's been working with a firm called Edison in a prototype car industry, and people are talking about big things happening there in the near future. It sounds like there'll be opportunities for young people like me who are prepared to work.'

'You'll be a stranger in a strange land,' said Abigail.

'Not necessarily,' said Paolo. 'There's a man at the place I work who's interested in doing the same thing. His name's Otto. He's in his twenties and has relatives in Detroit. He said we can stay with them until we get ourselves settled in. That's what we're thinking of doing. At the moment I'm working all the hours I can to save for the fare.'

Paolo then talked more about America, things he'd gleaned from letters friends of his had received from relatives in the States.

By the time bedtime arrived, it was obvious to Daniel and Abigail that Paolo's future was to be in America. 'After all,' he said, 'I have no family here any more.'

CHAPTER TWENTY-TWO

Wednesday 15th August

Santola Sciacci stepped down from the train and looked around at the Termini railway station. He was twenty years old and this was his first time in Rome. In fact, it was the first time he'd left Sicily.

The day before, his grandfather, Benedetto Sciacci, had summoned him to his villa set in his sprawling Sicily estate. Santola had often seen his grandfather at occasions like family weddings or island celebrations, but this was the first time he had been one-to-one with the old man. And Benedetto was old, there was no denying it. He was said to be in his eighties, but as Santola looked at him sitting by the fire in his favourite armchair, he thought that he'd never seen anyone of any age looking so vital and alive. Benedetto's eyes blazed with angry fire in his grizzled face.

'Fifty years ago my beloved son, Bartelo, was killed by two cowards,' Benedetto said.

'Yes,' nodded Santola. 'My father told me about the murder. A tragedy.'

'More than a tragedy,' growled Benedetto. 'Bartelo was my youngest, my dearest, my most loved. I swore at the time his death would be avenged, but the cowards fled from the island. No one knew where they'd gone. We demanded information from their families, but they claimed not to know. Even when we killed one or two as an example. All that happened was the rest of the families also fled. You know our code, Santola – the death of a loved one has to be avenged, no matter how long it takes. It has taken fifty years, but finally we have learnt what happened to the two villains. They fled to Rome and changed their names. They were Federico Alessio and Luca Casimiro and they changed their names to Federico Legato and Luca Capaldi. Both men are still alive, but old. I wish Bartelo's death to be avenged.'

'You want me to kill them?'

'Yes, but not yet. I want them to suffer as I suffered. Both men have sons in their forties, both successful, especially Legato's son, Rocco. Capaldi's son is called Lorenzo. He is a police sergeant.'

'A police sergeant?' echoed Santola, surprised.

'I expect it was done as a ruse. I believe the Legatos and the Capaldis are still close. You know we have a saying here in Sicily: revenge is a dish best eaten cold. This dish is very cold, fifty years cold, but before you deal with the two men who killed Santola, your task is to kill their sons, Rocco Legato and Lorenzo Capaldi.' Benedetto's eyes burnt even fiercer as he added, 'I want them to suffer as I suffered, to know their sons are dead. They will know their own deaths will follow, but I want them to be tortured in their own hell as they wonder where and when that will happen. Their sons dying will tell them that we know where and who they are. They will be tormented just as I have been these past fifty years.'

'I will not let you down,' Santolo promised him. 'Rocco Legato and Lorenzo Capaldi will die. After I've done that, I will return to Sicily and await your instructions on when to mete out the punishment to their fathers.'

Benedetto nodded and handed him an envelope. 'Here are the details of where they live, where they work, their families, everything about them.'

'Do you have contacts in Rome, should I need assistance with anything?' asked Santolo.

'I have contacts, but they are not to be contacted or used. No one can be trusted. There would be a danger of word of this being passed to the Legatos and Capaldis. Federico and Luca will know soon enough when they learn their sons are dead.' The old man passed a bulky wallet to Santolo. 'Here is money. You will also find the address of a bank in Rome at which I have an account. The details are there. If you need more money, I have arranged for you to withdraw it. Expense is no object here. The deaths of Rocco Legato and Lorenzo Capaldi are all that matter. But be careful. It is important you are not caught.'

'I will not be caught,' Santolo promised.

Now, as he stood in the Termini railway station, Santolo thought about his promise. Two men to kill, and then return to Sicily. Rocco Legato, a Cosa Nostra *capo*, would be well protected by his men. Lorenzo Capaldi, a police sergeant, would be protected by both his colleagues in the police force and by Legato's men. He needed to mount a watch on both and work out the best way of carrying out his task.

The ancient church was packed for the funeral. Daniel and Abigail recognised Giuseppe and Antonio and some other attendants, but the vast majority were people they didn't know. Giuseppe and Paolo acted as pall-bearers, carrying the coffins from the church out to the burial ground, along with other friends of the much-missed late couple. Daniel had no idea what the words the priest was saying during the ceremony meant, and he'd already told Abigail there was no need to translate – she could tell him about it later. The church was filled with wreaths expressing condolences and affection, among them one from Abigail and Daniel, which Abigail had arranged with a local florist.

After the ceremony everyone was invited to a large hall where refreshments had been laid on, and where fond memories of Giovanni and Sarah were exchanged. In the middle of these, Paolo approached Daniel and Abigail and slipped a piece of paper into Abigail's hand.

'This is my address in Milan, if you get any news. It will save you troubling Giuseppe to write or telegraph me; he really has enough to cope with at the moment with the Festival.'

'Thank you,' said Abigail. 'I promise you we'll keep you informed if we hear anything. You have our address in England?'

'I do,' said Paolo. 'It was in my mother's address book, along with her father's address. I now have those. One day I hope to get to England and call upon him. He is my grandfather, after all.'

'If you do get to England, please call on us,' said Abigail. 'There'll always be a welcome for you at our house. And let us know if you do decide to go to America.'

'I will,' he promised them. He looked at the crowds of people, chattering together solemnly, and said, 'I will say my goodbye to Giuseppe and then I must leave to get my train back to Milan.'

'Do you want us to come with you to the station?' asked Daniel.

'No thank you,' said Paolo. 'I'll just slip away quietly on my own.'

After Paolo had gone, Daniel said, 'I do admire that young man. Seventeen years old and he's coping with a lot.'

'You had to cope with a lot when you were his age,' Abigail reminded him. 'An orphan, not long out of the workhouse, working at God knows what.'

'Which is why I know how hard it can be,' said Daniel.

Soon after Paolo had departed, Abigail and Daniel also left, after saying their farewells to Giuseppe and Antonio and assuring them both they'd keep in touch with any developments.

Once they returned to the flat and made themselves a pot of tea, Abigail read through some of the articles that Giovanni had published.

'Giovanni was quite left-leaning in his views,' she told Daniel. 'He's critical of most of the large industrialists for the way they treat their workers. He's also critical of the current Prime Minister, Giuseppe Saracco. He compares him unfavourably with Garibaldi, for example.'

'Who's Garibaldi?' asked Daniel.

'You don't know much about Italian history, do you?' observed Abigail with a smile.

'I don't know anything about Italian history,' said Daniel, returning her smile, 'but I'm sure you're going to tell me.'

'For one thing, it's only fairly recently that Italy has existed as an independent unified nation. Until the 1870s it was a set of states who were either at war with one another, or with neighbouring countries. Austria, for example, and France, who ruled much of the territory. The largest state was the Bourbon Kingdom of the Two Sicilies, ruled by the Bourbon kings of France, and one of the most influential was the Papal States.'

'Which I assume meant the Pope's territory,' said Daniel. 'The Vatican.'

'Not just the Vatican, a whole central part of the country: Rome, Marche, Umbria. Garibaldi was one of those who advocated the unification of Italy. And not just advocated it – he fought for it, aided by his own military force. They were known as the Ragamuffins, and also as the Redshirts. They fought for the rights of the oppressed, as well as fighting for a unified Italy.'

'He sounds like an Italian Robin Hood.'

'Oh, he was much more than that. His influence was global. To show you how far his popularity spread, as a follower of English football I assume you've heard of a team called Nottingham Forest.'

'Everyone's heard of Nottingham Forest,' said Daniel indignantly.

'Yes, but what most people don't know is that when the team was formed in 1865, they adopted the colour red as their team's colours, in honour of Garibaldi's Redshirts.'

'You're joking!' said Daniel, incredulous.

'It's absolutely true. And when we get back to England, you can check with your football-loving friends in Nottingham – they'll confirm it. When Garibaldi came to England, he was celebrated across the country as a hero to working people because of his fights for freedom. I won't list for you all the battles he was involved in, but there were many. He was even involved in the American Civil War.'

'On which side?'

'The Union. He was fiercely opposed to slavery and any kind of prejudice against people considered oppressed or persecuted. In fact, the Thirty-Ninth New York Volunteer Regiment was named "The Garibaldi Guard" after him. He was offered a major general's commission in the United States army. This was in 1861. Interestingly, he turned it down, saying he would only take the commission if the Union government declared the abolition of slavery. This was a year before Lincoln issued the Proclamation of Emancipation.'

'My God, he was ahead of his time.'

'He was,' said Abigail. 'You can see why so many people considered him a hero. However, some large sections of the population opposed him, particularly the Papal States. Garibaldi made no bones about the fact that he was anti-Catholic and against the Pope. Any Pope. But by the late 1860s he'd amassed a formidable fighting force, which had been incorporated into the Italian army. It was in 1870 that Garibaldi's army forcefully entered Rome and annexed it in the name of the Kingdom of Italy.'

'Who was the King at this time?'

'Victor Emmanuel II. Effectively, once Rome had been conquered, Italy became a unified country, with all the different states accepting the fact, especially once the capital of Italy was declared to be Rome. Up till then the capital of Italy had been Florence.'

'And this was all down to Garibaldi.'

'Not completely. Giuseppe Mazzini played a major role, as did others such as Camillo Benso and King Victor Emmanuel II. But for most people, Garibaldi personified the successful struggle to unite Italy into one nation.'

There was a knocking at the street door. Daniel went to open it and Giuseppe breezed in, a look of triumph on his face.

'I have discovered where Julia was staying!' he announced delightedly. He produced a piece of paper from his pocket and put it on the table. 'Here is the address.'

'How did you find it?' asked Abigail.

'Through my contacts,' said Giuseppe. 'The photograph of Julia had been shared amongst them, especially local policemen, and one of them recognised her. His beat covers the market at Campo de' Fiori, and he was sure he'd seen her come out of a building close to the market where people rented rooms. He knows the landlady, a Signora Spinetti, so he went to see her and showed her the photograph. She recognised Julia and told him that about a fortnight or so ago she began renting one of her rooms to her.'

'Did she know that Julia had been killed?'

'No. She'd heard that a young woman had been found dead in a doorway, but never thought it was her tenant.'

'I'm surprised she didn't make enquiries when her tenant disappeared and the rent stopped being paid.'

'The rent had been paid a month in advance. But not by Julia. It was paid by a young man.'

'Did she get the young man's name?'

'No. The room was rented in the name of Julia Winstanley. That's the only name she had. She said the young man used to visit the girl.'

'Did she describe him?'

Giuseppe shrugged. 'I asked her and she said he was pretty nondescript. In his early twenties, neat and tidy. No distinguishing features. No beard or moustache or anything.'

'Did you have a look at the room?' asked Daniel.

'No. I thought I'd leave that to you. You're the detectives. I didn't want to mess things up.' He smiled. 'I got the feeling that Signora Spinetti may not have been telling me everything. Perhaps the sight of some lira might make her more forthcoming, but I decided to leave that up to you for when you meet her.'

Lorenzo Capaldi was doing his regular patrol on his patch when he became aware he was being followed. He turned, and saw that a young man he recognised as Niccolo Andretti was behind him. Niccolo immediately stopped and turned away and looked in a shop window. Capaldi strolled over to where Niccolo stood.

'Niccolo Andretti, isn't it?' he said genially.

Niccolo nodded.

'Yes,' he said.

'Did you want to tell me something?' asked Capaldi.

Niccolo hesitated, then nodded.

'Whatever it is, you can tell me,' said Capaldi with a friendly smile. 'Whatever it is, you won't be in trouble.'

Niccolo hesitated, then said awkwardly, 'There's a plot to kill the Prime Minister.'

Capaldi had to do his hardest to stop his face showing shock at these words. How did this boy know?

'Tell me,' he said, trying to appear as casual as he could.

'It concerns a friend of mine,' said Niccolo. 'I don't want him to get in trouble.'

'For killing the Prime Minister?' said Capaldi, indignantly.

'I don't know if he really means it, or if it's all just talk,' said Niccolo. 'But he said he's going to do it when the Prime Minister comes to the closing of this festival that's going on. The one at the Colosseum.'

'That's on Friday,' said Capaldi. 'I shall be on duty guarding the Prime Minister.'

'That's why I thought you were the one to tell,' said Niccolo.

'Who is this friend of yours? How is he planning to kill the Prime Minister?'

'With a gun,' said Niccolo. 'His name is Vito Volpetti. It may be just talk, but I wanted to let you know so that you could stop him if he really does try to do it.'

Capaldi studied Niccolo intently, then said, 'There's more, isn't there?'

Niccolo nodded. 'He's asked me to help him.'

'How?'

'I don't know, he hasn't said. Just be with him. I think he plans to run off after he's doing it and he'll want my help to get him away from the Colosseum.'

'Is anyone else involved?' asked Capaldi.

'Not as far as I know,' said Niccolo. 'Just me. And our friend Matteo knows about it.'

Capaldi looked thoughtful, musing over what he'd just been told. Then he said, 'You did right to tell me. I shall keep a close watch on this Vito Volpetti on the day, and if he tries anything I shall step in and arrest him.'

'He'll have a gun,' said Niccolo. 'He's a policeman with the railway police.'

Capaldi nodded. 'I shall be prepared.'

'You won't harm him?' asked Niccolo, concerned.

'No. I shall just arrest him,' Capaldi reassured him. 'Thank you, Niccolo. You have done a great service to Italy in telling me this. Your family will be proud of you.'

Yes, they will, thought Niccolo happily as he watched Sergeant Capaldi walk away. *I will have saved the life of the Prime Minister.*

CHAPTER TWENTY-THREE

Abigail and Daniel found the lodging house where Julia had been staying, and Signora Spinetti, the owner and landlady, was there. Daniel stayed back and let Abigail handle the dialogue, which was all very Italian with many florid hand gestures. Daniel could see from the woman's face that she was suspicious of them and reluctant to allow their entrance, but her manner changed dramatically when Abigail produced a bundle of banknotes. In a short while Signora Spinetti had led them upstairs to a dingy landing and unlocked one of the doors, then ushered them into a small and untidy room which smelt of stale sweat.

More conversation followed between Abigail and the landlady, and finally Abigail counted off ten banknotes and handed them to the woman, accompanied by more fluent Italian, which Daniel guessed to be promises of further money later.

Signora Spinetti took the banknotes, smiled, and left the room, leaving them space to explore it.

'Translation?' asked Daniel. 'A bribe, obviously, in order that we can examine the room.'

'Based on what Giuseppe told us, and the look in her eyes when I produced the banknotes, I knew the key to us getting what we wanted was money, as simple as that.'

'There was a lot of talking. Did she give you anything useful? The mysterious young man's name for example?'

'No, she said he never gave his name. It was sufficient to her that she had the girl's name in case any authority started asking questions. I got the impression that was unlikely, and – more importantly for her – he paid in cash. The one piece of information she did give up, for a few more lira, was that one day the young man was seen leaving the house wearing a police uniform.'

'Police?' repeated Daniel. 'So he was a policeman.'

'It would appear so,' said Abigail. 'I told her that we'd been asked by the girl's father back in England to try and find out what had happened to his daughter, and to achieve that he'd authorised us to pay whatever costs were needed if we could get that information. The money I paid her was an initial payment to allow us to search the room for clues, and anything belonging to Julia. I promised her more money when we'd finished.'

Daniel looked at the unifying sprawling mess that was the room.

'Right, so I guess we'd better start.'

'Yes,' said Abigail. 'If you find anything in English, check it out. Everything in Italian, leave to me.'

It was fortunate that the room was small and the amount of possessions limited in number, unlike Giovanni and Sarah's flat. In fact there were very few items in English, only a romantic novel and a diary. Daniel put the diary in his pocket.

For her part, Abigail had more to do, as there were a

number of sheets in handwritten Italian. She also found a small handbag, which contained money and a variety of used tickets, some from buses, some from theatres and other events. It was in the handbag that Abigail discovered a small bundle of envelopes tied up with a length of pink ribbon.

'Ah-ha!' she said.

'What have you found?' asked Daniel.

'If I'm not mistaken, her secret cache of love letters.' Abigail untied the ribbon and opened the first envelope. 'Yes,' she said. 'They're quite brief, and more practical than ardent outpourings of love. But they give us a clue to the sender. He signs himself "V".'

'V,' echoed Daniel. 'A policeman whose name begins with V. Volpetti, perhaps? If so, it would explain why he seems to be blocking our investigation.'

'Mrs Spinetti described him as a young man. Inspector Volpetti is not a young man, by any stretch of the imagination.'

'Yes, true,' agreed Daniel reluctantly.

Abigail put the bundle of envelopes into her own handbag. 'We'll take a proper look at them later.'

They continued searching the room. Daniel discovered some letters to Julia in English from her father, which seemed to be urging her to live a proper life of respectability. One of them ended with the remark that, unless she could achieve that and promise to be better behaved in the future, she would not be welcome to return to England.

'You think the answer to the mystery is in this room?' asked Daniel.

'I do,' said Abigail. 'At least, some of the answers. The important ones.'

'In that case, I think we should offer to rent the room from Signora Spinetti for a further week, in case we need to come back and search it more thoroughly,' he said. 'For that, she should let us have a key so we can come here whenever we want.'

Salvatore Fuschetti sat in his office at the stables. His right-hand man, Mario Torriano, was on the other side of the desk, expectant for orders from his boss.

Fuschetti had thought long and hard about this after he'd told Massimo Cassani about the threatening notes he'd sent to Giovanni Maduro. It had seemed a very minor thing at the time, done to satisfy the Sulli brothers, but the shooting of Maduro and his wife had given it a whole different dimension. The shootings had happened on Rocco Legato's territory, and Fuschetti had observed that this had caused his boss Massimo Cassani some concern. Territorial disputes sometimes occurred when one Cosa Nostra unit infringed on another's territory. That had not been the intention with Maduro, but something needed to be done to convince Rocco Legato of this. Cassani had told Fuschetti to leave it to him, but Fuschetti knew what the price was for a perceived territorial infringement, and he was determined that wouldn't happen to Massimo. So far, nothing had happened, but the problem was these Wilsons ferreting around – would they find the threatening notes? That was quite likely now they were staying at the Maduros' flat. Action needed to be taken to stop the Wilsons from nosing around further, and it was up to him, Salvatore Fuschetti, to do so. After all, he'd been the one who caused this situation. After he'd sorted things out, then he'd tell Massimo what he'd done, but not before. He wanted Massimo to feel confident in him.

He'd made enquiries about these Wilsons and had learnt from someone at the police station that Inspector Volpetti believed the woman, Signora Wilson, was the most dangerous of the two. It was for this reason he'd summoned Mario Torriano.

'I have a job for you. There is an English couple staying at the flat of Giovanni Maduro. They are called the Wilsons. I want you to capture the man, Daniel Wilson, and bring him here. Put him in one of the stables, under guard. No actual violence is to be used against him. He does not speak Italian, so you will have to make your intention clear by visual means. I suggest a pistol pointed at him will suffice.

'When you have him safely under lock and key, you will bring me his wallet, if he has one. If not, something that will identify him. Is that clear?'

'Very clear, Signor Fuschetti,' said Torriano.

'That blabbermouth Vito has been talking about the plan to shoot the Prime Minister at the Colosseum during the celebrations,' said Capaldi.

He and Rocco Legato were sitting in Legato's office in his olive oil exporter's shop.

'Who did you hear this from?' asked Legato.

'From Niccolo Andretti, a young man who's a friend of Vito's.'

'Who else knows?'

'According to Niccolo, their other friend Matteo Pucho has been told.'

'Anyone else?'

'Not according to Niccolo. What are we going to do?'

'We carry on exactly as planned. You are ready for Friday?'

Capaldi nodded.

'I would suggest keeping in touch with this Niccolo Andretti, before the day,' said Legato.

'I'd already planned to do that,' said Capaldi.

'Good,' said Legato approvingly. 'We don't want any unfortunate things happening unexpectedly.'

CHAPTER TWENTY-FOUR

When Abigail and Daniel got back to the flat, they took out the documents they'd discovered at the room: the bundle of letters, and the diary.

'Interestingly, a lot of the diary's in English,' noted Daniel as he turned over the pages. 'Even though Julia could write and speak Italian.'

'That's to stop anyone Italian reading it if they found it,' said Abigail.

Daniel began to read through the diary. 'There's quite a few bits that appear to be in some sort of code.' He showed a couple of them to her.

'Definitely interesting,' said Abigail thoughtfully. 'She had something to hide. It's a mixture of coded words, jumbled up with English and Italian. Were you any good with codes when you were at Scotland Yard?'

'Only the simplest ones,' said Daniel. 'I wondered if you might be better at it. After all, you've deciphered hieroglyphics at the pyramids.'

'Yes, but I had a lot of previous work by generations of archaeologists to build on,' said Abigail.

She handed the diary back to Daniel, then indicated the letters she'd been going through. 'There's evidence right here in these,' she said. 'V says in one that G and S have been dealt with, so she doesn't need to worry about that any more.'

'G and S,' said Daniel. 'Giovanni and Sarah.'

'Exactly. And there's another telling her to meet him at the Campo de' Fiori, and it's dated 12th August, the day she died.'

'So, it's the proof that this young policeman killed Giovanni and Sarah and then Julia,' suggested Daniel.

'Very likely, although a good defence barrister could put a different spin on them both.'

'I think we should take all this to Inspector Volpetti,' proposed Daniel.

'I'm sure he'll dismiss it, as he has done with everything we've brought to him so far,' said Abigail.

'Yes, I think that's quite likely. But I'd just like to see his reaction when we show him these two incriminating letters. As I've said before, I have my suspicions about the inspector.'

'You think he's involved in some way?'

'His reluctance to deal with it properly, and the way he's been obstructing our investigation, raise doubts about him for me. Certainly, if it hadn't been for the fact that Julia's policeman lover was a young man, I'd have put money on that V being for Volpetti. Especially now we know he's a dead shot with a rifle.'

Santola Sciacci walked slowly past Legato's olive oil shop, holding a sheet of paper on which he'd scribbled the name and address of a chemist further along the same street. He'd written it earlier and had it ready so that if anyone stopped him and asked him what he was doing, he'd tell them he was looking for this chemist because he was a stranger in town visiting his grandmother, who needed some particular tablets. He stopped to look in the window of the shop at the display of cans of olive oil, but mainly to see how many people were inside. There seemed to be about half a dozen, all men, and he could tell from the way their jackets hung that most of them were armed. He reached a corner and turned down it, then turned again and found himself in a narrow street that ran behind the shop. He walked along this, looking for any doors that might lead into the shop from the rear, but found only a large, blank brick wall that ran the whole length of the street.

So, the only way in was through the shop, which meant being confronted by Legato's bodyguards.

He needed to find another way.

Once again, Abigail and Daniel had called on Inspector Volpetti.

'What is it now?' he demanded wearily.

'We discovered where Julia was staying before she was murdered,' said Abigail. 'She rented a room in the Campo de' Fiori.'

'How did you find that out?' asked Volpetti.

'It's what we do,' said Abigail. 'We're detectives.' She produced the two letters from her handbag. 'We discovered these in her room.' She pushed them across the desk to him. They watched him attentively as he read the letters. There seemed to be no reaction showing on his face, no curiosity.

'What are these supposed to show?' he asked.

'That this V, who wrote them, had killed Giovanni and Sarah.'

'He does not say that,' said Volpetti. 'It says he has dealt with G and S. That could mean anything. It could refer to your great British musical geniuses, Gilbert and Sullivan. Perhaps he had managed to get tickets for a performance of one of their operas.'

'And the one telling her to meet him at the Campo de' Fiori, given to her on the day she died? There is no stamp on the envelope, so he must have delivered it by hand.'

'It just means they met later. Perhaps she did not turn up for this meeting. Perhaps she was already dead by then, slain by some unknown killer.'

'It's a bit of a coincidence, don't you think?' said Abigail. 'Aren't you going to try and find this young man called V? I'm sure you can do this, as we are told he is a young police officer.'

'There are plenty of young police officers, and many of them have names beginning with V,' said Volpetti. He tapped the two letters. 'However, I will take these and investigate them.'

With a swift movement Abigail reached out, took hold of the letters and pulled them back to her, putting them into her bag.

'Thank you,' she said, 'but we'll conduct our own investigation into them.'

'You cannot take them,' protested Volpetti. 'They are evidence, and as such the property of the police.'

'You have just dismissed them as evidence,' said Abigail. 'Also, they are not the property of the police, but of Julia's next of kin, her father, Brigadier Winstanley. If you disagree, you can take it up with the British Ambassador, with whom we shall be lodging these letters until they can be sent to Brigadier Winstanley.'

With that, Abigail rose and walked out of the office, followed by Daniel. At the door, Abigail stopped and turned back to face the inspector.

'There's one thing I've been meaning to ask, Inspector. The bullets that killed Giovanni and Sarah. Do you know what gun they were fired from?'

Volpetti looked momentarily disconcerted. Then he said, 'Unfortunately, they were lost at the hospital.'

'Lost?' echoed Abigail, incredulously.

'Yes. Apparently, a hospital orderly threw them away after the post-mortem had been carried out.'

'Did they match the gun that was found at the scene?'

'We did not check. It was obvious what had happened, as the gun was the weapon that had been used.'

'But it may not have been. It may just have been left there to implicate Sarah Maduro.'

Volpetti did not reply, just glowered at her.

'This case has been conducted appallingly, Inspector,' said Abigail. 'Vital evidence – in this case the fatal bullets – has been disposed of without being properly checked. I am surprised you still keep your position as inspector. I would not allow you to run a stall selling sausages.'

Inspector Volpetti stared after them as they left, an angry glare suffusing his face. Somehow, he had to get those letters from them. He knew who'd written them; he'd recognised the handwriting at once. Someone he'd sworn he would always protect. And now he had to take drastic action in order to keep his promise.

CHAPTER TWENTY-FIVE

Daniel stopped in the street outside the entrance to the police station and looked at Abigail, his expression angry at them being dismissed in such a derisory fashion.

'This is ridiculous,' he said. 'Translate to me what Inspector Volpetti said.'

After Abigail had told him the inspector's refutation of the evidence they'd presented to him, he looked even angrier.

'There is definitely something wrong here,' he said. 'Inspector Volpetti is hiding something big. He may even be involved in the actual murders.'

'That may be a bit extreme,' cautioned Abigail.

'I know it,' insisted Daniel. 'Call it my copper's nose, or my years of experience working at Scotland Yard, but I know it. It was in his eyes when you showed him those letters from V, and the way he tried to hold onto them. My gut tells me he was so worried by what he saw in those letters that he's going to do something about them.'

'What?' asked Abigail.

'I don't know, but something,' said Daniel. He pointed to a coffee bar across the road from the police station. 'I suggest you go back to the flat and do what you were doing, working your way through the documents in Italian for clues. I'm going to park myself in that café and watch the police station. I'm sure that the inspector is going to do something, and when he does, I'm going to follow him.'

'You don't speak Italian,' Abigail pointed out.

'I don't need to,' said Daniel. 'I'm just going to follow him and see where he goes and who he meets.'

'Say he spots you?'

'He won't,' said Daniel confidently. 'I learnt from all those years at Scotland Yard, following dodgy people.' He tapped his pocket where he kept his wallet. 'And I've got money in case I need to catch a cab, or something.'

'All right,' said Abigail. 'I'll see you back at the flat. Be careful.'

Inspector Volpetti was fuming with anger as he left the police station and headed for the house where his son, Vito, lived with his young wife and two children. He was so caught up in his thoughts over the letters the English couple had shown him, that he didn't notice the Englishman come out of the coffee bar opposite the police station. The inspector had always done his best for his son, ever since Vito's mother had died soon after the boy was born. The inspector's relatives had all urged him to get the baby boy adopted, or at least get him fostered while he was small, but Volpetti had refused.

'He is my son, and the son of my much-loved late wife, Helena, and I will bring him up and love him and care for him. It's what she would have wanted.'

He'd used his female relatives, his three sisters and his

cousins, as surrogate mothers when Vito was still a baby. The problems began when he started school. Different people used to collect him from school and take him home with them, until Volpetti could finish work. The problem was the boy was difficult. He had tantrums. He stole. He made life onerous for those who looked after him, so that they were keen to get him off their hands and handed to his father. Often, Volpetti was urged to marry again, but it soon became obvious that when any woman entered his life, she was scared off by the difficult child, and then the young teenager that Vito became. But still, Volpetti looked after him; every time he looked at Vito he saw Helena's features, her eyes, and he knew it was a burden he'd have to live with.

Although Vito seemed to behave when he was with his father, Volpetti heard many stories about his son's bad behaviour when he was away from him. He did so many bad things that it was hard to remember them all. Volpetti blamed himself for being too soft with his son, forgiving him, making excuses for him. And now, this was the result: the letters the Wilson woman had shown him, in Vito's handwriting, that they'd found in Julia's room. He didn't need to be a detective to understand what these letters meant.

Plus, with this damned festival he hadn't been able to get away with his friends, Enzo and Vittorio, to the mountains at weekends and hunt boar. It was the only thing that made life bearable.

He reached Vito's house and knocked at the door, which was opened by Valetia, Vito's wife.

'Inspector!' said Valetia, giving him a broad smile of welcome.

'Is my son at home?' asked Volpetti.

'Yes. Won't you come in?'

'No, I'm afraid I can't stay. I just need to tell him something.'

'No problem. I'll get him.'

Shortly after, Vito appeared in the doorway, an anxious look on his face.

'Valetia said you wanted to see me.'

'I do,' said Volpetti. 'But not here. Come outside and we'll walk to the corner.'

'Why?' asked Vito.

'Because I said so,' snapped Volpetti.

Vito looked at his father, perturbed. He wasn't used to being treated like this. He came out of the house, pulling the door shut after him, and followed his father to the corner of the street, where there was a patch of waste ground. No one was around.

'What is it?' asked Vito.

Volpetti turned on his son, angrily.

'You fool!'

Vito looked at his father, puzzled.

'What do you mean?' he asked.

'I've seen the letters you wrote to that English girl. Those English detectives have got hold of them. One tells her not to worry because you've dealt with the problem with G and S, which they know means Giovanni and Sarah Maduro. And the other telling her to meet you at Campo de' Fiori on the day she was killed.'

Vito's mouth fell open in shock.

'How did they get them?' he asked.

'That damned girl kept them, because she was a romantic.

161

The English couple found out where she was staying and searched the room.' He glared angrily at his son. 'You killed the Maduros, and then you killed the girl. Don't try and deny it.'

'I do deny it,' protested Vito. 'Yes, I wrote to Julia telling her that the problem of Giovanni and Sarah was over, but that was after I'd discovered they'd been shot. And I did arrange to meet Julia on the day she died, but she never turned up. I had nothing to do with those killings.'

'Liar!' exploded Volpetti. 'You've always been a liar and trouble. I gave you every opportunity. I got you that job at the railway police because I thought it would straighten you out, after all the trouble you've always been in. You have been a bitter disappointment to me. Not just this, but the women you carry on with behind Valetia's back, and especially consorting as you do with criminals like Rocco Legato.'

'I don't consort with him.'

'You do! I've had reports about you meeting him. And where else would you get the money to spend it the way you do? Not on a railway policeman's wages.'

'I didn't do the killings!' insisted Vito. He looked plaintively at his father. 'What are you going to do?'

'I don't know,' said Volpetti unhappily.

'You can't turn me in,' pleaded Vito. 'I didn't do it. I'm your son.'

From his vantage point further along the street, Daniel saw the inspector walk away from the young man. The inspector looked angry.

Which one to follow? pondered Daniel. *The inspector or the young man?* The inspector, he decided. He knew where the young man lived – he'd be able to discover who he was soon enough.

Daniel followed the inspector, being careful to keep his distance from his prey. Although it was obvious from Volpetti's manner, his speed of walking, that the inspector was a very upset man, too upset to bother to look behind him.

Daniel followed the inspector back to the police station, and once he'd seen Volpetti go in, he decided he'd learnt enough for the moment. His next task was to find out who the young man was, and for that he'd need Abigail's help. He'd show her the house and ask her to go and ask for some fictitious person there. When whoever opened the door told her there was no one of that name there, she'd ask who did live there, because she'd obviously been given the wrong address. Once they knew that, it was down to practical detective work to find out who the young man was and how he was connected to the murders.

As he made his way to the flat, Daniel felt quite pleased that he'd been able to find his way around. True, he'd been up and down these streets with Abigail, but he was glad that the sense of direction he'd built up over the years when walking through towns and cities was still with him, as it had been when he and Abigail had been in Paris, and before that in Manchester.

As he neared the flat, he saw a carriage parked on the other side of the street, and wondered if someone was calling on them. *It doesn't have to be for us*, he told himself; there were plenty of flats. But over the years he'd developed a sixth sense of watchfulness.

Inside the carriage, Mario Torriano and a colleague, Jobby, had spent the last hour watching the flat, waiting in the hope that

Daniel would appear. They had been just about to head back to the stables, when they saw Daniel walking towards the flat. Torriano and Jobby got out of the carriage, strolled across the street and fell into step behind Daniel. They then separated so that each was walking alongside their target. Daniel stopped, aware that something was wrong. He looked at the two men, and then down at the pistol that one of them was holding pointed at his ribs.

The man with the pistol put a hand on Daniel's arm to stop him, then pointed to the carriage parked at the kerb.

Daniel considered fighting back, trying to disarm the man, but as there were two of them and he was in a foreign city, he decided to take a chance that their purpose was to take him prisoner for some reason, rather than shoot him. At least, that's what he hoped. But why? he wondered as he walked to the waiting carriage. What was going on?

One of the men climbed into the driver's seat, and the man with the gun, Mario Torriano, got into the carriage with Daniel, that pistol trained on him the whole time. As the carriage trundled through the streets of Rome, Daniel looked through the window, trying to commit the route to memory for when he would be able to escape, but the horse and carriage seemed to go through many back streets rather than along a main route. Eventually it pulled up outside a stable yard. The man with the gun gestured for Daniel to get out. Daniel did so, and found himself being ushered by the gunman and another man into the yard and towards an empty stable. The men stopped by the stable door, and the man with the gun held out his open hand towards Daniel and said, '*Portafoglio.*'

'I don't speak Italian,' said Daniel.

The man reached into his pocket and took out his own wallet, which he showed Daniel, before putting it back in his jacket.

So, they want my wallet, Daniel thought. *Why? This has got to be more than just a robbery.*

He took out his wallet and handed it to the man, who put it in his pocket. Then Daniel was pushed into the stable and the door was shut. Daniel heard a bolt being slotted into place, securing it.

CHAPTER TWENTY-SIX

Abigail was using the stiletto-like paperknife to open some of the envelopes she'd found in Giovanni and Sarah's dresser, when there was a knock at the door. Daniel returning, she assumed. She went to the door and opened it, and found herself face to face with two men.

'*Buongiorno*, Signora Wilson,' said one, and he produced a wallet that Abigail recognised as Daniel's.

'What's happened to my husband?' she asked, alarmed.

'It will be better if we talk inside,' said Salvatore Fuschetti.

Abigail regarded him warily, then stepped back and let the two men enter. She closed the door, then returned to the table and sat down. She gestured at a chair next to her and the man who'd spoken took a seat. The other remained standing, silent, obviously the bodyguard. The man put Daniel's wallet on the table.

'I bring this as proof that we are holding your husband.'

'Why?' demanded Abigail.

'Because we want you to stop investigating the deaths of Giovanni and Sarah Maduro at the Colosseum,' said the man. 'If you do not, your husband will suffer.'

Abigail glared at him with open contempt. She reached out towards the wallet, but instead snatched up the paperknife and brought it up under the man's chin, the sharp point digging into the flesh, blood appearing from where the point had pricked him. Immediately, the other man, the bodyguard, pulled out a pistol from inside his jacket, but Abigail's voice snapped sharply, 'Put that pistol on the table or I'll kill this man here and now. And if you shoot me, my body will react and push the knife up into his brain.'

As Abigail put pressure on the knife, digging it deeper into Fuschetti's flesh, he cried out frantically, 'Do as she says!'

The man put the pistol on the table, then stepped back, watchful and apprehensive.

'Listen to me, you worm,' said Abigail to the man she held prisoner with the knife, her tone harsh, 'all I have to do is push this upwards. It will cut through your tongue, then up past your eyes and into your brain. You will be dead very quickly. Do you understand? And I suggest you don't nod your head. I will ease the pressure off to allow you to talk.'

She lowered the knife slightly, although the point still stayed in the flesh beneath Fuschetti's chin.

'Yes,' said Fuschetti hoarsely.

'Right,' said Abigail. 'You obviously know who we are, so what's your name?'

When Fuschetti hesitated, Abigail pushed the knife upwards. Fuschetti yelped.

'My name is Fuschetti,' he said.

Fuschetti. Abigail remembered the name scribbled on the threatening note from the Cosa Nostra.

'Good,' said Abigail. 'Well, Mr Fuschetti, your man is going to bring my husband here.' She looked at the bodyguard. 'Go. Now. And leave the street door on the latch.'

The man looked at Fuschetti, who said hoarsely, 'Do as she says. And see that the English man is not harmed.'

Inside the stable, Daniel sat on a bale of hay and weighed up his situation. His main concern was for Abigail. If the men had picked him up outside their flat, then it was quite likely they were holding her prisoner there for some reason. But why? The removal of his wallet gave him the answer. Whoever these men were, they wanted answers. But they knew that Daniel, with his lack of Italian, wouldn't be able to understand their questions, or give them answers. The wallet was to prove to Abigail that they were holding him prisoner. What other sort of pressure would they put on her? The thought of her being at their mercy filled him with a deep anger. He had to get out of here and back to her. But how? The men were armed, and he wasn't. He also didn't know how to get back to the flat from here. For that he'd need to get a taxi. It was lucky for him that he'd taken the precaution of writing down the address of the flat in case he got lost, as he'd done when they were in Paris. But even if he managed to get out of this stable, without his wallet he had no money for a taxi.

I have been so stupid, he cursed himself. But the main thing at this moment was to get out of this stable. After that, he'd play it by ear.

Once Fuschetti's man had departed, with her free hand Abigail picked up the pistol and pointed it at Fuschetti. She laid the knife down on the table, relieved not to have to hold it in that uncomfortable position any longer. Abigail looked intently at Fuschetti. 'I must warn you, I am a deadly shot with a pistol. Any attempt by you to attack me, and you'll be very dead. Now, you will answer some questions. Why do you want us to stop looking into who killed Giovanni and Sarah Maduro? Is that because you killed them?'

'No,' said Fuschetti fervently. 'I swear on my life and that of my children that we had nothing to do with it!'

'Then why all this?' Abigail demanded. When he didn't answer, she said, 'You threatened him, didn't you. You're worried that we would find out and think you were the ones who killed Giovanni and Sarah.'

'We did not kill them,' repeated Fuschetti firmly. 'I swear—'

'On the life of your children,' said Abigail sarcastically. 'Why did you threaten them?'

'Giovanni was writing bad things about some people we knew. These people asked us to get him to stop. But we did not kill him. Or her.'

'Then who did?'

'I don't know,' said Fuschetti.

'Another of your compadres in the Cosa Nostra, perhaps?' asked Abigail.

Fuschetti looked at her with alarm in his eyes. 'There is no Cosa Nostra,' he said.

'Well that's a lie,' said Abigail. 'Which makes me wonder if everything else you've said is too.'

Daniel looked around the stable. He couldn't see anything that could be used as a weapon against a pistol. There was a broom, that was all. In that case, he'd have to rely on a ruse he'd used earlier in his career to get out of similar tight spots. He fell to his knees and began to groan, at first just feeble moans, then slowly getting louder. At the same time he began to thrash around on the ground, his flailing feet striking the walls and door.

There came a banging from outside, and the man on guard shouted, '*Silenzio!*'

Daniel began to increase the volume of his moans and groans and his thrashing about, hoping the sounds would convince the man outside that he was in genuine gut-aching pain. As his groans turned into a scream of agony, he heard the bolt being drawn back. Daniel continued with his convulsions, clutching his stomach as he yelled and screamed. The man approached Daniel, his pistol pointed at his prisoner, a torrent of angry abuse spilling out of his mouth. Daniel made his screams louder, his writhing more frantic. The man was obviously losing his temper, and bent down over the Englishman and struck at him with the barrel of his pistol.

This was the moment Daniel had been waiting for. He reached out, caught the man's pistol hand and pulled the man down towards him, at the same time lifting his shoulders from the ground and ramming his forehead as hard as he could into the man's face. The man fell back, blood spurting from his broken nose. Daniel jerked the pistol from his hand and struck him over the head with it. The man collapsed in a heap on the ground. Daniel pushed himself to his feet. As he saw the man twitching, he kicked him hard in the head, and the man fell still.

Daniel looked out at the stable yard. It appeared to be empty. He guessed the others had gone off in the carriage to the flat. Daniel went to the unconscious man and rifled through his pockets. He needed money to be able to get a taxi back to the flat. He found some notes and coins, which he stuffed into his pocket, along with the pistol.

'I swear we were not involved in the killings at the Colosseum,' Fuschetti appealed to Abigail. 'All we did was write him letters to try to persuade him to stop writing his articles. We worried that if you found out about that, you might think we'd shot them.'

'We did find out about you threatening them,' said Abigail. 'And we still think it's possible you did kill them.'

'No!' said Fuschetti. 'You have my word!'

'The word of a criminal?' said Abigail in disbelief. She looked at the clock on the wall. 'Very well, we'll wait until your man arrives and hope he brings my husband with him. Then we'll decide what to do.'

CHAPTER TWENTY-SEVEN

Daniel descended from the taxi and handed over some notes and coins to the driver. He looked at the flat, and up and down the street. There was no sign of any carriages parked nearby. What had happened after they'd abducted him? Had they taken Abigail? Or was she still in the flat, possibly with some armed thug watching over her? He pulled the pistol from his pocket and held it firmly in his hand, then made for the door. Gently, he tried the handle, and found the door was unlocked. He listened, and heard voices: Abigail's, and a man's. Thank God she was alive! They seemed to be talking conversationally, no sound of panic or threat in their voices. But better to be on his guard.

Daniel opened the door and stepped into the living room, the pistol in his hand, then he stopped in surprise. Abigail was sitting at the table, a pistol in her own hand aimed at a man.

'Daniel!' she said, relieved. 'They told me you were a prisoner.'

'I was. I got away.'

'Did they harm you?'

'No,' said Daniel. 'What about you? And who's this?'

'This is Mr Fuschetti,' she said.

'The Cosa Nostra man,' said Daniel, remembering.

'He insists there's no such thing, which we know is a lie. He has told me why you were kidnapped – it's to do with them not wanting anyone finding out that they'd threatened Giovanni.'

'For the articles he wrote?' suggested Daniel.

'Exactly so,' said Abigail. 'The question is, what do we do with him?'

Daniel looked at the man thoughtfully, then said, 'We could kill him and dump his body somewhere. But his men would come after us.'

It was obvious that Fuschetti had understood what Daniel had said, because he looked visibly alarmed.

Suddenly there was the sound of a horse's hooves and a carriage drawing up outside, doors slamming, voices raised in alarm, then the door burst open and the two men who'd taken Daniel prisoner rushed in, pistols in their hands. They stopped when Daniel pointed his own gun at them, and Abigail levelled hers at Fuschetti.

'Drop your guns or I'll blow his brains out,' barked Abigail.

'Do it!' shouted Fuschetti urgently.

The men hesitated, then dropped their guns on the floor.

'I'm guessing they were coming here to tell you I'd got away,' said Daniel.

'I believe this is what we would call in chess "stalemate",' Abigail said in Italian to Fuschetti. 'We kill you all now, more of your men kill us later. Far better for us all to stay alive. We now know what you wanted, but it's irrelevant. We will continue our investigation into the deaths of our friends the Maduros. Take this as a warning not to threaten us again. You may go, but leave your guns behind.'

Fuschetti got to his feet, then stopped, unsure if Abigail meant it. When she pointed to the door, Fuschetti hurried to it and out into the street, followed by his men. They waited before they heard the sound of the carriage driving off, then Abigail collapsed on the settee.

'My God!' she said. 'That was terrifying!'

'Really?' said Daniel. 'You didn't seem terrified. You looked completely in control.'

'That's because you weren't here for the whole thing. Believe me, how I maintained my composure is beyond me. These were proper gangsters! Giuseppe told us they are ruthless!'

'Are you worried they might come back?' asked Daniel. 'Should we report what happened to the police?'

'No,' said Abigail firmly. 'I don't trust the police here. Again, remember what Giuseppe said about many of them being in the pay of the Cosa Nostra. I'm hoping Mr Fuschetti will have been scared off by what happened.'

'It would have scared me off,' said Daniel. 'You are the most courageous person I've ever known.'

'I didn't feel it.' She looked thoughtful. 'I think we ought to tell Giuseppe about it, just in case something nasty does happen as a result.'

'What can he do?'

'Be on his guard,' said Abigail.

'Before we see Giuseppe, do you feel up to coming with me on something else?'

'Where to?'

Daniel told her about his following Inspector Volpetti to a house, and the inspector going off with a young man and having an angry discussion.

'We need to find out who the young man is. If you could call at the house . . .'

'I know, and ask for some fictitious person who they'll tell me isn't there, and that way I can ask who does live there.'

'Exactly,' said Daniel. 'And then, after that, we can go and see Giuseppe.'

CHAPTER TWENTY-EIGHT

Daniel watched from a distance as Abigail knocked at the door of the house he'd indicated. When there was no answer, she knocked again, then a third time. Abigail then moved to the neighbouring house. This time the door was opened by a middle-aged woman. Abigail explained through words and gestures that she was looking for a person whom she'd been told lived next door. The woman shook her head, and replied to Abigail's questions. After which, Abigail thanked her and returned to join Daniel.

'The people who live at that house are called Volpetti,' she told Daniel.

'Volpetti!' exclaimed Daniel.

'He and his wife have two young children. Apparently, he's a policeman with the railway service, and his father is a police inspector.'

'She told you all that?' said Daniel indignantly. 'Do these people not keep secrets?'

'Be glad they don't,' said Abigail.

'Anyway, I think we've found our connection,' said Daniel. 'Julia was having an affair with a young policeman. Inspector

Volpetti's son is a young policeman. He's obviously the V who wrote those letters to Julia, which is why the inspector came to berate him.'

'You think it was Volpetti's son who killed Giovanni and Sarah? And Julia?'

'I do,' said Daniel. 'And I think the inspector either knows that, or suspects it. Which would explain why the inspector has been so keen to obstruct our investigation at every turn.'

'What are we going to do about it?' asked Abigail.

'Find out more about Inspector Volpetti and his son. To do that I suggest asking Giuseppe. He seems to know a lot of policemen, and some of them are bound to know something about the Volpettis. We can talk to him about them when we go to see him to tell him about Fuschetti's attempt on our lives. He needs to be warned.'

In his office at the Forum, Giuseppe stared at Daniel and Abigail in horror as Abigail recounted her experience with Fuschetti.

'My God, Abigail, what were you thinking of?!'

'I was thinking of Daniel in the hands of those thugs and was determined to get them to release him unharmed.'

'But this was someone important in the Cosa Nostra!' Then Giuseppe's face clouded over and he said unhappily, 'Although he may not be for much longer.'

'What do you mean?' asked Daniel.

'He has let himself be diminished,' said Giuseppe. 'He surrendered. And to a woman. The Cosa Nostra will not like that.'

'You think they'll come after Abigail?'

'No,' said Giuseppe. 'They'll go after Fuschetti.'

'Why?' demanded Abigail. 'Women have always held a strong position in Italian society. Look at Lucrezia Borgia.'

'Who?' asked Daniel.

'I'll tell you about her later,' said Abigail. 'My point is they could not expect me to let them harm my husband and do nothing. Anyway, I'm now pretty sure this Fuschetti didn't have anything to do with shooting Giovanni and Sarah. So that leaves us with Angelina Condotti, and this young policeman called V, who we now know to be Inspector Volpetti's son.'

'Inspector Volpetti's son?' repeated Giuseppi. 'Are you sure?'

'A lot of things point to it being him. But we don't even know his name. All we know is he works as a policeman for the railway. We were wondering if, among your acquaintances, you know someone who knows Inspector Volpetti and his son.'

'I can ask around,' said Giuseppe. 'In the meantime, I'd be very careful, both of you. What happened to you with Fuschetti means you're marked people.' He looked at Abigail, concerned. 'After your ordeal today, do you still feel up to doing your Forum talk tomorrow?'

'Of course,' said Abigail. 'In fact, as we're here I was going to show Daniel over the Forum ahead of it.'

'At the moment the university students are doing their show there, the debates,' said Giuseppe.

'That's no problem,' said Abigail. 'Daniel and I can watch that, and then afterwards we can walk through the site.'

As they walked towards the Forum, Daniel said, 'One thing strikes me. The murders are different. Giovanni and Sarah were shot. Julia was strangled. Could there be two different killers?'

Abigail thought it over, then said, 'It's a possibility. We do have two people in the frame, Angelina Condotti and Volpetti's son. We know that Angelina can handle a gun.'

'So Angelina shoots, and Volpetti's son is the strangler?' said Daniel.

'It's something to work on,' agreed Abigail.

Abigail and Daniel took their seats at the back of the Forum to watch the debate by the university students. A temporary wooden stage had been erected amongst the ruins, on which the action was played out. The speakers and those playing the senators all wore white togas, some of which had decorated patterns on them.

'Is this how the debates would have been in classical Roman times?' murmured Daniel.

'Not exactly,' whispered back Abigail. 'Then, they would have been debating in Latin. Today they're using contemporary Italian. Most of today's audience would soon tire of listening to an ancient language they don't understand.' She looked enquiringly at Daniel and whispered, 'Or, in your case, listening to a modern language you don't understand.'

Daniel gave an apologetic sigh. 'I'm sorry about that,' he said, adding quickly. 'But I'm happy to stay and watch, and you can explain to me later what it was all about.'

'Well, give it another ten minutes and then we'll make a discreet departure,' said Abigail. 'We can wander in the other parts of the Forum without disturbing the performers, providing we talk quietly. That's what other people are doing.'

Daniel nodded and started to look more closely at the ruins that covered the large area. The temporary stage had been set up in a grove surrounded by towering ancient stone columns, and with what looked like ruined temples everywhere.

On the stage, one of the performers was orating loudly and expressively. Behind his back, six toga-wearing figures approached him, each clutching a long knife.

'Here comes the climax,' said Abigail. 'The end of Julius Caesar.'

The six armed figures moved in on the performer playing Caesar and began to stab at him. The actor was obviously wearing balloons filled with red ink or paint beneath his toga, because as he was stabbed the white became stained with deep crimson, and he fell slowly to the floor, still emoting, finally calling out, '*Et tu, Brute?*' before expiring.

The actors, including the slain Caesar, then lined up at the edge of the stage and bowed, and the audience began to applaud loudly, many shouting 'Bravo!' and similar expressions of approval.

'When did all that happen?' asked Daniel as he and Abigail rose, along with the rest of the audience.

'Julius Caesar was assassinated in 44 BC.'

'And he still dominates literature almost two thousand years later.'

'Thanks to Shakespeare,' said Abigail.

While most of the audience made for the stage to congratulate the performers ('Proud family members,' murmured Abigail), Daniel followed Abigail on a winding path that took them between various ancient ruins which Abigail identified. 'The Temple of Vesta,' she said, indicating a row of large plinths from which three tall columns reached up to the remains of a roof. 'And over there is the Temple of Castor and Pollux.'

'You've mentioned them before,' said Daniel. 'I've only

remembered them because they sound like a music hall comedy act. Who were they?'

'They were originally Greek, but like quite a bit of Roman mythology, Greek heroes were absorbed into the culture. They were twin brothers, but they had different fathers.'

'Interesting,' observed Daniel.

'Castor was the son of a mortal called Tyndareus, who was King of Sparta, and Pollux was the son of Zeus, king of the Gods, who seduced their mother, Leda, while he was disguised as a swan.'

'Nothing's straightforward in these old myths,' said Daniel.

As they left the Forum, Daniel commented, 'What I don't understand about this country is what went wrong.'

'Wrong?' asked Abigail.

'You've told me about all the different warring states before Italy became Italy not so long ago. Yet we are here celebrating a festival of classical Rome, surrounded by all the relics of the past glories: the Colosseum, the Palatine Hill, the Forum. I've been told that the Roman Empire was the largest empire there's ever been.'

'Of its time,' Abigail clarified. 'At the moment the British Empire is the largest ever, with much of Africa included in it, plus India, Australia, Canada – and think of how much bigger it was when the United States of America was part of it, before the War of Independence.'

'So what went wrong for Rome?' asked Daniel. 'Why did it go from the most powerful country in the world, to a dysfunctional place with no real power?'

'Many scholars still argue over the reasons,' said Abigail. 'But the general consensus is that the empire was badly managed.

For a start, it was huge, from Hadrian's Wall in Britain in the north, to North Africa in the south. All the countries around the Mediterranean were part of it, and it extended into Turkey and other parts of Asia in the east. To keep order in these far-flung parts, and stop any rebellion against Roman rule, required a massive army. Most of the soldiers in the army weren't from Rome but from wherever Rome had conquered. So, for example, you had Moroccan soldiers in the army, and some of those were sent to protect Hadrian's Wall.'

'Moroccans at Hadrian's Wall?' said Daniel, stunned. 'Are you sure?'

'I am,' nodded Abigail. 'I did a dig at the remains of the second-largest fort on Hadrian's Wall, at Bowness-on-Solway in Cumberland, and we found relics from Moroccan soldiers.

'The point is that a huge army like this, stretching across the known world, was very costly to maintain – wages for the soldiers, for example. And supplies for the outposts. As time went on, there were problems with paying the troops. You have to remember that the Roman Empire lasted from about 30 BC until roughly 470 AD. That's 500 years. And towards the end, one of the big problems was financial. Most of the wealth discovered in the far-flung provinces had been sent back to Rome, where the emperors spent it on their own pet projects. Often statues of themselves and ornately decorated palaces. This led to discontent among the populations in those distant provinces who remained in poverty while the Romans lived a life of luxury. Or, at least, the ruling class did. The ordinary Romans remained poor. Often the wages for the soldiers at the distant outposts didn't arrive, so they got discontented, and towards the end many of them walked away from the army. Morale and pride in Rome disappeared.

So when the barbarians decided to attack and plunder the Roman settlements, there was little strong resistance. Then the barbarians – and that means any tribe or nation that wasn't Roman – moved in to attack mainland Italy, and Rome itself. And there you have the collapse of the Roman Empire. Weak and selfish government at the centre in Rome, and resentments in the distant countries that Rome had conquered.

'It's said that Britain should remark on this, unless it wants its own empire to go the same way.'

'What do you mean?' asked Daniel.

'Well, there are parallels. I've just said that the British Empire is the largest ever, with much of Africa included in it, along with India, Australia and Canada and lots of other territories. We've already lost America because our army over there was inadequate against the local militias, and the Americans rose up in rebellion because they didn't like the heavy taxes the British government had imposed on them. What happens if India decides to revolt because the mineral wealth has been taken from them and sent to England, while most of their people languish in poverty? There are parallels with the collapse of the Roman Empire.'

'Hmm,' said Daniel. 'Surely our politicians will have learnt from history, and will make sure the same doesn't happen to us.'

Abigail sighed. 'If only that were true. Unfortunately, most politicians are only interested in their own local votes.'

Daniel chuckled. 'And you're the one who usually accuses me of being cynical.'

'There's a famous phrase,' said Abigail sombrely. 'Learn from history if you don't want to commit the same mistakes.'

CHAPTER TWENTY-NINE

Angelina Condotti sat on the low wall that edged the Lungotevere in Sassia, the riverside walkway that ran along the north side of the Tiber, not far from St Peter's Basilica in the Vatican. She felt she'd be safe from discovery here; most of the people milling around were pilgrims hoping to get sight of the Pope. Angelina had no interest in seeing the Pope, nor did most of the people she knew, which was why she'd chosen to seek refuge in this area.

She'd known she was in trouble when Lucia had told her about the Wilsons. 'They want to get hold of you and talk to you,' Lucia had said.

'Why?' Angelina had asked.

'They didn't say,' Lucia replied. 'But I got the impression they wanted to talk to you urgently.' She handed Angelina a piece of paper on which an address had been written. 'They said this is where you can find them. Or you can get hold of them through Giuseppe Saredo at the Forum. I guess they're something to do with this Classical Rome Festival that's happening there.'

So Angelina had sought out Dario, a friend of hers who'd got a job as a steward at this festival.

'Do you know a couple called Wilson who are something to do with the Festival?' she'd asked.

Dario had nodded. 'Abigail and Daniel Wilson,' he said. 'They're English. She's giving some talks at the Festival about the Roman ruins. She's an archaeologist who was here about fifteen years ago, working at the Colosseum.'

'What are they like?'

'A nice couple. In fact, as well as being an archaeologist, she and her husband are detectives.'

'Detectives?'

'Private ones,' said Dario. 'I don't know if you heard, but one of the organisers of the Festival, Giovanni Maduro, and his wife, were shot dead at the Colosseum a few days ago.'

'Shot dead!' said Angelina, looking suitably shocked.

'It was dreadful,' said Dario. 'Anyway, Giuseppe Saredo, who's organising the Festival, has asked them to investigate the deaths. And not just the Marudos, but her English sister as well, who was over here staying with them.'

'Was she shot as well?'

'No. It seems she was strangled.'

As soon as she heard this, Angelina gave notice at the room she was renting near the Spanish Steps and looked for one near the Vatican. She'd taken the room close to the Spanish Steps because it was near to where Giovanni lived. Now she needed to be as far away from there as possible.

How had they got her name? she wondered. The only ones who suspected her feelings for Giovanni were his wife, Sarah, and the archaeologist, Antonio Perucci. But Antonio didn't know where she lived. How had the English couple heard about her having coffee with Lucia? Alessandro, she realised.

So it was important she stayed away from any part of Rome where Alessandro or Lucia might see her. No more coffees at the Termini station. No more target practice at the Shooting Gallery. Not that she'd be able to, anyway, since her pistol had been stolen. And she knew who had done it.

The important thing now was to lie low, keep out of sight.

That evening, Daniel and Abigail examined the coded sections in Julia's diary, trying to decipher them.

'It doesn't help she's done it in a mixture of English and Italian,' complained Daniel. 'We need a codebreaker.'

'Antonio!' said Abigail suddenly.

'He breaks codes?' asked Daniel, surprised.

'No, but he was at university here. He might know a fellow student who studied such things.'

'It's a bit of a long shot,' said Daniel doubtfully.

'Have you got any better ideas?'

'No,' admitted Daniel.

CHAPTER THIRTY

Thursday 16th August

Early the next morning, they paid a visit to Antonio.

'We're sorry to call so early,' Abigail apologised, 'but we wanted to get hold of you before your day got too busy.'

'How can I help?' asked Antonio.

Abigail showed him some of the coded sections in Julia's diary.

'We've tried to crack the codes and find out what she was writing about, but we can't. We wondered if you knew anyone who was good at cracking codes.'

Antonio gave a chuckle and smiled. 'It's possible I might be able to help,' he said.

'You?' said Daniel, surprised. 'You crack codes?'

'It was something we learnt to do when studying documents from classical Roman times. Most senators and the like were terrified of being accused of treason and executed, so many of their documents were kept in code.' He looked at Abigail. 'Did you do the same when you studied classical Rome at your university?'

'Alas, no,' said Abigail. 'The course we did at Girton was mostly about architecture and the history of the time, but the idea of breaking codes passed us by. I suppose our tutors would have considered it frivolous.'

'Fortunately, our tutors considered it essential if we were to discover what the key people in Rome at that time were really thinking,' said Antonio.

He took the diary and sat down at a table with it.

'Shall I make us some coffee?' asked Abigail.

'Yes, please,' said Antonio.

'I can do it,' offered Daniel. 'You might want to work on the language with Antonio.'

Abigail shook her head.

'I don't wish to hurt your feelings, Daniel, but you make terrible coffee. Lovely tea, but you haven't yet mastered the art of Italian coffee.'

'In that case, I shall watch and learn as you do it,' said Daniel.

While Abigail made the coffee in a pot, with Daniel observing, Antonio set to work with a pencil and paper, copying out the coded sections in Julia's diary and then juggling the letters around.

By the time the coffee had brewed and they sat down with the pot and three cups, Antonio had covered two pieces of paper with notes and annotations.

'I think I've got it,' he said. 'Fortunately, it's quite a simple code. Nothing too elaborate. It's a transition, one letter for another, but reversed to make it harder. Also, it's in a mixture of English and Italian. There's a section here made on Monday 6th August, which I translate as "Angel has a gun". Does that mean anything to you?'

'That's four days before Giovanni and Sarah were shot,'

said Daniel. 'I suspect Angel could be short for Angelina?'

'Yes, that's possible. Then there's another section in code, on 11th August, that translates as "No more G and S".'

'The day after Giovanni and Sarah were shot,' said Abigail.

'It seems pretty clear from this,' said Daniel. 'Julia got this Angelina to shoot Giovanni and Sarah.' He looked gratefully at Antonio. 'Thank you, Antonio. We've been puzzling over this for ages, and you've solved it just like that.'

'Thanks to my university lecturers.'

'But why would Angelina do that?' asked Abigail. 'I remember you told us, Antonio, that Angelina was obsessed with Giovanni. Why would she shoot him?'

'Only she can answer that,' said Antonio.

'We need to find Angelina,' said Daniel.

Santola Sciacci was in his hotel room, going through the equipment he'd brought with him to Rome. A stiletto knife and a good pistol, but the one he was proudest of was the rifle that came to pieces and could be screwed together. The long barrel was in two parts, and the wooden butt had been hollowed out to make it lighter to carry. It fired just one shot at a time, but that was all he needed. He had spent time practising with it in Sicily until he could hit the smallest of targets from a good distance.

He'd spent the time since he'd been in Rome watching the two men who were his targets, making sure he kept his distance from them and wasn't spotted. Rocco Legato had a shop in the industrial area. He always seemed to be surrounded by bodyguards, even in his shop. They accompanied him when he travelled home, and were with him again when he returned.

I need to find a high location somewhere on the route along which he regularly travels, he decided. *I need to find out when his head will be exposed, because it would require a head shot.*

The other, Lorenzo Capaldi, was not surrounded by bodyguards, but he was always with people and always on the move. The rifle would be difficult to use on Capaldi; it would have to be up close with the pistol or the stiletto.

Santola had seen the posters advertising the Festival of Classical Rome, and had discovered that on Friday the Prime Minister would be attending the celebrations, and to ensure his security and safety, members of the local police had been engaged on bodyguard duties. Santola had made a point of walking around the area of the Colosseum and the Forum, listening to the talk about it, and had learnt that Sergeant Capaldi was going to be one of the guards taking care of the Prime Minister. Which meant that any attempt on Capaldi during the actual Festival would be too risky. It would be better to wait until the Prime Minister had departed, and Capaldi and the other officers detailed to guard him were going about their business.

Santola had already checked out the house where Capaldi lived with his wife and children. The best place to make his move would be as Capaldi walked to his home after the Festival had finished. Walk up close behind him. Depending on how many people were around, stab him in the back or shoot him and then disappear into the maze of streets. Quick and direct. Even if people were around, they would be so shocked that he should be able to make his getaway before anyone raised the alarm.

A disguise would be a good idea. Something he would wear

when he made the attack, but then get rid of immediately.

He looked at the costumes he'd brought with him. The postman's outfit would take too long to undo. The priest's robe, the cassock, would be best. Just pull it over his head as soon as he was out of sight and stuff it in his briefcase.

There would be confusion when people reported a priest had been there when the crime was committed. People wouldn't believe it. They'd say it must have been a mistake.

The pistol or the knife? he wondered. The knife, he decided. The sound of the pistol going off would certainly draw attention. A simple stab with the knife in the back was the answer. The stiletto was the perfect knife for that with its long, thin, strong blade and very sharp point.

Daniel and Abigail had once more called on Giuseppe in his office at the Forum to see if he had any news.

'I talked to a policeman who's worked with Inspector Volpetti for the past few years,' Giuseppe told them. 'He says the inspector is a very private man. He's a widower – his wife died soon after his only son, Vittorio, who everyone calls Vito, was born. The inspector never remarried. Rumour has it that Vito is a ne'er-do-well who was always in trouble, which some people say is why he never married again.'

'And this Vito is a policeman?'

'Yes, with the railway police. The inspector wangled him a job with them in the hope it would put him on the right track. Straighten him out.'

'And did it?'

'You'll need to talk to his colleagues at the railway. The policeman I was talking to professed not to know anything about Vito's activities, and whether he was straightened out. The only other thing I learnt is that the inspector likes shooting wild boar. He goes hunting with some friends of his in the mountains.'

'So, a marksman,' mused Daniel.

'Actually, we need another favour, Giuseppe,' said Abigail. 'We need to get hold of an artist, one who specialises in drawing portraits. And realistic ones, not impressionist. We need it to look like the person we are after.'

'Who is it?'

'That woman Angelina Condotti you told us about.'

'Angelina? You think she had anything to do with what happened to Giovanni and Sarah?'

'It's highly possible, if the coded entries in Julia's diary have been translated properly. But we need to get hold of her. Our thought is that if we can find a good artist, we'll take them to meet Alessandro, Angelina's former boyfriend, and also Angelina's friend, Lucia, and they can give a description of her, and the artist will draw an image of her. We'll show it to Antonio and he can say whether it's an accurate likeness, and if it is we'll have copies made of it for you to distribute to your various contacts. Policemen and such.'

'This sounds a good idea,' said Giuseppe. 'I know such an artist – he has done good work for us here, making drawings of various statues. Very lifelike. Very accurate. He calls himself Tinto.'

'Tinto?'

Giuseppe smiled. 'He wants to be the new Tintoretto. I will find him and get him to come here for when you've finished your talk. Will that be all right?'

CHAPTER THIRTY-ONE

As he had done at the Colosseum, Daniel sat and watched as Abigail moved around in front of her audience at the Forum, pointing at different parts of the huge ruin while she enlarged on its history and its overall story. Even though he couldn't understand the language she was using, he'd been given an overall picture of the Forum's history by Abigail, along with specific examples of the most interesting aspects of the place, so he had a good idea of what she was telling her audience. Her story began with the Comitium, which was where the Senate and its different offices had their beginnings before, over time, they transplanted to the larger space nearby that developed into the Forum, mainly as the result of the efforts by Julius Caesar. This new Forum became a busy city square, where the people of Rome gathered for their pursuits: commercial, political, religious and judicial. Over the centuries it developed as more buildings were added, a variety of temples prominent among them – the Temple of Castor and Pollux, the Temple of Saturn, and the Temple of Vesta, whose columns still stood, dominating the skyline. The Temple of Saturn functioned as much more than a religious site where rituals and animal sacrifices were made; it was also a bank for prominent citizens.

In the front row, Massimo Cassani sat alongside Mario Torriano, watching and listening to Abigail.

'She's good,' commented Cassani. 'She tells it well.'

'She does,' agreed Torriano.

At this moment, Torriano was feeling very uncomfortable. It wasn't often that the Capo dei Capi summoned a foot soldier like Mario to meet him.

'And she is the woman who forced Salvatore to back down?'

'She is.'

'Tell me what happened. I have heard stories, but you were there.'

Torriano told him about the kidnapping of Daniel, then going to see Mrs Wilson at the flat. 'Salvatore told her that if she wanted her man back safely, she had to stop looking into the deaths of the couple at the Colosseum, Giovanni Maduro and his wife. And then, before we knew what was happening, she'd snatched up a letter-opener from the table and pushed it into the fleshy area beneath Salvatore's chin, and said she'd push it right in and kill him unless her husband was returned to her immediately, unharmed.'

'And you? What did you do?'

Torriano looked shamefaced. 'I took out my gun and aimed it at her, and told her to put down the knife. She said if I shot her, it would make her body react and the knife would go up into Salvatore's brain.'

'And then?'

'Salvatore told me to put the gun down and bring her husband to the flat. So I went to the stables to collect him.

But he'd escaped. I returned to the flat to let Salvatore know, and found her husband there, with Salvatore. Both the man and the woman were armed with pistols. I thought she would blow Salvator's brains out unless we did what she said.'

'What did the man say?'

'Nothing. He cannot speak Italian. She did all the talking.'

Cassani looked at Abigail as she pointed towards different artefacts and bits of ruins and talked confidently about them.

'And after all that, here she is today giving this talk.'

Torriano nodded. 'She is an unusual woman.'

'Where is Salvatore today?'

'At the stables.'

Cassani nodded. 'Very well,' he said. 'We shall talk again.'

'It was not his fault!' burst out Torriano. 'It was the woman. No one expected her to act the way she did. Nor the man with her. They were English visitors. What they did was against common sense. It was not Salvatore's fault.'

Cassani nodded, then rose to his feet. Torriano watched Cassani depart with a sense of grim foreboding. It had been a humiliation. Salvatore had backed down. He'd held all the cards – the husband as a prisoner, his bodyguards armed with pistols – and yet he'd surrendered to a woman armed only with a paperknife. He had been dishonoured and the organisation's reputation made a laughing stock. Torriano knew there was only one thing to be done, but he hoped his appeal might stop that. Salvatore was more than his boss, he was his best friend.

After Abigail had finished, Daniel walked over to congratulate her.

'But you didn't understand a word,' she laughed.

'No, but the audience did and I saw how bewitched they were by you.'

'Bewitched?'

'It's a good word and it sums up how they looked. But I want to talk about today. We're about to meet this artist, Tinto, and then we'll take him to the Shooting Gallery to get the description of Angelina from Alessandro so he can make a drawing.'

'That's right,' said Abigail.

'The problem with that is, as I don't understand Italian, I shall be hanging around like a spare part. I think my time might be more productive if I seek out Vito and follow him, see where he goes and the people he meets. After all, he's at the centre of this case because of Julia.'

'But, as you say, you don't understand Italian so you could well get lost wandering around the streets.'

'I shan't be wandering. I shall be following Vito. And as we've made our way around these last few days, I've got a good idea of where some places are. I won't get lost. And if I do, I've got some money, so I could always hail a cab and show him the flat address.'

Abigail nodded. 'All right, it sounds plausible. But how are you going to find Vito? He could be anywhere in Rome.'

'He's a policeman with the railway service, and he seems to spend a lot of his time around the Termini station, so I shall start there. If he turns up, that's good. If not, I shall go back to the flat.'

'All right,' said Abigail. 'I'll see you back at the flat.'

Daniel kissed her and made off. As he walked away, Abigail remonstrated with herself. *I should have thought of this before we came*, she told herself sternly. *I should have insisted Daniel had some basic Italian lessons. Or at least brought an English–Italian phrase book with us he could use.* Then she told herself off for being too overprotective. *He's a grown man in his forties*, she told herself. *He's survived in difficult places without a nursemaid. He's intelligent. He'll be fine.*

Abigail made her way to the temporary office that Giuseppe was occupying. A young man was with him as she entered – slim, handsome, with long wavy hair. *This has to be the artist*, she thought.

It was, but she was pleasantly surprised to find Tinto was exceedingly well mannered, courteous, polite, unlike some so-called artists she'd encountered.

'This is Tinto,' Giuseppe introduced him. 'He is the artist I told you about.' To Tinto he said, 'This is Abigail Wilson, the famous English archaeologist.'

'My pleasure,' smiled Tinto, offering his hand to her, which she shook.

Abigail noticed that Tinto had a large portfolio on the table next to him, and enquired, 'Are these some examples of your work?'

'They are indeed,' smiled Tinto.

He undid his portfolio, opened it and spread some of his work out on the table for her to see. To Abigail's great delight, many of them were sketched portraits in charcoal or pencil, done in a realistic style. She tapped them.

'These are wonderful,' she said. 'This is exactly what we are looking for. I'd like you to accompany me to a place called the Shooting Gallery. I don't know whether you know it.'

Tinto shook his head. 'No,' he said.

'It's a place people go to practise firing guns.'

Tinto gave a shudder. 'The kind of place I would never go. I loathe firearms.'

'Unfortunately, the person we need to give a description of the person we're looking for works there. Do you think you can cope?'

Tinto gave a bow. 'For my art, I will go anywhere.'

CHAPTER THIRTY-TWO

Daniel went to the Termini station and hung around for about an hour. At least it was possible to do that kind of thing at a railway station without drawing too much attention to himself; railway stations were always filled with people just hanging around, waiting for trains or people. He was just on the point of calling it a day and making for the flat, when he saw Vito walk in. Immediately Daniel moved to a stall selling books and magazines and began rummaging casually through them, while at the same time keeping a watch on the young railway policeman. Vito wandered to the coffee bar and spoke to Lucia briefly, then did a circular tour of the station, before making for the exit. Daniel followed, keeping a discreet distance, but also not letting Vito get too far ahead of him.

Vito's route took him to a part of Rome Daniel was unfamiliar with. It looked like an industrial district, with lots of small factories and a few shops, most of which seemed to be selling hardware. Daniel was curious as to where Vito was making for in this area, and was puzzled to see him head towards a shop that bore a sign saying 'Lugato L'olio d'oliva'.

The windows were filled with displays of cans of different sizes painted pale green with pictures of olives on them. So, a shop selling olive oil, thought Daniel. But what was Vito doing there? He thought it unlikely the young policeman was here to buy a can of olive oil – it would be cumbersome for him to carry through the streets. *I bet it's to do with collecting a bribe*, Daniel thought. Vito had already shown he had criminal tendencies, and picking up a bribe seemed the most logical reason for him being here.

Daniel watched the young railway policeman enter the shop, then looked around for a place to secret himself. There was a factory directly opposite the shop, and the metal door in its doorway had an iron bar across it, closing it off. Daniel wandered over to the doorway and placed himself in it, leaning against a wall. He hoped that Vito wouldn't be in the shop long. If he was collecting a bribe, it would surely just be a case of picking up some money and then leaving. At which point, Daniel would resume his following.

Inside the shop, Vito sat in the office at the back, facing Rocco Legato across his desk.

'Thank you for coming in,' said Legato. 'I need to assure myself that everything is in place for tomorrow.'

'Everything is,' said Vito.

'It's all to plan?'

Yes, to my plan, thought Vito. Aloud, he said, 'Exactly as discussed with Sergeant Capaldi.'

'And your friend, Niccolo, is still involved?'

'He is,' confirmed Vito. 'Nothing can go wrong.'

There was a tap at the door, which opened, and a man looked in and gave Legato a quizzical look of concern. Legato understood immediately, and said to Vito, 'Can you wait in the shop for a moment. There's something I need to discuss with Bruno.'

Vito nodded, got up and went out of the office and into the shop. The man came in and shut the door.

'There's someone watching the shop,' he said.

'Who is it, Bruno?' asked Legato.

'I don't know,' said Bruno. 'It's no one I know. I pointed him out to some of the others, and no one recognised him.'

Legato thought it over. 'Very well,' he said. 'Bring him in and put him in the stock room. Put a couple of men to guard him. I'll talk to him after I've finished with Vito.'

Bruno nodded and left, leaving the door ajar so that Vito could return.

Across the street from the shop, Daniel stood in the factory doorway and pondered on the fact there had been no sign of Vito coming out. That suggested his visit was not just to pick up a bribe, which would have taken minutes at the most. What then? Was he socialising, drinking coffee and chatting?

He was just running these thoughts through his head when he saw the door open and four men come out and start to cross the road towards him.

Oh-ho! Time to leave, he decided, and he left the doorway and began to walk along the street – but he'd barely walked a few steps before two of the men sped up and headed him off, cutting off his pathway. He stopped and turned to head in the opposite direction, but the other two men had already set a course to cut off his escape that way. And one of them, Daniel noticed, had a pistol in his hand, which he was pointing at Daniel.

Daniel stopped and put his hands in the air. The four men gathered round him, and the man with the pistol rapped out something at him in Italian.

'No Italian,' said Daniel. 'English.'

The men exchanged looks, then two of them took hold of Daniel's arms and they steered him across the street in the direction of the olive oil shop.

Now we have a problem, thought Daniel ruefully.

Inside the Shooting Gallery, Abigail watched, impressed, as Tinto translated the spoken details of Angelina's facial appearance that Alessandro gave him into a charcoal drawing composed of strokes and smudges. Before her eyes the picture of the woman came alive. Even though Abigail had never met her, she knew she was looking at an image which resonated with life. The eyes, especially, had a vitality of their own. As the portrait emerged on the page, Alessandro caught his breath and exclaimed, 'That is brilliant! That is Angelina!'

'One more thing,' Abigail said to Tinto as they left the Shooting Gallery. 'We have to show this to someone else who knew her, to make sure that both people who were close to her agree. But I have to tell you, Tinto, that you have a major talent. If I ever decide to have my portrait done, you will be the one I'll select.'

'I would be delighted to do it,' said Tinto.

Abigail laughed. 'For that I'm grateful, but we have to wait and see how things turn out here for us. We still have a job to do.'

'To discover a murderer,' said Tinto.

'Perhaps more than one,' said Abigail.

Once Tinto had carefully stowed his portrait inside his portfolio, they walked to the Termini station and found Lucia. When Tinto opened his portfolio and showed her the portrait, Lucia let out a gasp of astonishment.

'My God! You have captured her! That is Angelina!'

CHAPTER THIRTY-THREE

Daniel was ushered into the olive oil shop, and then into a storage room where cans of olive oil were stacked one on top of another. The man with the pistol, Bruno, pointed at a chair. Daniel sat. Bruno nodded to two of the men, and one of them produced his own pistol which he trained on Daniel, while Bruno and the fourth man left the room.

What next? wondered Daniel. After his experience with Fuschetti and his men, he realised that once again he was in the clutches of the Cosa Nostra. A different gang, perhaps, but the same sort of gangsters, even to the ill-fitting suits they wore. He idly wondered if the Cosa Nostra all went to the same tailor.

While he sat, he had time to reflect on what he was going to say in order to talk his way out of this situation and get safely back to Abigail. Assuming he *could* talk his way out, of course. The fact that they hadn't shot him yet, or even roughed him up, gave him hope.

He sat there, under the baleful watchful eyes of the two burly men, for about half an hour. Then the door opened and Bruno reappeared. He gestured for the two men to lift Daniel off the chair, which they did. Daniel was then escorted out of the store room and through the shop to another door. Bruno tapped on it, then opened the door, and Daniel was ushered into an office where a well-dressed man in his forties sat behind a desk. The man pointed at the empty chair opposite him, and again Daniel sat. The man barked out something in Italian.

'I'm sorry, I do not speak or understand Italian. English. I am English,' responded Daniel.

'*Inglese*,' muttered Legato's man.

'Yes, I got that,' said Legato. 'Go and fetch Carlo Moroni, the tobacconist. He understands English.'

Daniel was grateful for the delay in them finding someone to translate for them; it gave him time to embellish the cover story he'd come up with while in the store room.

The tobacconist arrived, and it was obvious from his humble and deeply respectful attitude that the man behind the desk was someone to be wary of – a fact Daniel had already ascertained after observing the way the surrounding men treated him. Respect and fear.

The man fired a question at the new arrival, Carlo Moroni, who nodded and said obsequiously, '*Si, Signor Legato*.'

So, his name's Legato, noted Daniel. *He owns this shop.*

'What is your name?' Moroni asked.

'Daniel Wilson,' replied Daniel. 'I am a visitor from England.'

'Why were you watching this shop?'

'I was waiting for the young policeman who came in to come out, so I could speak to him.'

'Why?'

'I work in England as a private investigator. An Italian

friend of mine in London heard that I was going to Rome and asked if I would do him a favour. His father, who also lived in London, has recently died, and he left some money he wanted to go to his great-grandson who lives in Rome. Unfortunately, he does not have his great-grandson's address in Rome, just his name: Luca Perroni, and he believes he's a policeman here.'

'Luca Perroni?' said Legato thoughtfully.

'When I saw that young policeman, it struck me how much he resembled my friend in London, and I wondered if they could be related.'

'What is the name of your Italian friend in London?'

'Auguste Marchisi. So I decided to wait until he came out of the place and then ask him if he was Luca Perroni, or if he was related to Auguste Marchisi who lived in London. But before I could do that, your men arrived and brought me in here and put me in a back room under guard.'

'You were not watching my shop for any other reason?'

'No. I don't know who you are, or anything about your shop, except that you sell olive oil, to judge by the cans in the store room where I was kept.'

'How long are you going to be in Rome?' asked Legato.

'A few more days,' said Daniel. 'We are here for this Festival of Classical Rome. My wife is one of the speakers – she is giving talks about the Colosseum and the Forum.'

'Your wife is Italian?'

'No, she's an English archaeologist. She was part of the team that worked at the dig at the Colosseum about fifteen years ago. She's also been engaged in other archaeological digs here in Rome over the years, although her primary work has been in the pyramids of Egypt. Two years ago, she was the first woman to lead an archaeological expedition to the pyramids.'

'And what is her name?'

'She's Abigail Wilson. She used to be known as Abigail Fenton until we married. If you ask at the Forum where the Festival is being held, you'll see her name in the programme of events.'

Legato looked at Daniel thoughtfully, then said, 'It seems an error has been made. My men were under the impression that you were a rival in the olive oil business, keeping watch on us.'

'Absolutely not,' said Daniel. 'I know nothing about olive oil. My interest is in the Classical Rome Festival, and while I am here seeing if I can locate Luca Perroni. Do you know of a young police officer called Luca Perroni?'

Legato shook his head. 'No, but I shall make enquiries. If I find out anything, where can you be contacted?'

'At the moment we are staying with friends, but it's a temporary arrangement. The best way to get in touch with me is through Giuseppe Saredo at the Festival. He has an office at the Forum, and my wife and I are there most days.'

Legato nodded, then rose from his chair and held out his hand towards Daniel.

'In that case, I can only apologise for the mistake my men made in detaining you. Thank you for your explanation, and I wish you well in your search for this Luca Perroni.'

Daniel shook Legato's hand and said, 'Thank you.'

Legato turned to one of his men. 'You will please escort Signor Wilson to the door.'

The man nodded and touched Daniel's elbow, then led him to the door and the street.

I don't know who I've just met, but I suspect he was someone very dangerous, thought Daniel. *Luckily I'm leaving his shop alive.*

Rocco Legato waited until he was certain that Daniel had left the shop, then he turned to Bruno and asked, 'What do you think? Was he telling the truth?'

'He seemed to be,' replied Bruno. 'But then, good liars always appear to be telling the truth. Although I'm fairly sure he's not Italian.'

'Check him out,' said Legato. 'See if he really has a wife who's giving a talk at this festival. Find out if he really is English.'

'And if we find out he was lying?'

Legato shrugged.

'In that case we see him as a potential danger, and there's only one way to deal with danger.'

In the small back yard at the rear of his house, Vito aimed his pistol at the target he'd fixed to the wall. He'd measured his distance, ten paces, which should be enough. Lorenzo Capaldi would be close to him so that should be a safe enough shot, but Niccolo might be further away. It was important he hit both of them, killing them both. He pulled the trigger and the pistol exploded with a loud bang, the bullet tearing into the centre of the target.

'What are you doing?' demanded a woman's anxious voice behind him.

He turned and saw that Valetia had come out from the kitchen and was looking at him in distress.

'I'm getting in some pistol practice for tomorrow,' he said.

'It's the last day of the Festival, remember, and I'm part of the police guard protecting the Prime Minister. We don't want anything to happen to him like what happened to the King.'

'Do you think that's likely?' she asked fearfully.

'Who knows in these troubled times,' said Vito. 'The thing is, we have to be prepared for anything.'

'Well, how long will you be doing this practice for?' she asked. 'I'm about to go and collect the children from Caterina. I don't want you firing that thing when they're here. It'll scare them.'

'Don't worry, I'll stop shortly,' he said. 'I'll have finished by the time you get back with the kids.'

She left.

And tomorrow, he thought, *your husband will be a hero. The man who shot the assassins who were gunning for the Prime Minister.* It was a pity he also needed to shoot the Prime Minister, but if he didn't, Rocco Legato wouldn't pay him the balance of the money. And this was all about the money.

Vito aimed the pistol again, and pulled the trigger. The bullet this time hit the target right in the centre of the bullseye.

Excellent! he told himself proudly.

CHAPTER THIRTY-FOUR

When Daniel returned to the flat, he found a note from Abigail saying she was at the Forum. He made his way there and found her with Giuseppe.

'Where have you been?' asked Abigail. 'I've been worried about you.'

'I was taken prisoner by someone called Legato and held in his olive oil shop while he questioned me.'

'Rocco Legato?' said Giuseppe, shocked.

'I never got his first name. A man in his forties, grey-haired.'

'Mother of God!' exclaimed Giuseppe and he crossed himself.

'Not good?' asked Daniel.

'You tell me you encountered Salvatore Fuschetti, which was bad. But this! Rocco Legato is one of the most feared figures in the Cosa Nostra in Rome, if not Italy.'

'Did he harm you?' asked Abigail anxiously.

'Not at all,' said Daniel. 'It was all very civilised. He asked me what I was doing watching his shop, and I told him I was looking for a young policeman called Luca Perroni, and I thought I'd seen him go into the shop.'

'Who's Luca Perroni?' asked Abigail.

'I have no idea. I just made the name up. But it seemed to satisfy him.'

'Rocco Legato is very, very dangerous,' said Giuseppe.

'Yes, I got that impression,' said Daniel.

'But what were you doing watching his shop?' demanded Abigail.

'I was following young Vito Volpetti. I wanted to see who he met and what he did. He disappeared into this olive oil shop, and I was just waiting for him to come out so I could follow him again.'

'You have to stop this, Daniel,' said Abigail. 'This is a dangerous city, and you don't know what you're doing or who you're going to come up against.'

'I do know what I'm doing,' said Daniel. 'I'm looking into Vito Volpetti. I'm convinced he's involved in the murders. He may actually be our murderer. If he isn't, he'll lead us to the person who is.'

'Someone like this dangerous character, Legato,' said Abigail ominously.

'Perhaps,' said Daniel.

'I think you ought to drop it,' said Giuseppe. 'I know I was the one who asked you to look into the murders, but that was before you'd uncovered the connections to the Volpettis, and now Rocco Legato. Your lives are at risk. Both of your lives.'

'We've survived so far,' said Daniel. He looked at Abigail. 'What do you think?'

'I think we have a perfect image of Angelina Condotti,' said Abigail. She produced Tinto's portrait and showed it to him. 'I'm going to show it to Antonio to see if he thinks it's a good likeness. If it is, we'll get copies printed and have them distributed.'

'This is magnificent,' said Daniel admiringly. He looked at Abigail. 'Do you think he'd do a portrait of you?'

'I believe he would,' smiled Abigail.

'In that case, let's sign him up.'

Mario Torriano sensed something was wrong as he entered the stable yard. For one thing, no one was around. The horses were in their stables, but there was no sign of any of Fuschetti's men. Nor was there any sign of Salvatore, and Salvatore usually let Torriano know if he would be out. He walked to the centre of the yard and called out, 'Where is everyone?'

Immediately he heard a banging coming from one of the stables, the door of which was closed. He walked to the stable and saw the bolt had been slid shut.

'Who is in there?' he demanded.

'Alberto!' came the reply.

Alberto, one of the men who looked after the horses. Torriano slid the bolt and pulled the door open. Alberto, a man in his late fifties, looked out at him disconsolately.

'They came and ordered me in,' he said unhappily. 'They pointed guns at me.'

'Who were they?' asked Torriano.

'I don't know,' said Alberto. 'I never saw them before. There were two of them.'

'Where's Salvatore?' asked Torriano.

'I don't know,' said Alberto. 'But I heard a shot.'

'Where from?'

Alberto pointed along the line of stables. 'From there.'

Torriano began to walk along the row of stables, some of which had horses in, while others were empty. Alberto followed him. Torriano looked into every stable. He found Salvatore Fuschetti in the one at the end of the row. He was sprawled on the straw which covered the floor, his dead body slouched against a bale. He had been shot in the back of the head.

Torriano turned angrily on Alberto. 'Who did this?' he demanded.

'I told you, I'd never seen them before,' said Alberto, his tone defensive and pleading.

'Where was everyone else?' demanded Torriano.

'I don't know,' said Alberto. 'I was the only one here, apart from Signor Fuschetti. Then those two men walked in.'

Torriano looked at the dead body of Salvatore Fuschetti. *Cassani*, he thought bitterly. *He has done this. He as good as told me he was going to when we talked at the Forum, but I didn't believe he really would. Not to Salvatore. I cannot let this pass.*

CHAPTER THIRTY-FIVE

Friday 17th August

When Daniel and Abigail arrived at the Colosseum for the last day of the Festival, they found the place a hive of activity ahead of the Prime Minister's visit. Giuseppe was at the centre of it, directing his people to the different points where they'd be needed.

'There's Antonio,' said Abigail.

The young archaeologist was in conversation with some dignitaries, but as soon as he saw Daniel and Abigail he made his excuses and hurried to join them.

'You're here for the last day,' he said. 'That's great. I was hoping you would be, so I could catch up on what's happened about the murders. What's the latest?'

'The latest is that we've got a portrait of Angelina,' said Abigail. 'We wanted to show it to you to see if you think it's accurate.'

She took the rolled-up portrait from the protective cardboard tube she'd put it in, and unrolled it to show Antonio.

'My heavens!' he said, obviously impressed. 'Whoever the artist is, he or she has got her to perfection. That is the living image of Angelina.'

'I'm so glad you think so,' said Abigail. She rolled the picture up and replaced it in the cardboard tube. 'We're going to give it to Giuseppe and ask him if he can get it copied, so we can distribute it.'

'Please, let me organise that,' offered Antonio. 'Giuseppe will have a lot on his plate today. I can get it copied and printed off at the university.'

'Are you sure?' asked Abigail.

'Absolutely,' said Antonio. 'It will be my pleasure towards doing something for this case. Sarah and Giovanni meant a great deal to me.' He held out his hand for the carboard tube. 'In fact, I can get it done today.'

'In that case, thank you,' said Abigail. She handed him the tube with the portrait, then asked, 'But don't you want to be here for the celebrations?'

Antonio chuckled. 'I've shown my face, that's enough. This many dignitaries in one place I find overwhelming, and not in a good way.'

With that, he bowed and headed for the exit.

'What a nice young man,' said Daniel.

'He is indeed,' agreed Abigail.

'Abigail! Daniel!'

They turned and saw the figure of Giuseppe bearing down on them.

'What was Antonio doing?' he asked. 'Where's he off to?'

'On an important errand,' explained Abigail. 'He's gone to the university to get the portrait of Angelina printed off so we can distribute copies to as many people as possible.' Then she spotted that Giuseppe looked worried, and she asked, 'Is anything the matter?'

'Salvatore Fuschetti has been shot dead,' he told them.

They stared at him, shocked.

'Shot dead?' repeated Abigail, stunned. 'Who by?'

'The full details are not known. All that's known is his body was found at the stables he owns. He had been shot in the back of the head. It is a signature punishment. He had betrayed the code of the Cosa Nostra.'

'How?'

'By allowing you to defeat him.'

'Me?'

'With a paperknife. If you – a woman – can do that, then anyone can. He had to be made an example of to recover the organisation's reputation.'

'What about Abigail?' asked Daniel. 'Where does that leave her? Will they come after her?'

'I don't know,' admitted Giuseppe unhappily. He looked at the crowds gathering and said, 'I'm sorry, I have to go. There are people to organise.'

They watched him hurry off towards a temporary platform that had been erected, on which were rows of chairs ready for the Prime Minister and the other dignitaries.

Daniel looked at Abigail, concerned. 'We have to do something to keep you safe,' he said.

'What?' asked Abigail. 'By all accounts, the Cosa Nostra seem to bump people off with impunity.' Then she added thoughtfully, 'But only those people who are a direct threat to them, it seems to me.'

'You don't think they see you as a threat?' asked Daniel. 'Because of you, one of their top people is dead.'

'Because of his own actions,' countered Abigail. 'Or inaction.'

Daniel shook his head. 'You are at risk,' he said. He looked around at the crowd gathering and said, 'Anyone could be here today with instruction to kill you. I'm not going to let that happen.' He made for where Giuseppe was standing, saying to Abigail, 'Come with me.'

'Why?' asked Abigail.

'You'll see,' replied Daniel.

As they neared Giuseppe, Daniel gestured for him to join them, which Giuseppe did.

'Giuseppe,' said Daniel, 'we need a favour. If the Cosa Nostra are intent on revenging themselves on Abigail because of what they had to do to Fuschetti, we need to keep her safe today.' He gestured around the crowd that was gathering. 'The platform where the dignitaries are being sat seems the safest place for her. I can't see anyone making a move against her while she's there. Can you arrange for her to have a seat on the platform? After all, she is one of the speakers at the Festival.'

Giuseppe nodded. 'Yes. That's a good thought. I shall fix up two chairs for both of you. That way you can keep an eye on her. If you go onto the platform and wait, I'll sort that out. If any of the stewards question you, tell them it's been arranged with me.'

'So, special privileges,' commented Abigail disapprovingly as Giuseppe went to arrange two more chairs.

'You are a guest speaker at this festival, an internationally renowned archaeologist,' said Daniel. 'You deserve to be on this platform.'

'I still don't think the Cosa Nostra will target me,' said Abigail. 'I'm not a danger to them.'

'Let's agree to disagree,' said Daniel.

CHAPTER THIRTY-SIX

Rocco Legato sat in his office and pondered on what was happening at the Colosseum. He had arranged for half a dozen of his men to be in the crowd watching the celebrations, the processions, taking turns to report back to him every half hour with the latest news. It was important that when the event happened, he, Rocco Legato, was nowhere near it.

This would be a momentous day for Italy. Francesco Bastigna had told him that the future of the country lay in the balance and that what was planned for today would decide the country's future. And he and his Cosa Nostra would be integral to that future, inextricably bound up with the politicians who controlled the country, which meant the country's money, its international alliances and its power in the world. The society that would unfold depended on the plan today succeeding. This one incident today at the Colosseum would send shock waves all around Europe, even more so than the assassination of the King.

There was the sound of running footsteps outside in the shop, then a knock at his door, which opened to admit Bruno. Legato looked at him enquiringly.

'No news, boss,' reported Bruno. 'Everything's the same. The processions are still taking place.'

'The Prime Minister is there?'

'He is,' confirmed Bruno. 'I'll get back there. Leo will be next with the latest.'

Giuseppe had placed Daniel and Abigail in seats one row from the back on the platform and four chairs in, so they were protected on all sides from attack. This also meant that they were hemmed in and unable to escape from watching the processions that were parading through the Colosseum in a final farewell celebration.

The organisers had waited until everyone else, all the other dignitaries, were in place on the podium, before the frail figure of the elderly Prime Minister was escorted from a carriage towards the platform. He was accompanied by a tall, distinguished-looking man.

'Giuseppe Saracco, the Prime Minister,' Abigail whispered to Daniel. 'The distinguished-looking gentleman with him is his right-hand man, Francesco Bastigna.'

'Saracco looks pretty old,' said Daniel.

'He is. He's almost eighty.'

As Saracco was helped up the steps onto the platform, the dignitaries already on it rose to their feet and applauded him. Abigail joined in.

'You as well,' she ordered Daniel.

Obediently, Daniel got to his feet and joined in the applause. Saracco bowed to the people on the platform, then took his seat in the front row. Bastigna took the seat next to him.

The dignitaries stopped applauding and resumed their seats.

'Now it can begin,' said Abigail.

For the next two hours, the procession, which included dancers, acrobats, musicians and of course children, went by. It had begun at Palatine Hill and proceeded to the Forum, passing the rostrum before assembling in its separate groups on the sandy surface of the Colosseum.

'This is interminable,' groaned Daniel as yet another wave of young children waving flags passed in front of the podium.

'Shhhh,' Abigail reprimanded him. 'This is very important for these children. And the locals. And especially for Giuseppe – he's put a huge amount of work into it.'

'Yes, but how long does it go on for? We've already seen about two thousand children march past.'

'Ninety,' Abigail corrected him. 'I counted them. And we had a marching band.'

'Who didn't play in tune,' complained Daniel.

'They're amateurs and children who are just learning. It would be the same in any English village when some big event is on. And the Prime Minister of Italy is here.'

The front few rows were occupied by local dignitaries, including the Mayor, along with various church men, some wearing very ornately adorned robes. In the middle of the very front row sat the Prime Minister, Giuseppe Saracco, with various men in dark suits ranged on either side of him. The nuns who were present were accompanying the children as they marched or danced past.

Another marching band appeared, this one made up of military cadets looking splendid in their uniforms. They were followed by a troop of choirboys wearing surplices and carrying candles, who sang hymns as they did a slow march under the supervision of four priests.

'Was it like this when you were here before?' asked Daniel. 'All these displays of religion?'

'Yes,' said Abigail. 'It's very important to the Italian establishment. They are very worried about the rise in socialism and communism that's been happening in the country.'

'Your friend Garibaldi,' said Daniel.

'He was not a communist,' said Abigail. 'He was a liberal with a social conscience.'

'Who opposed the Catholic Church,' said Daniel. 'I can't imagine him sitting watching all this without protesting in some way.'

'You are not Garibaldi,' said Abigail. 'Just sit and tolerate it. It won't last much longer.'

'How do you know?'

'I've seen these sorts of things before. You'll see a little girl holding a small bunch of flowers. She's going to present them to the Prime Minister, and after that all the children and performers and bands will assemble in the arena and give three cheers for the Prime Minister.'

'Or not,' murmured Daniel.

'What do you mean?' asked Abigail.

'A police sergeant and another policeman are making their way towards the Prime Minister. I can't see who the other policeman is properly, but the way he moves makes think it might be Vito Volpetti.'

'How strange,' said Abigail, puzzled.

As they watched, the police sergeant said something to Giuseppe Saracco.

'We are sorry to interrupt the occasion, Your Excellency,' said Sergeant Capaldi, 'but we have reliable information about a possible security threat, which it would be irresponsible to ignore.' He pointed towards where a young man stood, near to a four-wheeled carriage. 'That is our informant,' he said. 'We will accompany you in the carriage.'

Saracco turned to Bastigna.

'What do you think, Francesco?' he asked.

'I think you should take their advice, Your Excellency,' said Bastigna. 'This is their job, after all. If they have information, it must be acted upon.'

The Prime Minister nodded, then pushed himself to his feet and walked with the two uniformed officers to the steps at the edge of the podium. The officers helped him down to the ground, then the three walked off along the front of the podium, and made towards the exit.

'Where are they going?' asked Daniel.

'I have no idea,' said Abigail. 'I assume it's some kind of emergency that requires the Prime Minister's presence.'

As they drew near to where Niccolo was standing, Vito felt his stomach tighten with apprehension. At all costs he had to keep his nerve.

Sergeant Capaldi took a pistol from inside his tunic and passed it to Vito.

'This is the one,' he said.

Vito nodded. It felt very different from his own pistol. Lighter. More than ever he felt this was a set-up. Instead of aiming the pistol at Giuseppe Saracco, he swung it to point at Sergeant Capaldi and pulled the trigger.

Nothing happened.

Puzzled, he pulled the trigger again, and as it again clicked on an empty chamber, he found himself staring down the barrel of a pistol in Capaldi's hand.

I've been . . . the thought began in his shocked mind, and then the gun in Lorenzo Capaldi's hand fired and the bullet took Vito in the face.

Vito toppled to the ground. Niccolo stared at the fallen Vito, horrified, and as Capaldi pointed the gun at him, he shouted, 'No!'

It was the last word he uttered. Capaldi fired two bullets, the first into Niccolo's body, the second into his head.

As people came running, alarmed by the sound of shooting, Lorenzo turned to Saracco and asked urgently, 'Are you all right, Your Excellency? Those two were going to kill you.'

The Prime Minister stared at him, and at the bodies of the two dead men lying on the ground, in a state of deep shock.

Daniel and Abigail had been among the first to rush from their seats and make for where the shooting had happened, joining the uniformed officers, most of whom had drawn their weapons. The majority of those in the dignitaries' area on the podium had rushed in the opposite direction, away from the sound of shooting.

As Abigail and Daniel reached the centre of the action, they saw the police sergeant who'd taken the Prime Minister away from the podium putting his pistol back in its holster and raising his hands above his head as the armed officers appeared.

'They were going to shoot the Prime Minister!' he shouted.

'Good heavens!' exclaimed Abigail, catching sight of the two young men lying dead. 'That's Inspector Volpetti's son, Vito.'

By now a crowd of men, whom Abigail assumed were the Prime Minister's bodyguards, had gathered around Giuseppe Saracco. Giuseppe Saredo had also appeared and rushed up to Abigail and Daniel.

'What's happened?' he demanded. 'Someone said they'd shot the Prime Minister, but he's there.'

'From what we can gather, that police sergeant was the one who did the shooting,' said Abigail. 'He shot the two men on the ground because they were going to shoot the Prime Minister.'

'But why?' asked Giuseppe.

'Who knows?' said Abigail. 'I suppose it will come out in time.'

Giuseppe looked at the police sergeant, who was now talking to the other policemen.

'I know him!' said Giuseppe. 'His name's Lorenzo Capaldi.'

'So he really is a policeman?'

'Oh yes. He's a sergeant at the local police station. I expect he was one of the local police who volunteered to act as security for the Prime Minister.'

'Lucky he did,' said Daniel.

Santola Sciacci stood apart from the group gathered around Sergeant Capaldi, weighing up his course of action. He would have to wait a little longer before making his move against Capaldi; to attempt anything at this time would be too risky.

Tomorrow, he decided. When all the fuss had died down and Capaldi would be on his own again.

CHAPTER THIRTY-SEVEN

Inspector Volpetti was at the reception desk talking to the duty sergeant, when a constable rushed in.

'There's been a shooting at the Colosseum!' he burst out in a panic.

'A shooting?' exclaimed Volpetti.

'Someone tried to assassinate the Prime Minister, but someone shot him. They shot two of them. Both would-be assassins are dead.'

'Who were they?' demanded Volpetti.

The constable hesitated, his expression showing his anguish.

'Who were they?' repeated Volpetti, harsher this time.

'One was your son, Vito, Inspector,' said the constable awkwardly.

Immediately Volpetti rushed out of the police station, running as fast as he could for the Colosseum.

Deciding there was nothing they could contribute, and that they would only be in the way while the emergency services sorted things out, Abigail and Daniel decided to go with the obviously distressed Giuseppe to his office at the Forum. He had told the people in charge, the police and medical people, where he would be if they wanted him.

'This is a disaster!' he repeated hollowly for the eighth time.

'It could have been worse,' Abigail commiserated. 'The Prime Minister is alive, that's the main thing.'

'It will be known as the Death Festival,' groaned Giuseppe. 'It started with a double murder on the first day, and ends with another double shooting at the same place. They'll say the Colosseum is cursed.'

'None of this is your fault,' stressed Abigail.

'But I am the Festival Director!' burst out Giuseppe.

'But not the Festival murderer, or the Festival shooter,' said Abigail firmly. 'It has been a success.'

'With four dead people?' cried Giuseppe.

'Which is a small number for a major event in Italy,' insisted Abigail. 'Trust me, Giuseppe, when people talk about this they'll talk about its successes, not four dead people. And only two of them died at the actual Festival. Giovanni and Sarah died before it started.'

Giuseppe shook his head. 'I should never have suggested it.'

In the Palazzo Chigi it was Francesco Bastigna's turn to watch as Giuseppe Saracco paced agitatedly around the palatial office. Although 'paced' might have been exaggerating – as befitted a man of advancing years, the Prime Minister took a few steps, then sat. Bastigna's first act had been to get the Prime Minister into a carriage, along with his bodyguards, and make full speed for the Palazzo. The carriage which Saracco had been ushered towards when the shootings took place had been impounded and the driver arrested, despite his plaintive pleas that he'd had no idea of anything to do with shooting the Prime Minister.

'Why?' Saracco asked. 'Why me? What have I done that would make anyone try to kill me?'

'It is not you, Your Excellency,' said Bastigna, 'it's your office of state as Prime Minister. It attracts all sorts of lunatics and anarchists. Remember, it happened to the King.'

'Who were the assassins?' asked Saracco. 'One of them was wearing a uniform.'

'He was a railway policeman,' said Bastigna.

'A policeman!' said Saracco, shocked.

'With the railway. Fortunately, there was a real policeman there, the one who saved you. The one who shot the would-be assassins.'

'Who was he? What was his name?'

'Sergeant Lorenzo Capaldi.'

'He ought to be given a medal for his bravery. He will be given a medal.'

'I'll make the arrangements,' said Bastigna. 'The King will present it.'

'I'm not sure if we need to trouble His Majesty,' said Saracco uncertainly.

'It will be no trouble, I am sure. He will be pleased to commend the brave officer who saved the life of his prime minister.'

Saracco frowned, thoughtfully. 'The odd thing was that it looked as if the assassin had aimed his gun at the sergeant, not at me, when he was shot.'

'No,' said Bastigna firmly. 'You are mistaken. After all, it all happened so quickly, you got confused.'

227

'What about the other assassin? I didn't see if he was holding a gun.'

'He must have been. The police sergeant must have seen it, or seen him reaching for it. Altogether, it was a dreadful experience. Just be thankful the police sergeant acted so swiftly.' He hesitated before adding, almost as a throwaway thought, 'There is one positive thing that will come out of this. Your popularity will soar.'

'Soar?' repeated Saracco, bewildered.

'Of course. An attempt has been made on your life, which you survived. It shows that the elements in Italy who wish to undermine what we have, our democracy, fear you. The public will know that we are on the right path to prosperity and security with you as Prime Minister, rather than the anarchy and chaos that has gone before. At the next election they will rally round you.'

'This is not the time to talk about the next election,' said Saracco.

'It is always time to talk about the next election,' insisted Bastigna. 'Your political enemies have been talking about nothing but ever since you were made Prime Minister. We must use this attempted assassination as the springboard to boost your popularity.'

CHAPTER THIRTY-EIGHT

Saturday 18th August

The following morning, every newspaper bore the story of the attempted assassination in banner type on their front pages. At breakfast, Abigail read the piece in the newspaper about the shooting at the Festival to Daniel.

'They've named the would-be assassins who were shot dead at the scene. A young man called Niccolo Andretti and a young railway policeman called Vito Volpetti. The son of Inspector Volpetti, according to the paper. Inspector Volpetti has refused to talk to the press.'

'I'm not surprised,' said Daniel.

'It seems that the other young man, Niccolo Andretti, was not armed. But Sergeant Capaldi, the one who shot them both, said he thought Andretti was going for a gun hidden in his jacket.'

'It's all very confused,' said Daniel. 'We know Vito Volpetti was the young police officer who rented the room for Julia.'

'And who also killed her,' said Abigail. 'Which was why Inspector Volpetti was always trying to block our investigation. His son was the killer.'

'Did he know for certain?'

'He suspected,' said Abigail. 'I'd like to go and see Inspector Volpetti,' she added.

'Why?' asked Daniel.

'To offer our condolences on the death of his son.'

'I doubt he will want to talk to us,' said Daniel.

'Nevertheless, I feel it's important. Especially as we both feel, from the way he obstructed our investigation at every turn, that he was aware something was going on with his son. We thought it was something to do with Giovanni and Sarah and Julia, but, according to the papers, it was something much more. The inspector will be feeling devastated this morning. There is a danger he could take his own life. We have a duty to stop that happening.'

'I'm still not sure about you walking round Rome after what happened to Fuschetti,' said Daniel.

'After what happened at the Festival yesterday, I think the Cosa Nostra will be keeping a low profile,' said Abigail. 'Anyway, I refuse to be imprisoned. We still have three murders to solve.'

Santola, dressed in his priest's long black cassock, hovered in the street where Lorenzo Capaldi lived, waiting for him to appear. He would be going to work, of that he was sure, a fact confirmed when the front door opened and Capaldi appeared wearing his police sergeant's uniform. However, he was accompanied by his wife, Sophia, who had apparently decided to parade around the streets with her husband, who would now be a celebrity after shooting the two would-be assassins and saving the life of the Prime Minister.

Damn, he thought. Still, he followed the couple. As they

neared the Palatine Hill, Sophia Capaldi took her leave of her husband.

At last, thought Santola. However, he kept his distance from Capaldi as the police sergeant walked further up Palatine Hill. It was just as well he had, he decided, when he saw the figure of Rocco Legato walking towards Capaldi. As always, Legato had his bodyguards for protection, five burly men who walked alongside him and who, when Legato and Capaldi met, fanned out to stay distant but at the same time keep a protective eye on their master.

Now is not the time, Santola decided. *I need to get to Capaldi when he is on his own, unprotected. As for Legato, I have to get a fix on him from a higher point, and with a rifle.*

Santola turned and walked off, heading for his hotel.

Time to organise his next move.

At the Palatine Hill, Legato fell into step beside the police sergeant.

'A difficult job, perfectly executed,' said Legato. 'Exactly what our client asked for.'

'Fortunately, young Volpetti had become predictable,' said Capaldi. 'He was greedy and duplicitous. As we suspected, he was going to shoot me.'

'He was a fool,' nodded Legato. 'However, he was not completely predictable. There may be some loose ends to tie up. Niccolo is dead, but there is this other friend of his, Matteo. How much did Vito tell him?'

'It will be dealt with,' said Capaldi.

'There is also the issue of Vito's father, Inspector Volpetti. How much did he suspect of his son's activities?'

'There was some estrangement between them,' said Capaldi.

'But the father may have guessed his son was up to something. He may even have asked him and got enough of an answer to make him suspicious. It could be a dangerous loose end in the future.'

'It will be dealt with,' said Capaldi.

'In a way that will not involve us,' said Legato quietly.

'Of course,' said Capaldi.

'Inspector Volpetti is not seeing anyone today,' the duty sergeant at the police station told Abigail and Daniel.

'We understand that,' said Abigail. 'We are prepared to wait. We feel sure he will see us.'

The sergeant looked at them thoughtfully, then said, 'I do not believe he will, but if you are prepared to wait, I shall inform him that you are here. You can wait in the room opposite his office, so if he decides to see you he can summon you in.'

'Thank you,' said Abigail.

The duty sergeant escorted Abigail and Daniel along a corridor, eventually arriving at a small waiting room. The sergeant indicated a bench in the waiting room for them to sit, then pulled the door shut and returned to his reception desk. Abigail got up and opened the door.

'We'll leave the door open so that Volpetti will see us if he leaves his office,' she said.

Lorenzo Capaldi weighed up the situation. Two loose ends to tie up: the boy, Matteo, and Vito's father, Inspector Volpetti. Of the two, Inspector Volpetti was the most pressing. As an experienced policeman of many years, he would surely be set on investigating what had really happened. And as a father, he would be determined to rescue his son's reputation. At the moment he would be in shock, but once that had passed he would dig away to try and prove his son had not been an assassin. Capaldi had worked with Inspector Volpetti long enough to know that he might be slow, but he was tenacious.

Capaldi headed for the police station. He knew that Inspector Volpetti was there, effectively hiding from questions from the press and police authorities. He had sent word out that he was not to be disturbed, but Capaldi was guessing he would make an exception for his old comrade, Sergeant Capaldi. Especially as it was Capaldi who had killed his son.

He entered the police station, nodding at the duty sergeant at the reception desk, then passing on down the corridor towards Inspector Volpetti's office. He would tell him he was here to offer his condolences for the death of the inspector's son, and also give his apologies for being the one who was forced to shoot him. And then he would shoot the inspector in the head, put the gun in the dead man's hand and call for help from the other officers.

'I was talking to him, apologising for what I did, and suddenly he took his gun and shot himself in the head,' he'd say. They'd believe him. Why shouldn't they? Everyone knew the inspector would be devastated at what had happened to his son.

As Capaldi walked down the corridor, he took the pistol from its holster so it was ready in his hand. He reached Volpetti's office door, knocked, and at the command 'Enter,' walked in. The inspector was sitting at his desk looking at papers strewn across it, although he did not appear to be concentrating on them. He looked up at Sergeant Capaldi.

'Inspector, what I did weighs heavy on my heart, but I had no choice. I hope you can see that,' said Capaldi.

'I do,' said Volpetti sadly.

'I also apologise for this,' said Lorenzo, and he pointed his pistol at the inspector's head.

'What on earth . . . !' came a woman's shocked voice. Capaldi turned and saw that the English couple had just come into the office. He swung the gun round to point at them, and as he did, the man kicked out, striking his hand upwards. The gun went off, the bullet smashing into the ceiling. Capaldi brought the gun down and aimed it again, but this time the woman kicked him hard in the groin and he let out a scream and collapsed to the floor.

The half-open door of the office burst fully open as three uniformed officers rushed in, alarmed, pistols in their hands. They saw Capaldi doubled over in pain, the pistol on the floor, the inspector sitting in shock at his desk, and a man and a woman standing over the sergeant. Immediately, the officers swung their pistols to point at Daniel and Abigail, but a shout from Inspector Volpetti of 'No!' made them hesitate.

Volpetti pointed at the agonised figure of Capaldi writhing on the floor. 'There is the assassin. Sergeant Capaldi. Handcuff him immediately. Bring shackles for his legs.'

CHAPTER THIRTY-NINE

Once Capaldi had been taken away in shackles to a cell, Inspector Volpetti gestured to Abigail and Daniel to sit with him. He looked like a man who wanted to get things off his chest, and Daniel could only sit, watch and listen as the inspector and Abigail conversed in Italian.

'Why did that sergeant want to kill you?' asked Abigail.

'I do not know,' admitted Volpetti. 'I can only guess. It must be something to do with what happened yesterday. Capaldi claimed he shot Vito because he was about to shoot the Prime Minister. But say that wasn't how it was. Say something else was going on, which Vito knew about, and he had to be silenced.'

'What?' asked Abigail.

Volpetti shook his head. 'We have to hope that Capaldi will tell us.'

'Will he?' she pressed.

'I don't know,' admitted Volpetti. 'It depends who he was working for.' He looked at the pair, then said, 'You think it was Vito who killed the Maduros and Julia Winstanley, don't you.'

'The letters we found indicate that's the most likely,' said Abigail.

'I asked Vito about them. I challenged him. He swore he did not. He told me that he discovered the Maduros were dead, and that was what he meant when he wrote to Julia telling her the problem had been solved.'

'And the killing of Julia? We saw his letter to her arranging to see her on that day.'

'He said she never turned up.'

'Did you believe him?'

'I did. It may sound ridiculous in view of what happened, that he was shot trying to kill the Prime Minister, but after what we've seen with Sergeant Capaldi, that comes into doubt. And I know my son. He was bad right from childhood, always in trouble. Vito stole from the other children at school. He was cruel. But he was my son. My only son. I did my best to try and put him on the right path, but it was no good. He hung around with bad people. I thought if he went into the police force, it would put him on the right path. I pulled strings and got him into the railway police. But even there I heard tales of him hanging around with bad people. Men like Rocco Legato. He is a powerful Cosa Nostra chief.'

'Yes,' nodded Abigail. 'We know about Rocco Legato and the Cosa Nostra. Could they have been involved in the attempted shooting of the Prime Minister?'

'If they had been, the Prime Minister would be dead,' said Volpetti grimly. 'They do not fail so easily. But back to Vito and that woman, Julia. I cannot believe he killed her. One day I saw him with her. They were embracing. It was obvious they were lovers. I was angry. I told him he was a married man. He was dismissive to me. He told me she was what he wanted. She was exciting, a real woman. Fiery. Passionate. He refused to give her up. He was obsessed with her. Why would he kill her?'

'Perhaps he found out she was seeing someone else,' suggested Abigail. 'You say he was obsessed with her. Obsession is a powerful emotion. Jealous obsession can turn to murder.'

Volpetti shook his head.

'She was an unstable person. I'd already suspected she was involved in the killings of her sister and her sister's husband, and I thought perhaps she did it to hide her affair with my son. Then I thought: say he was part of it? The way they were shot, it was professional. Someone who knew how to use a gun. Say she had persuaded him?'

'So that's why you tried to block our investigation?'

Volpetti nodded. 'But now, I'm uncertain. You may think I'm being foolish, but I believe he was telling the truth when he said he did not kill the Maduros or Julia.'

'So who did?' asked Abigail. 'Could it have been connected to Sergeant Capaldi?'

'How?' asked Volpetti. 'Why?' He shook his head. 'I don't know, any more. All I know is there is something rotten in this city and my son is dead.'

Abigail and Daniel left the unhappy inspector dwelling on his misery. After they'd left the police station, Abigail filled Daniel in on what Volpetti had said.

'I think he's being delusional,' said Daniel. 'His son committed the murders and tried to shoot the Prime Minister, but he refuses to believe it.'

'Unless Vito isn't the murderer,' mused Abigail thoughtfully. 'There's still the involvement of Angelina Condotti. We know she knows how to use a gun, and she was obsessed with Giovanni.'

'Then why shoot him?' said Daniel frustratedly.

'I don't know,' admitted Abigail. 'We won't know that until we talk to her. So let's hope that picture we had Tinto make of her gets some results, and someone finds her.'

At the police station, Volpetti roused himself from his feeling of misery and walked to the cell where Capaldi was imprisoned. *I have to know why*, he thought. *Why did he try to shoot me? And why was he so sure that Vito intended to shoot the Prime Minister?* There was something not right with this.

Capaldi was sitting on a bench. He was handcuffed and his legs were shackled. His face bore the bruises from when the police officer had overpowered him. He looked up as the cell was unlocked and Volpetti walked in.

Capaldi held up his handcuffed hands.

'Do I have to have these on?' he asked.

'You know the rules,' said the inspector. 'You've carried them out yourself often enough. A dangerous person has to be restrained.'

'I am not a dangerous person,' said Capaldi.

'You tried to shoot me,' said Volpetti. 'If it hadn't been for that English couple – the Wilsons – you would have.'

'It was a mistake,' said Capaldi. 'I was confused.'

'I don't believe that,' said Volpetti. 'Why did you do it?'

'I've just told you, I was confused. I don't know what happened.'

'Who paid you to do it?'

'No one.'

'Someone must have. Or was it personal? Something I've done that angers you.'

'No. You've done nothing to make me angry at you. As I

say, it was a mistake. Confusion in my head.'

'Why did you shoot Vito?'

'Because he was going to shoot the Prime Minister.'

'How can you be sure?'

'He had a gun and he was aiming it at the Prime Minister.'

'But he didn't fire it. The gun did not go off.'

Capaldi shrugged. 'Perhaps it jammed. That sometimes happens with guns.'

In the Pucho household, Donna Pucho came down the stairs and walked into the kitchen where her husband, Lucio, was reading a newspaper.

'You have to talk to him,' she berated her husband.

'To who?' asked Lucio.

'Who do you think I'm talking about. Your son, Matteo, of course. He refuses to come out of his room. He refuses to get out of bed. When I tried to make him, he began to howl and wail, saying they were going to kill him.'

'Who was going to kill him?'

'That's why you have to talk to him.'

'He never listens to me,' protested Lucio. 'If you can't make him get up, he won't get up just because I tell him.'

'In that case, I'm going to get someone who he will listen to,' snapped Donna.

'Who?' asked Lucio.

But his wife had already left the room, and Lucio heard the front door slam shut.

Francesco Bastigna had summoned Carmine Ventari, the Direttore Generale della Pubblica Sicurezza, also known as the

Capo della Polizia, the Head of Police, to the palazzo.

'We need the attempted assassination of the Prime Minister investigated,' he told him. 'It needs to be done at the highest level.'

'Of course,' nodded Ventari.

'The would-be assassin was the son of Inspector Volpetti, the senior police inspector in the Colosseum district,' said Bastigna. 'Obviously, Inspector Volpetti must take no part in the investigation. We cannot afford any accusations that there has been a cover-up to protect his son, Vito Volpetti.'

'Should Inspector Volpetti be suspended while the investigation is going on?' asked Ventari.

Bastigna shook his head. 'No. Morale is bad in the police right now. To suspend a long-serving senior officer because of what his son did would only damage the service even more. We know what the facts are: we know who the would-be assassins were. We know the name of the hero who intervened and saved the life of the Prime Minister, Sergeant Lorenzo Capaldi. We need to find out why the assassins attempted to kill His Excellency Saracco. Were they anarchists, acting on their own, or were other people involved? Was there a conspiracy?'

'I shall find out,' Ventari assured him. 'I shall leave no stone unturned.'

'And we must not let this investigation drag on,' continued Bastigna. 'We need a swift conclusion. I look to you, Direttore Generale, to provide one.'

After Ventari had left, Bastigna reflected on the assignment he'd given him. It had been important for Bastigna to move quickly before anyone else suggested an inquiry. This way he, Bastigna, would be in charge of what was uncovered in the way of evidence. It was important, for example, that there should be no mention of Rocco Legato or any association with the Cosa Nostra. He'd already decided what the outcome would be: a small group of troubled anarchists set on undermining the state. Fortunately, because of good work by the security services, the attempt to assassinate the Prime Minister had been foiled. It was now a case of sifting through whatever Carmine Ventari came up with to make sure everything led to the same conclusion.

At the police station, Inspector Volpetti walked back to his office. *I have to get to the bottom of this*, told himself. *There will be questions asked and we need to have the answers. Why did Vito and his friend Niccolo try to assassinate the Prime Minister?* The fact that Lorenzo Capaldi had shot them at the scene, and then come to the police station to kill the inspector raised serious doubts about the whole affair. Who had Capaldi been working for? Who else might have been involved? If his son had been entangled in the assassination attempt, he wanted proof, not allegations.

He walked past his office and continued along the corridor until he came to the door of the officers' rest room. He opened it and marched in. Two constables and a sergeant were in there, and they leapt to their feet and stood to attention.

'What happened at the Colosseum yesterday needs full investigation,' snapped Volpetti. He looked at one of the constables and said, 'I want you to go and see the family of this Niccolo Andretti, the boy who was killed. Find out how much they knew about what he was up to. Who were his friends? Who did he mix with? Did he have a gun? I want to know everything there is to know about him.'

He looked at the sergeant. 'Sergeant, you are to go to the railway police headquarters. You are to find out everything about my son's activities during his time with them. What rumours there were about him. Who his associates were, both inside the force and outside.'

He turned to the other constable. 'You are to go to the Colosseum and find out who saw the Prime Minister around the time of the attempt on his life. Talk to Giuseppe Saredo, who organised the stewards at the event. Ask them what they saw just before the shooting began. We know my son Vito, this boy Niccolo Andretti and Sergeant Capaldi were with him. Who else was with them? Why were they walking out of the arena?' He looked at his watch. 'You will get to work now. I want reports on my desk by the end of the afternoon.'

With that, Volpetti returned to his office and pulled on his outdoor coat. He had one important task to do – to call on Lorenzo Capaldi's family and inform them of what had happened. They would be shocked, and although it would appear cruel, that would be the time to ask them about Capaldi's associations outside the police force, before they had time to concoct a defence of the late sergeant.

CHAPTER FORTY

Volpetti called at the home of the Capaldis and found Lorenzo's wife, Sophia, there. The children were out, which was one blessing. Sophia beamed proudly as she opened the door to the inspector and invited him in, but then she remembered the story of the assassination attempt in that morning's newspaper which named the inspector's son as one of the assassins, and replaced her broad smile with a solemn look.

'I am sorry for your loss, Inspector,' she said as she led him to the living room.

Volpetti merely nodded. Sophia, now unable to hide her pride, showed him the cards displayed on the mantlepiece, the posies of flowers in vases scattered around the room.

'From grateful people,' she said proudly. 'Lorenzo is a hero. He saved the life of the Prime Minister.'

'He did,' nodded Volpetti.

'He will get a medal from the King, I expect,' she said, smiling.

'That's likely,' said Volpetti. 'Although there is a problem.'

Her smile vanished and was replaced by a look of suspicion.

'What problem?' she asked.

'Lorenzo tried to kill me this morning. He is in a cell under arrest.'

Her mouth dropped open in shock.

'No! What are you saying?'

'Exactly what I have just said. He came into my office this morning and pointed a gun at my head. Luckily for me, someone interrupted him and the bullet missed. He was overpowered and shackled and is now a cell. He will be charged with attempted murder.'

'No!' she shrieked. 'It cannot be so.' She gestured at the flowers and the cards. 'He is a hero!'

'A hero who tried to kill me, his commanding officer. I want to know why.'

'You are wrong!' she burst out angrily. She rushed out into the passage and took her outdoor coat from the peg. 'You must let me see him.'

'No one is seeing him until he tells us why he did it,' said Volpetti.

'He didn't do it!' insisted Sophia. 'You are lying.'

'There were other people who saw him do it. Police officers. We want to know why. Did someone pay him?'

'Pay him?'

'To kill me. If so who, and why?'

'This is madness,' she said firmly.

'The madness is in Lorenzo,' said Volpetti. 'Either he went mad this morning, or he was carrying out orders from someone. If the doctors say he is not mad, then what made him do it?'

Antonio Perucci sat in his comfortable living room reading through the notes he'd made. Not notes for the talks he was giving at the Festival, but of the events that had happened during it.

This would make a wonderful novel, he decided. The murders of Giovanni and Sarah Maduro. The murder of Sarah's sister, Julia. The assassination attempt on the Prime Minister, Giuseppe Saracco. Daniel and Abigail being taken hostage by members of the Cosa Nostra. The shooting dead at the Colosseum of two young anarchists by a police sergeant. And now, if the stories were true, the latest bizarre event: the attempt by that same police sergeant to shoot dead the police inspector in charge of the investigations.

He'd have to change the names, of course, but he'd make sure the words 'based on true events' were writ large on the cover.

It would be a sensation. Yes, Antonio loved archaeology, especially of classical Rome, but it didn't pay very well. A lurid sensational crime novel like this would make a massive difference to his financial situation.

He'd have to avoid using the words 'Cosa Nostra', or he'd find himself in serious trouble with them. Something like The Mob, or the Castiglio Gang.

Yes, he thought. This would be a book that would sell, and sell well.

Sophia Capaldi's mind was in a turmoil. Lorenzo in jail, for attempting to kill Inspector Volpetti! It wasn't possible, not after what had just happened, with Lorenzo saving the life of the Prime Minister. But the inspector said it was true. And there were witnesses.

Rocco Legato, she thought. He had to be involved somewhere.

Lorenzo and Legato were as close as any two people could be. She knew that Rocco was a criminal, and there had been rumours that it had been Rocco who had got Lorenzo to join the police force, but she had turned a blind eye and a deaf ear to that sort of talk. What mattered was that she and Lorenzo had a good life. The two of them and their children were well provided for. She knew that Rocco and Lorenzo often met, and that when they did money appeared, but that was nothing to do with her. Lorenzo and Rocco were very old friends – they had been since childhood. One thing was sure: if Lorenzo really had tried to kill Volpetti, then Rocco was involved in some way.

She took her coat from the peg in the hall and slipped it on. She didn't care how important Rocco Legato was; she needed to protect her husband and her family. Something had to be done about this situation, and Rocco Legato was the one man who could fix it.

CHAPTER FORTY-ONE

Inspector Volpetti stood in the shadows at the corner of the street watching the Capaldis' house. He stepped further back into the cover of a doorway when he saw the door of the house open and Sophia appear. He'd been sure that Sophia would do something as a result of his visit, see someone. The question was: who? There was only one way to find out, and that was to follow her – so that was what he did now. She strode forward, looking neither to left nor right, set on where she was going. Her children hadn't been at home when he'd called, so perhaps she was going to find them. Or maybe she was going to see a relative. Or a priest. She'd been obviously distressed, so he didn't expect her to do anything ordinary, like shopping. Her determined manner showed she was set on wherever it was she was going. Would she hail a cab? he wondered. If so, his intention to find out where she was going would die a death. But he knew from Lorenzo that Sophia had a preference for walking. He hoped that would be the case today.

Sophia walked, unaware of Volpetti tailing her while keeping his distance. It was fortunate for the inspector that Sophia was a tall woman, and one who favoured wearing a red hat, so he was able to watch her without getting too close, just in case she should turn around.

It wasn't long before Sophia arrived at the industrial area, and he scowled as he saw her make for Legato's oil exporter's shop. She went in.

Volpetti waited to see if she came out straight away, but she didn't. So she had business there.

Volpetti knew it was dangerous to stand watching Legato's place, especially as he was wearing his uniform, so he moved off, back the way he'd come. The main thing was he had proof of the connection between Legato and Lorenzo Capaldi. He remembered the doubts some senior officers had expressed when Capaldi joined the police force. 'He's friends with criminals,' said one. 'Everyone knows he's close pals with Rocco Legato. They were always getting in trouble as teenagers. How come he suddenly wants to be in the police force?' But over time those stories had faded as Capaldi developed a reputation as a good police officer.

'People change,' someone had observed. 'Look at St Paul. He was Saul, the persecutor of Christians. And then he had a conversion on the road to Damascus. And he became one of the most important Christian saints ever. People change.'

Not in this case, thought Volpetti. *It looks like Capaldi and Legato are still connected*, he mused as he walked away, heading back to his police station.

Rocco Legato was behind Capaldi's attack on him, he was sure. Which was linked to the supposed assassination attempt on the Prime Minister. Which meant Legato was behind the killing of his son, Vito.

* * *

Inside Legato's shop, Sophia had pushed past Legato's bodyguards and entered his office.

'Lorenzo has been arrested,' she told him, her expression showing her confusion and anger.

Legato looked at her, stunned.

'What. Why?'

'Inspector Volpetti says Lorenzo tried to shoot the inspector this morning.' She looked at Legato accusingly. 'What do you know about this?'

'Nothing,' said Legato. 'Why would I?'

'Because Lorenzo and I have been together since we were children. I know you and he were as close as any two people could be. I know the kind of things you both got up to. I know you and he still see one another.'

'It's a mistake,' said Legato. 'It must be.'

'Why did Lorenzo join the police?' demanded Sophia.

'Because he wanted to,' said Legato. 'It was his choice.'

Sophia shook her head. 'I thought it was strange at the time. But he assured me it was for the best for him to have a proper career away from crime, to provide properly for me and the children.'

'That's what he said to me,' said Legato.

'But you and he still saw one another. And you gave him money.'

'As an old friend. A police sergeant does not earn a great deal.'

'Did you tell him to shoot Inspector Volpetti?'

'No, of course not!'

'Then who did? Lorenzo would not have done it on his own.'

'He must have had some sort of breakdown. Where is he?'

'In a cell at the police station.'

'Have you seen him?'

'No. The inspector says no one is to see him until he's said why he did it.'

Legato looked thoughtful, then he said, 'Leave this to me, Sophia. I will sort it out.'

Donna Pucho made for the local church where she found the priest, Father Borelli, engaged in making arrangements with his curate for the funeral of Niccolo Andretti. Normally, Donna would have waited politely for the two men to finish their conversation, but these were not normal times.

'Father!' she said, her distress obvious as she burst into their conversation. 'You must come urgently. It's my Matteo. He's acting like he's possessed.'

'Possessed?'

'By the devil. You have to come and see him. Find out what's going on? We cannot control him.'

'Is he being violent?' asked Father Borelli, apprehensively.

'No,' said Donna. 'He is hiding in his room and refusing to leave his bed, or his room. He wails and kicks out if we try and force him.'

Father Borelli nodded. 'I will come at once.' He turned to his curate and said, 'Continue with the arrangements for the funeral, so we are ready when we talk to the Andrettis.'

Constable Fontane found himself facing an atmosphere of deep grief and bewilderment when he was admitted into the Andretti house. Signora Andretti had taken to her bed and was refusing to see anyone. Signor Andretti sat in a stunned stupor beside the stove in the kitchen. The stove had gone out, but no one was bothered about getting a fire going in it. The only one of the family who seemed able to hold a conversation was Niccolo's twenty-year-old sister, Marissa.

'It's all lies,' she told Constable Fontane. 'Niccolo never owned a gun. There was nothing in the papers about him being armed. He was just there, with his friend Vito. He had no part in what happened. You should talk to his friend Matteo. Niccolo was always hanging around with Vito and Matteo. Where was Matteo when it happened? Why wasn't he there with the others?'

'Matteo?' asked Constable Fontane, opening his notebook.

'Matteo Pucho,' said Marissa.

'Where does he live?'

Marissa gave him the address, and he wrote it down in his notebook.

'Who were Niccolo's other friends?' asked Fontane.

'He had none,' said Marissa. 'Just Vito and Matteo. They were always together.'

'Did Niccolo get involved in politics?'

Marissa shook her head vigorously. 'Never!'

'What did he and his friends talk about when they were together?'

'How do I know?' she said aggressively. 'I wasn't there. You need to ask Matteo.'

CHAPTER FORTY-TWO

Father Borelli arrived with Donna Pucho at the Pucho family home.

'He's upstairs in his room,' she said. 'He refuses to leave his bed.'

The priest climbed the stairs behind Donna, then followed her into Matteo's bedroom. The boy lay in his bed, the blanket pulled up over his head.

'Father Borelli is here to see you,' she said.

The blanket was thrown off and Matteo sat up, a hunted look on his face.

'Go away!' shouted Matteo.

Incensed that her son should dare to abuse a priest in this way, Donna Pucho let fly with her open hand, slapping her son hard around the face.

'How dare you!' she shouted.

The slap seemed to do the trick, the shock of it making Matteo stare at her in astonishment. He was even more shocked when his mother struck him again, even harder.

'Signora,' appealed the priest. 'There is no need for this.'

'There is every need,' Donna raged. 'In my house, a son

of mine shouts at a priest? Never!' She leant towards her son and shouted, 'You must be mad! Or possessed. I'll have you locked up.'

Matteo looked at her in agonised appeal.

'It is not my fault,' he said.

Father Borelli looked at Donna. 'Signora, please, let me talk to the boy on my own. I am sure we can get to the bottom of this mystery.'

Donna hesitated, glared at Matteo, then said tightly, 'You will talk to Father Borelli or, I promise you, you will be locked up for ever.'

With a last angry scowl at Matteo, she left the bedroom.

Father Borelli pulled a chair close to the bed.

'You are suffering, my son,' he said. He looked around the room. 'Think of this room as a confessional while I am here. Whatever you say to me remains here. You know the confessional is sacrosanct.'

Matteo sat up in bed and looked at the priest. His pale face was marked red where his mother had struck him. He looked at the priest's face, and thought, *I have to talk to this man. There is no one else I can unburden myself to. Maybe he can protect me from those who killed Vito and Niccolo; keep me alive.*

Aloud, but in a voice that was little more than a whisper, he said, 'You know my friends Niccolo and Vito were shot dead yesterday.'

'Yes,' said the priest. 'I saw it in the newspaper. They say they were shot while trying to kill the Prime Minister.'

'I was with them,' sobbed Matteo.

'When it happened?' asked Father Borelli, horrified.

'No, before. We used to meet, me and Niccolo and Vito. It was Vito's idea.'

'What was?'

'To shoot the Prime Minister.' He shook his head. 'I didn't want to go along with it. That's why I wasn't there when they did it.' He started to cry. 'They shot Vito and Niccolo because of it. Now they will shoot me.'

'Why would they shoot you?'

'Because I knew about it.'

'Who do you think will shoot you?'

'The same people who shot Vito and Niccolo.'

'It was a policeman doing his duty,' said Father Borelli. 'He shot them to stop them from killing the Prime Minister. You weren't even there. There is no reason for him, or anyone else, to shoot you.' He looked at Matteo, intently but sympathetically. 'Look, you need to tell the police everything you know.'

'No!' exclaimed Matteo, alarmed. 'It was a policeman who shot Vito and Niccolo.'

'As I said, he was doing his duty,' repeated Father Borelli. 'But the police need to know why Vito and Niccolo were doing what they were doing. Neither is alive to tell anyone. You're the only one who can.' He looked even more intently at Matteo. 'I will come with you. You don't need to be afraid. I will be there.'

Matteo looked doubtful. 'I don't know,' he said uncertainly.

Suddenly the bedroom door slammed open and Donna Pucho burst in. 'Go with him!' she shouted. She turned to the startled priest and said apologetically, 'I didn't mean to listen at the door, but he's my only son.'

* * *

So Lorenzo screwed up, thought Legato angrily. Something he'd thought would never happen. What had gone wrong?

This needed to be fixed. Lorenzo must never come to trial. Lorenzo would stay silent, Legato was sure, but as long as he remained alive there was a chance someone would find out the truth. He dared not risk using one of his own people to carry out the hit on Lorenzo. His people were known to the police. If it went wrong – and the fact that Lorenzo had failed meant it could go wrong – then it would be traced back to him.

Matteo sat in Inspector Volpetti's office, his head hanging down, unable to look the inspector in the face. Beside him sat Father Borelli.

'Matteo has something to tell you, Inspector,' said the priest.

Volpetti looked at the boy, who kept his head obstinately looking downwards.

'Well?' asked the inspector.

Matteo stayed silent.

'You need to tell him if your soul is to be saved,' said the priest to Matteo.

It was the mention of his soul that brought Matteo's face up to look at the inspector.

'Vito and Niccolo were planning to shoot the Prime Minister,' he said.

'Why?' asked Volpetti.

'Vito said it was to save Italy and make the country great and powerful again, as it used to be.'

'How would that make us a great and powerful country?'

'He never said,' admitted Matteo. 'I thought it was wrong, so I never went along with them.'

'Had Vito been talking to anyone?' asked Volpetti. 'Anyone involved in politics, for example.'

'No,' said Matteo. 'At least, not as far as I know.'

'Someone must have put that idea in his head.'

Matteo shrugged. 'If they did, I don't know who. He never said.'

'Did Vito ever mention Rocco Legato?'

Matteo shook his head. 'No,' he said.

'Do you know who Rocco Legato is?'

Matteo scowled. 'Everyone knows who Rocco Legato is. He's a gangster.'

'Did Vito have anything to do with Rocco Legato?'

Matteo thought about it, then said, 'Not as far as I know. But Vito always had money. More money than I think he got paid as a railway policeman.'

'Where did he get this money from?'

'I don't know. He never said and I never asked him.'

Volpetti fell into a thoughtful silence, broken by the priest asking, 'Is there anything else, Inspector? Only I have a funeral to organise.'

'No,' said Volpetti. 'Not for the moment.' He looked at Matteo and added, 'Thank you for coming in, Matteo.'

CHAPTER FORTY-THREE

Massimo Cassani looked up at the very tall, muscular man in the ill-fitting suit who had delivered the envelope to him and was now standing on the other side of his desk. Cassani recognised him as one of Rocco Legato's men. Cassani read the letter again.

Dear friend, it began. *I would be grateful if we could meet. I suggest the arena at the Colosseum as neutral territory, if you agree. Today at three o'clock, if that's convenient. I shall be alone and will be grateful if you arrive alone.*

The Colosseum was hardly neutral ground, thought Cassani. It was just inside Legato's patch. And why did Legato want to meet? Was it to do with the two people found shot dead at the Colosseum? Or the attempt on the life of the Prime Minister?

The language puzzled him, all this talk of being 'grateful'. This was unlike Legato.

Cassani weighed it up. To turn down the invitation would be dangerous. It would be taken as an insult, and Rocco Legato was not a man who took insults lightly. Cassani also couldn't imagine that Legato would really be alone. He would have his men dotted around the Colosseum, ready to be called in if needed.

Very well, thought Cassani. It would be courting suicide to refuse the invitation, but it could also be courting death to attend. Rocco Legato's reputation for utter ruthlessness had been well earned. Cassani would attend and arrive alone, but he'd do the same as Legato – send some of his own men ahead, suitably armed, with orders to disperse themselves among the ruins, close enough to be called but far enough away to avoid causing suspicion.

Cassani nodded at the tall man.

'Please tell Signor Legato that I will be delighted to meet him at the time and place he suggests.'

The man nodded, then left.

Cassani waited a moment to make sure the man had really gone, then he called in Dominico, his right-hand man.

'I shall be going to the Colosseum at three o'clock this afternoon to meet Rocco Legato,' he told him. 'We have agreed that both of us will be alone for this meeting. However, neither of us would be foolish enough to leave ourselves open to risk. I want six men, suitably armed, to go to the Colosseum and wait around the area. They are to do their best to look like tourists. I imagine Legato's men will be doing the same. They are to keep their distance from myself and Legato, unless they are summoned.' He produced a pistol from inside his jacket. 'The firing of this will be the signal.'

'I was thinking,' said Abigail.

'So was I,' said Daniel, concern on his face.

'You're still thinking about Fuschetti,' said Abigail.

'Aren't you?' asked Daniel.

'To be honest, I'm trying to forget it. But I've had one thought that I believe might help.'

Daniel looked at her enquiringly.

'You feel that if we keep to well-populated areas, I'll be safe,' she said. 'Like at the Festival closing ceremony when we sat on the platform with those others.'

'Which I'm now rethinking after someone tried to assassinate the Prime Minister.'

'But it's still a good thought,' said Abigail.

'What's your point?' asked Daniel.

'Let's go to one of the busiest places in Rome. The Vatican.'

'You're going to ask the Pope to protect you?' said Daniel with a hint of sarcasm.

'No, but it's always very busy. Especially the Sistine Chapel. You really ought to see the magnificent ceiling there before we leave Rome.'

Daniel studied her. 'You're serious?'

'I am,' said Abigail. 'It's very unlikely we'll come back to Rome. And you really need to experience Michelangelo's masterpiece. This is a once in-a-lifetime opportunity.'

Carmine Ventari faced his senior assistant, Pietro Annigoni, across his desk, a stunned expression on his face.

'Say that again,' he said.

'I began my investigation by going in search of Sergeant Lorenzo Capaldi to get his eyewitness report on the assassination attempt, and discovered he had been arrested and was in a police cell, charged with the attempted murder of Inspector Volpetti.'

Ventari studied Annigoni, a look of incomprehension on his face.

'I do not understand,' he said. 'This must be some mistake.'

'No mistake,' said Annigoni. 'There were witnesses to the attempt, two English people who were at the police station at the time. It was they who prevented Capaldi from shooting Volpetti. We also have evidence from three police officers who were present.'

'But this was the man who saved the life of the Prime Minister!' exclaimed Ventari. 'The hero of the hour! It makes no sense. Why would he try to kill a senior police officer?'

'We do not know,' said Annigoni. 'I will send someone to question him.'

Legato and Cassani sat together at the Colosseum. Their bodyguards remained at a distance from the pair, doing their best to appear unobtrusive and failing miserably, something that neither man chose to comment on.

'I need assistance which only you can give,' said Legato. 'If you do this for me, successfully, you will have my undying gratitude.'

'Anything I can do will be done,' Cassani assured him.

'An associate of mine, Lorenzo Capaldi, has been arrested and is in a cell at police headquarters. It is important he does not come to trial, or even be questioned. You understand what I am saying?'

Cassani nodded.

'I cannot use one of my own people for this, because they are known,' continued Legato. 'You have your own people, different to mine.'

Again, Cassani nodded. 'It will be an honour to assist.'

Legato held out his hand and the two men shook hands.

'I am sure this will lead to many co-operations between us,' said Legato. 'It is what is needed in these uncertain times.' He then added, slightly awkwardly, 'I also offer my condolences on Salvatore Fuschetti. It was not my men who were involved in what happened to him. The decision was taken at a Council. To avoid local embarrassments, two men were dispatched from out of the city. I was only informed after the fact.'

'I understand,' said Cassani. 'It could not be avoided.'

The young man wearing the long black robe with a white dog collar and carrying a briefcase walked through the prison gates and made his way to reception. The warder on duty made a slight bow of reverence to show he acknowledged the priest's importance. The priest produced an envelope.

'My parishioner, Signora Capaldi, has asked me to talk to her husband Lorenzo to give him comfort, and also to give him a message from her.'

'Of course, Father,' said the warder. He summoned another warder and ordered him, 'Escort the father to the prisoner Lorenzo Capaldi.'

The young priest followed the warder out of the reception area and along some corridors until they came to a row of barred doors. The warder walked to one and rattled his baton across the bars. Lorenzo Capaldi appeared from the sheltered end of the cell.

'A priest to see you with a message from your wife,' he announced.

Capaldi nodded. The priest turned to the warder. 'I am here to take his confession,' he said sternly. 'Which, as you know, is always done in private.'

The warder suddenly became apologetic; he knew how

tough these priests could be and how many of them took every opportunity to cause trouble. He recognised this priest as one such.

'Of course, Father,' he said contritely.

He unlocked the door and the priest entered the cell.

'The rules say I have to relock it, Father, until you are ready to go,' he said awkwardly.

'Then do it,' said the priest tersely. 'You may go. I will call you when I am ready to leave.'

The warder relocked the door, then walked away along the corridor.

The priest gestured towards the bench in the cell that served as a bed.

'We shall sit,' he said.

They sat.

'You have a message from my wife,' said Capaldi.

The priest shook his head. 'The message is from an old associate of yours.'

Rocco Legato, realised Capaldi. He looked at the priest's briefcase and asked, 'You have things to help me get out of here?'

'I have,' answered the priest. He opened the briefcase and took out a silk scarf, which he draped to hang loosely from his neck.

'We must go through the appearances,' he murmured.

'Of course,' Capaldi whispered back in response.

The priest rose to his feet.

'We will stand and face one another,' he said quietly.

Obediently, Capaldi stood, facing the priest. The priest took a long, thin stiletto from his briefcase.

'This is for you,' he said.

Capaldi frowned. 'I will need more than this,' he said.

'No,' said the priest. And before Capaldi could react, he slid the long, thin blade into Capaldi's chest and into his heart. As Capaldi toppled forward, they priest caught him, taking his weight.

'The Sciacci family say may you rot in hell,' he murmured.

He pulled the knife out, then laid the dead man down on the bench and rolled him so that his face was to the wall. He then adjusted Capaldi's legs and arms so he looked like he was sleeping, and pulled the thin blanket over him.

He wiped the blade of the knife and put it in his briefcase, along with his communion scarf. That done, he walked to the barred door.

'Warder!' he called imperiously. There was a pause, then the warder appeared. He unlocked the barred door and looked at the prisoner lying on the bench.

'He is not to be disturbed,' the priest told him firmly. 'He is overcome with grief and needs solitude. I repeat, he is not to be disturbed in any way. Do you understand me?'

'Yes, Father,' said the warder.

'Good,' said the priest.

He walked out of the cell then waited for the warder to follow him, his gaze on the man to make sure he didn't attempt to touch the prisoner.

The warder came out of the cell and locked the door, then escorted the priest back through the prison to the main gate.

The Council decided, thought Torriano bitterly. Torriano did not know anyone on the Council; he was too far down the pecking order. He doubted if Cassani knew who was on the Council either. Legato, possibly, knew some of them. After all, they had informed him after Salvatore had been killed.

But Torriano could not let the killing of his greatest friend pass unavenged. Cassani claimed Legato was not involved. Neither, he claimed, was Cassani himself, nor any of his people. The Council were anonymous. But someone had to pay!

The woman, he decided. It had happened because of the woman holding Salvatore hostage with that damned stiletto. She was the cause of what had happened to Salvatore. Abigail Wilson. The motto Torriano had lived by since he joined the Cosa Nostra was simple: blood for blood. Very well – Abigail Wilson's for Salvatore's. She would pay the price.

Abigail and Daniel were once more going through the documents they'd found in Julia's room, looking for clues, when there was a knock at the door of the flat. The visitor was Giuseppe, who handed them an envelope.

'This came to the festival office at the Forum. It's addressed to you. The envelope says it's from the office of the Direttore Generale della Pubblica Sicurezza.'

'Sounds impressive,' said Daniel.

'It is,' said Abigail, opening the envelope. 'It's the Rome headquarters of the Italian police force.'

She took out the letter and read it.

'We are required to present ourselves for an interview with the Direttore General, Carmine Ventari, at the earliest opportunity.'

'Both of us?' asked Daniel.

'That's what it says. Signor Daniel Wilson and Signora Abigail Wilson.'

'Do they tell us when we should go? An appointment time?'

'No. Just "at the earliest opportunity".'

'This is a letter from the very head of the police,' said Giuseppe. 'I would advise you to respond straight away.'

'Send a letter asking for an appointment?' asked Daniel.

'No, go to the offices. It will show you are taking them seriously. These are not people you want to annoy.'

Daniel and Abigail arrived at the palatial building in the via di S. Vitale that was the headquarters of the police force. Abigail presented the letter from the Direttore to the smartly uniformed man on duty at reception and told him who they were, and that they were responding to this summons. The receptionist returned the letter to Abigail, then hailed another officer and rapped out instructions to him.

'Impressive,' Abigail murmured to Daniel. 'I thought we'd have to wait, or they'd arrange an appointment, but we're being taken straight to the Director, this Carmine Ventari, now.'

They followed the uniformed officer up a wide marble staircase to the first floor, then along a richly carpeted landing before stopping at a large oak door. The uniformed officer knocked, and then on receiving a summons in Italian from within, opened it.

'Signor and Signora Wilson,' he announced.

The room they entered looked like the highly decorated rooms they'd encountered when they'd been invited to Buckingham Palace to meet the Queen. Large oil paintings, landscapes and portraits, adorned the walls. The furniture, too, was expensive-looking and appeared to be antique. Three uniformed officers stood to attention by the door. Either bodyguards or attendants, thought Abigail, to the two men wearing the dark uniforms of the police who stood behind a large desk, their clothing heavily adorned in gold braid on the sleeves and elsewhere on the jackets. One was tall and the other shorter and round. The taller, thinner one came towards them and bowed, and introduced himself and his companion in Italian. Abigail translated to Daniel. 'The tall one is Carmine Ventari, the Direttore; the other is his most senior assistant, Pietro Annigoni.'

Daniel returned their bows with a bow of his own, then he and Abigail sat in the two gilt-edged chairs facing the two policemen across a large desk.

'We understand that you were the ones who intervened when Sergeant Capaldi tried to shoot Inspector Volpetti,' said Ventari.

Daniel turned to Abigail, who in turn said in Italian to the two policemen, 'My husband does not speak or understand Italian. Either I can speak for both of us, or we will need a translator.'

Ventari thought this over, then rapped out an order to one of his staff, who bowed and left the room.

'He's gone to find a translator,' Abigail explained to Daniel. 'I get the idea they need to have statements from both of us.'

'What about?' asked Daniel.

'About what happened when the police sergeant tried to shoot Inspector Volpetti.'

'Surely your word is as good as mine,' said Daniel.

'Apparently not.' She looked at Ventari and asked, 'Is this because I am a woman and my husband's word carries more weight?'

'Absolutely not, *signora*,' Ventari assured her. 'It is just that this investigation is so important that we need to show it has been conducted with complete impartiality and transparency. You were both witnesses. We need statements from both of you.'

The door opened and a small, round man in a neat pinstriped suit entered, who was introduced to them as 'Signor Calleri, who will translate Signor Wilson's replies in Italian.'

It was Ventari who asked the questions while Annigoni wrote their answers down on a large pad. After each question, in Italian, Abigail translated it for Daniel's benefit, and if Daniel was the one who responded, Signor Carelli translated his English.

'What were you doing at the police station when you intervened to stop Sergeant Capaldi shooting Inspector Volpetti?'

'We were there to see Inspector Volpetti.'

'Why?'

'Because we'd been involved with him as the result of a case we were working on.'

Ventari frowned. 'A case?'

'Yes. Two friends of ours had been murdered at the Colosseum. We were investigating to find out who did it.'

'Why? That was a matter for the police.'

'Because in our own country we work as private detectives.'

Ventari frowned.

'But we have seen the Festival programme,' he said to Abigail. 'You are here to give talks on Roman classical sites, not to investigate murders.'

'That was how it began,' Abigail told him. She told him how

she'd been contacted to give talks during the Classical Rome Festival, and two of their friends had been shot dead. 'Our friend Giuseppe Saredo, the organiser of the Festival, knows that we have established a reputation for investigating murders in museums. The Colosseum is a museum. We usually work with the local police so there is no conflict. Here, in Rome, we have been working with Inspector Volpetti. We went to see him to commiserate with him after what happened at the Colosseum, involving his son. It was while we were waiting to see him that we were aware of Sergeant Capaldi entering his office with a pistol in his hand. It looked suspicious to us, so we went in to see what was happening.'

'Fortunately,' added Daniel.

'You intervened against a man who was armed?'

'Yes.'

'But you, yourselves, were not armed.'

'No.'

'Were you not afraid?'

'No. Someone we knew was in danger.'

'And you overpowered him.'

'We did.'

As Annigoni wrote this down on his pad, Ventari asked, 'What do you know about the attempt on the life of the Prime Minister?'

'Nothing,' said Abigail. 'Except that we saw it.'

'You were there? At the Colosseum?'

'We were on the platform, sitting a few rows behind the Prime Minister. We saw the sergeant say something to the Prime Minister, and Signor Saracco go with him towards a waiting carriage. We then heard shots. We couldn't see what happened because there were people in front of us. But afterwards we rushed to where it had happened and saw the two young men lying dead, and Sergeant Capaldi putting his pistol back in its holster and putting his hands up. He said, "They were going to shoot the Prime Minister."'

'Did you know either of the assassins?'

'We knew of Vito Volpetti because we suspected he may have been involved in the murders of the Marudos, Giovanni and Sarah,' said Daniel.

'But we never actually met him,' added Abigail. 'The other boy, we didn't know him at all.'

The conversation continued, with Ventari asking Abigail and Daniel what their plans were, and when they would be returning to England.

'When we have discovered who murdered Giovanni and Sarah Maduro, and Sarah's sister Julia Winstanley,' replied Abigail. 'Julia was found strangled near the Campo de' Fiori a few days after the Maduros were shot.'

'Do you believe the murders are connected?'

'We do,' said Abigail.

'Do you have any thoughts about who may have been responsible?'

'I did have one thought,' said Daniel. 'I wondered if the Cosa Nostra might be involved.'

Ventari glowered at him.

'There is no such thing as the Cosa Nostra,' he said.

'Yes,' said Daniel, 'so we keep hearing. But interestingly we met with a man called Salvatore Fuschetti who is said to be a member of this non-existent organisation. He held me hostage for a while. Later, he was shot dead. We were told that was because the Cosa Nostra believed he had let them down. I was also held for a while by a man called Rocco Legato, who we were also told was a senior Cosa Nostra chief. A *capo*, I believe they are called.'

Ventari shook his head and told them firmly, 'I do not know of such men. I repeat again, there is no such thing as the Cosa Nostra.'

The conversation continued in a stilted manner for a further half hour, then Ventari and Annigoni rose to their feet. Taking the hint, Abigail and Daniel did the same.

'We thank you for coming in at such short notice,' said Ventari. 'We hope the rest of your stay here in Italy is less exciting than it has been to date.'

Hands were shaken, and one of the attendants escorted Daniel and Abigail out of the ornate room and down the marble staircase to the exit.

When they were out on the pavement, Abigail asked, 'Why on earth did you tell him all that about the Cosa Nostra?'

'Because I'm still not convinced that you are safe from them,' said Daniel. 'By throwing those names in, I think they'll keep a watch on us to see what we do and where we go. Think of it as ensuring we have protection. The Cosa Nostra will undoubtedly know who these people are. I'm hoping they'll stay away from us.'

Inside the Direttore's grand office, Ventari mulled over the interview, then said to Annigoni, 'I want you to find out all you can about the Wilsons. And put a watch on them. A careful watch. Unobtrusive, but careful.'

CHAPTER FORTY-FOUR

Daniel and Abigail stood outside the police headquarters looking up at the impressive building.

'Well, that was an experience I never thought we'd have when we talked about coming to Rome,' said Abigail.

'It seems that whenever we go anywhere, we are caught up in a murder,' said Daniel ruefully. 'I bet you if we went to the North Pole, we'd find ourselves with least one dead body.'

'Well, as we've had the last few days filled with deaths, attempted assassinations and being kidnapped by gangsters, I think it's time to take things calmly,' said Abigail.

'What do you have in mind?'

'The thing I mentioned before. The Sistine Chapel. You can't come to Rome and not see it.'

'It had better be good,' said Daniel.

As Abigail and Daniel walked to the Vatican along the towpath running alongside the River Tiber, Abigail suddenly stopped and grabbed Daniel's arm.

'There she is!' she whispered urgently.

'Who?' asked Daniel, bewildered.

'Angelina Condotti. There. On that bench.'

Daniel followed her gaze. Sure enough, Angelina Condotti was sitting on a bench reading a newspaper.

'How do you suggest we do this?' asked Daniel.

'We go and introduce ourselves.'

'And what happens if she runs off?'

'We sit down on the bench either side of her. If she tries to escape, we grab her. But she shouldn't, if she hasn't done anything wrong.'

Abigail strolled casually to the bench where Angelina was sitting and settled herself down on one side of her, while Daniel sat on the other side. Angelina looked at the pair, wary.

'Angelina Condotti?' said Abigail, giving a friendly smile that she hoped would allay the girl's fears. 'My name is Abigail Wilson . . .'

At this, Angelina leapt to her feet and ran off, hurling the newspaper aside.

'Wait!' called Abigail, and she and Daniel set off after the running woman. Abigail caught up with her and reached out to grab Angelina's shoulder. In response, Angelina swung her arm out, her elbow catching Abigail in the face. Abigail stumbled. Daniel raced past Abigail and caught up with Angelina, reaching for her with both hands. Again, Angelina swung her arm backwards, her elbow smashing into his throat. Daniel stumbled and fell, choking and coughing, but Abigail had recovered and once more launched an attack on the running girl, this time sticking out a foot and tripping her. Angelina stumbled, then righted herself and turned to face Abigail, her fists ready to swing a punch. Abigail threw herself at Angelina, wrapping her arms around the young woman, the force of Abigail's move sending both women to the river's edge, where they tottered momentarily – and then suddenly both fell into the Tiber with a splash which brought all the passersby running to see what had happened. Daniel had got back to his feet and ran to the river's edge. The two women had disappeared beneath the surface of the water, but soon their heads appeared, both choking and spluttering. Angelina was swinging her arms at Abigail, striking out. Daniel leapt into the river and swam the few strokes to where the two women were struggling together. He grabbed Angelina's hair and pulled her off Abigail, then began to haul her to the river bank. Abigail followed, and helped Daniel pull Angelina out of the water and onto the walkway.

By this time a uniformed policeman had appeared and waved his baton menacingly at the three soaking wet culprits who'd invaded the sacred river. It was Abigail who rescued the situation with a torrent of urgent Italian towards the policeman, in which she told him the woman was a fugitive. She and the man with her, she told him, were working with Inspector Volpetti. They needed to have the woman placed under arrest and taken to Inspector Volpetti at once, along with the two of them.

The policeman looked at them, then at Angelina, who lay writhing on the paving slabs as Daniel lay on her, holding her down, both of them soaked. Then he put his police whistle to his lips and let out three shrill blasts to summon reinforcements.

CHAPTER FORTY-FIVE

The short, tubby, balding figure in the clothing of a priest, carrying a battered leather briefcase, entered the police station and walked up to the reception desk.

'I have come to see my parishioner, Lorenzo Capaldi,' he said. 'I have been told he is being held here.'

'He was,' said the sergeant on duty. 'He has been transferred to prison to be held on remand.'

'Which prison?' asked the priest.

'The new one on Lungara Street,' said the sergeant. 'Regina Coeli.'

'Thank you and bless you, my son,' said the priest.

The priest knew Regina Coeli. It had been a convent until the powers that be decided to turn it into a prison. The work to carry out the necessary refurbishment had not long been completed, and now Regina Coeli had taken over from the Carceri Nuove as Rome's primary prison.

The priest arrived at the Regina Coeli reception area and demanded to be taken to see his parishioner, Lorenzo Capaldi. The warder on duty at reception was about to say 'Another one?' and remark on the fact that a priest had only just visited the prisoner, but this being Rome, where the Church was all-powerful, in a short time the priest was walking along a corridor towards the cells. He was accompanied by the same warder who'd escorted the young priest earlier. This warder was less reticent than the one at reception, and couldn't resist saying, 'You are the second priest in just a few minutes to come to see Capaldi. The first one had a message from his wife, and also came to give him communion.'

The tubby priest looked uncomfortable on hearing this. Inside the battered briefcase he carried was a communion scarf, along with a packet of communion wafers and a bottle of communion wine laced with a deadly poison.

When they reached Capaldi's cell, they saw the prisoner lying apparently asleep.

'Unlock the door,' said the tubby priest.

'The last priest said he wasn't to be disturbed,' said the warder.

'Where was this priest from?' demanded the father.

'He didn't say,' admitted the warder. He then looked questioningly at the current priest and asked, 'Which parish church are you from?'

'St Ignatius,' the priest answered. He knew this was the parish church that the Capaldis attended because he'd been given that information by Massimo Cassani, just in case he was asked. 'Now open this door. I wish to see my parishioner.'

'Yes, Father. I meant no disrespect,' said the warder humbly. 'It's just it's unusual to get two different priests come to see the same person within the space of a few minutes.'

'I shall make enquiries,' said the tubby priest flatly. 'Now open this door.'

The warder unlocked the door and the priest entered the cell.

He approached the sleeping prisoner and gently prodded him.

'Signor Capaldi,' he said.

There was no response. The tubby priest took hold of Capaldi's shoulder and pulled him towards him, causing the thin blanket to roll off.

'Mother of God!' exclaimed the priest in horror.

The warder joined him and they both looked down at the dead face of Lorenzo Capaldi, the blood on the front of his prison uniform. The tubby priest looked in shock at the warder and demanded, 'Did you not check on this man?'

'The priest said he wasn't to be disturbed under any circumstances,' stammered the warder.

The tubby priest looked down at the dead Capaldi and crossed himself. 'There has been the devil's work here,' he said angrily. 'I must leave and report this to my bishop for investigation.'

'Don't you want to report it to the prison governor?' asked the bewildered warder.

'That is your job,' snapped the priest. 'Mine is to explain this to God.'

Inspector Volpetti sat at his desk, doodling. He had written the same two words on his blotting pad six times: *Capaldi* and *Legato*. Each time he had drawn an arrow through the words.

There was a knock at his door, which opened, and a constable entered.

'Excuse me for interrupting you, Inspector,' said the constable, 'but we have had disturbing news from Regina Coeli.'

'What news?'

'Lorenzo Capaldi is dead. He was found dead in his cell. He had been stabbed through the heart.'

'How did this happen?' demanded Volpetti.

'It seems a priest arrived to give Capaldi communion. We believe it was this person posing as a priest who killed him.'

'Who was this priest? Where was he from?'

'The staff did not ask, sir. He said Capaldi was a parishioner of his and he demanded to see him.'

Volpetti sat still for a moment, then said, 'Very well.'

He was about to dismiss him when the constable added, 'There is another thing, sir.'

'Yes?'

'The two English people who were with you yesterday, the Wilsons.'

'Yes? What about them?'

'They were pulled out of the Tiber near to the Vatican.'

Volpetti looked at him, bewildered.

'What do you mean, pulled out? How did they get in the river?'

'They were chasing after a woman they suspected of being involved in the murders at the Colosseum. They, and the woman, fell into the river.'

'Are they all right?' asked Volpetti, rising to his feet. 'Where are they?'

'They are in reception,' said the constable.

'For God's sake, why didn't you tell me immediately!' exploded Volpetti angrily. 'Bring them to me at once!'

Santola Sciacci returned to his hotel room, where he took off the priest's cassock and put on the postman's outfit he'd brought. It was time to explore the buildings near to Rocco Legato's olive oil shop, in particular the roof accesses. A postman climbing the stairs of the different buildings would not be questioned. Postmen were invisible.

Angelina and Abigail were both wearing loose, long grey flannel smocks, the kind worn by prisoners. Daniel wore a pair of trousers that were too short and a shirt that was too big. Their own wet clothes were hanging on a clothes line in the rear yard of the police station. Now the three of them sat in Inspector Volpetti's office around his desk. Angelina wore handcuffs, which were attached to the wooden chair on which she sat. Three uniformed constables stood, keeping guard over the prisoner.

Volpetti, in the new spirit of positive co-operation that was the result of Abigail and Daniel saving his life, had said that he was happy for Abigail to lead the questioning. Abigail began with a name that she felt would strike a chord with Angelina.

'Tell me about your relationship with Julia Winstanley.'

Angelina stared at her with undisguised hostility. 'We had no relationship,' she said. 'I hated her.'

'Enough to kill her?' asked Abigail.

'Yes.'

'Did you kill her?'

'Yes.'

The answer was so stark, so simple and uttered with such satisfaction that there was no mistaking the fact that Angelina felt she was telling the unvarnished truth.

'You strangled her,' said Abigail.

'I did. With a length of cord. She struggled, but I was too strong for her.' She gave a smile of pride and added, 'I'm very strong.'

'Why didn't you shoot her?' asked Abigail. 'You had a gun.'

'I *had* a gun,' stressed Angelina indignantly. 'That bitch stole it from me.'

'Why did she do that?'

'To shoot Giovanni and his wife.'

'So it was Julia who shot them?'

Angelina nodded, and looked with scorn at Inspector Volpetti. 'I came to the scene as soon as I heard the terrible news and I saw my poor Giovanni there, with the gun lying beside Sarah. I recognised it as mine. It had been taken from where I kept it the day before. Julia had been there. She came to the house when I was out. One of the other girls told me she'd been there. She told them she wanted to talk to me. It was only later that I checked on my gun and found it gone. I went to Giovanni's flat to see her, but no one was there. Giovanni must have been getting ready for the Festival.'

'And so you killed her because she'd killed Giovanni and his wife.'

'I couldn't care less about his wife. It was Giovanni I cared for.'

'But why did Julia want to kill Giovanni?'

'Because Giovanni had seen her with her lover, that railway policeman. She worried Giovanni might tell his wife, and she might pass it on to her father. I was determined to take my revenge for what she'd done. I found out where she was staying and killed her.'

Daniel and Abigail walked back to the flat, unaware they were being shadowed. The man who followed them was Mario Torriano. In his pocket he carried a pistol, his intended instrument of vengeance for the death of Salvatore Fuschetti.

'So, all three murders solved,' said Daniel. 'Julia, and Angelina Condotti. Though we don't know why Vito Volpetti and his friend were killed. They said it was because they were going to shoot the Prime Minister, but I have my doubts about that.'

'It doesn't matter,' said Abigail. 'We weren't asked to investigate anything to do with that. The fact is we can now go home.'

'Excellent!' said Daniel.

'But before we do, there is one more place to go,' said Abigail. 'The Sistine Chapel.'

'It had better be as good as you say it is,' said Daniel doubtfully.

'It will be,' promised Abigail.

She unlocked the door to the flat and they went in.

Behind them, Mario Torriano took the pistol from his pocket and approached the door. This would be straightforward, he decided. Knock on the door, and when the door was opened, shoot the one who opened it. The sound of the shot would bring the other one running, at which point he'd shoot them too.

It didn't matter in which order they died; both of them were culpable for what had happened to Salvatore.

He reached for the door knocker, but before his fingers could touch it, he was grabbed from behind and yanked forcefully backwards. Arms were wrapped around him and a bag pulled over his head, and a punch to his throat prevented him from calling out.

CHAPTER FORTY-SIX

Sunday 19th August

Abigail stood beside Daniel in the Sistine Chapel as he looked up at the astonishing ceiling fresco.

'Well?' she asked.

'Incredible,' he said. 'Truly incredible. And you say one man painted this?'

'Yes. Michelangelo. Originally he wanted to use assistants to help him, but in the end he decided none of them were up to the task of doing it how he saw it.'

'How long did it take him?'

'Four years, from 1508 to 1512. But he wasn't here the whole time. He and Pope Julius, who'd commissioned the ceiling, had a few arguments. They were both very temperamental. At one point Michelangelo went off in a huff to Florence after a row with Julius, and was finally persuaded to come back to continue the work by the Florentine government.'

'But how did he actually do it?'

'He had scaffolding erected and boards laid across the top level, just below the actual ceiling. There have been disagreements as to whether he lay on the boards and worked, or stood on them and painted. Vasari says that Michelangelo painted in a standing position, while Paolo Giovio claimed he did the work lying down.'

'Either way, his neck and arms must have ached,' said Daniel.

'Not just his arms,' said Abigail. 'Michelangelo wrote a poem about how painful the process was for him.' She then recited:

'My beard turns up to heaven; my nape falls in.
Fixed on my spine my breast-bone visibly grows like a
harp; a rich embroidery
Bedews my face from brush-drops thick and thin.
My loins into my paunch like levers grind;
My buttock like a crupper bears my weight; my feet
unguided wander to and fro.'

'Which suggests he was standing up,' said Daniel.

Abigail nodded. 'I've always preferred Vasari's histories of the artists to Giovio's,' she said.

Daniel looked up at the magnificent ceiling again.

'I'm glad you insisted I saw this,' he said.

'You can hardly come to Rome and not come and look at it,' she said.

Daniel nodded. 'Talking of art,' he said, 'there's one thing we need before we return to England. Tinto. I'd like him to do a portrait of you. It will make this trip something we'll always remember.'

'We already have a lot to make this trip memorable,' said Abigail. 'We've explored the wonders of classical Rome, and we solved three murders.'

'I'm not sure if we can claim the credit for solving the

murders,' mused Daniel. 'Angelina confessed, very proud at what she'd done.'

'But she wouldn't have, if we hadn't found her.' She produced an envelope. 'I've written to Paolo to tell him what's happened. That Julia shot his parents. And Angelina Condotti killed her, and is now in custody.'

'Good,' said Daniel. 'But let's finish this trip on a memorable note. Tinto, and your portrait.'

Abigail frowned. 'Why just me?' she asked. 'Let's ask him if he can do a double portrait. You and I. Now that would be something.'

In his olive oil exporter's shop, Rocco Legato listened as one of his men imparted the news about Lorenzo Capaldi.

'He was found dead in his cell at Regina Coeli,' the man told him. 'They say he was stabbed to death. They believe it was done by a man posing as a priest who had come to give Lorenzo communion.'

Legato thanked his man and sat for a moment in contemplative silence after the messenger had left. So this was the way it ended. His closest friend for all of his life. A man he would have died for but instead, who had died to protect him.

He got up. He needed to go to his own priest and take confession. But first, he would call on Sophia and give her his consolation, and assurances that everything that could be done would be done. Money was not an issue. It never had been, and it would continue to be taken care of as long as Rocco was alive.

He walked out of his office and into his shop, where four of his bodyguards were waiting. He would not need all four, he decided. Two would be sufficient.

He gestured for two of the men to accompany him and then opened the door of his shop and stepped out into the street. He stood for a moment, deliberating how best to break the news to Sophia, before he moved off. He barely made one stride before the bullet took him between the eyes and blew his skull apart, scattering blood and brains onto the pavement. The two bodyguards threw themselves to the ground, pulling out their pistols and scanning the street for the assassin.

On the roof of the factory opposite, Santola Sciacci took the rifle apart and put the sections into his satchel, then made his way to the roof opening. He was wearing the uniform of a postman. From his satchel he lifted a few envelopes and held them in his hand. When he descended the stairs and went out into the street, he would appear to be a postman on his round.

Lorenzo Capaldi and Rocco Legato both dead. *The first part of my mission is completed, Grandfather*, he thought.

AUTHOR'S NOTE

For those interested in Italian political history, Giuseppe Saracco was forced out of the Italian premiership in February 1901 by a vote in the chamber condemning his weak attitude towards a dock strike in Genoa. He was succeeded as Prime Minister by Giuseppe Zanardelli.

JIM ELDRIDGE was born in central London towards the end of World War II, and survived attacks by V2 rockets on the Kings Cross area where he lived. In 1971 he sold his first sitcom to the BBC and had his first book commissioned. Since then he has had more than one hundred books published, with sales of over three million copies. He lives in Kent with his wife.

jimeldridge.com